FIRE & CHASM

CHELSEA M. CAMPBELL

SKYSCAPE

SKYSCAPE

Text copyright © 2015 Chelsea M. Campbell
All rights reserved.

Published by Skyscape, New York

www.apub.com

Amazon, the Amazon logo, and Skyscape are trademarks of Amazon.com, Inc., or its affiliates.

ISBN-13: 9781477827987
ISBN-10: 1477827986

Book design by Cyanotype Book Architects

Library of Congress Control Number: 2014953210

Printed in the United States of America

For Apples. You know why.

CHAPTER ONE

The scents of pine needles and damp, newly turned earth hang heavy in the air. Leora and I make our way past the graves of the dishonored as the warm glow from the oil lamp she carries sways back and forth, sending long shadows up the narrow path leading to the mausoleum. It's pitch black out and well past curfew. No one is supposed to be here.

Especially not supposed to be creeping around all the fresh graves, all the deep, dark holes the Chasm-bound are buried in, where their bodies rot away in the cold, lifeless dirt. It's not exactly a secret that wizards have been disappearing around town late at night and that the same number of new graves appear afterward, dug along the farthest edge of the graveyard, as far from the church as possible. The Church might have to take in all the dead, according to the law—no matter how wicked they were in life, or how unnatural their magic—but they don't have to honor them.

The gravestones are flat and unmarked, but Leora's eyes move to them anyway, as if she could see who lurked underneath if only she stared at them long enough. "Do you think . . ." She shakes her head and forces her gaze away from the stones. "No, he's not one of them. I'm sure of it."

But she's not sure, not at all. "You hate wizards," I remind her. Because she does. She hates them as much as I do. Well, almost. Enough to not care if some of them have gone missing.

"I know that, Az. I didn't say I don't hate him. And I shouldn't be worrying about him, not today, but . . . He's still my father."

I watch the path in front of me, avoiding stepping on a loose rock, my footsteps silent. Today's the anniversary of her mother's death—hence our visit to the mausoleum—and she hasn't seen her father in years. I've never seen my parents. Not that I know of. But even if I don't know anything about having a family, I know Leora deserves better than the one she's got. Or at least what's left of it.

"He's in the capital, in Newhaven, not here," Leora whispers, still trying to reassure herself. A twig snaps under her foot, making her jump. "He's at the High Guild's headquarters. I mean, he would have written to me if he was coming. He knows where I am. He's paying for me to be here. By the Fire, it's not like he doesn't know where to find me."

"Maybe that's the problem. A letter from a wizard at the High Guild? Sent here, to the church?" I roll my eyes. "*That* would go over well." Though from what she's told me about him, I'm not so sure he would have written either way.

She holds out her lamp, hesitating as she scopes out the next part of the path. She's not used to lurking in the shadows and finding her way in the dark. Not like I am. "Do you think he could have tried to contact me, and . . . and one of the Fathers or the Mothers threw out his letter instead of giving it to me?"

"It's possible." But they don't throw out his money when that shows up. Apparently a wizard's coins are as good as anyone's.

"No one's disappearing in the capital. I mean, no wizards. Ordinary people are disappearing from their homes at night—I know that—and it's not like I don't know the High Guild is behind it. *Everyone knows.* So maybe it's wrong for me to be worried about him when . . . when so many other people are in danger. But I am anyway."

I take her hand, letting my thumb brush against her wrist. My skin tingles where we touch, and sparks zap up my spine and back down to my toes. Ever since the first day I met her, being around her has made my chest warm and achy. And I wonder if she feels the same, if the little glances she gives me when she thinks I'm not looking mean what I want them to mean. If every second we're apart is as painful for her as it is for me.

I've lost count of how many times the words have been on my lips, of all the times I've been so sure I wouldn't be able to stop myself from telling her the truth. Not about *what* I am, but about who I am when I'm with her.

But a chilly gust of wind rustles past us, unusually cold for late spring, filling my nose with the scent of fresh earth again, and a suffocating guilt crawls through my chest. Because Leora might not know who's in these unmarked graves, or who put them there, but *I* do. I remember each and every one of their faces, how they twisted in agony as their life drained out of them.

And she's right, everyone knows about the wizards from the High Guild who've been prowling around after the last bell, terrorizing people in their homes and taking what's not theirs to take. The Monarchy sanctions their late-night visits, turning a blind eye to the cruelty they inflict on innocent people. Everyone might know about the wizards' crimes, but no one has the means to fight back.

Well, almost no one.

For all the wizards' power, they're still only human. It's so easy for them to lose track of one of their own in the dark, of a partner they thought was just behind them. They never notice one of their brethren slipping off into the night without a sound.

Except sometimes there's a sound. Sometimes I'm not quick enough, and they get a chance to scream. It's blood-curdling and beautiful—the only beautiful thing about them.

I shouldn't feel that way. I shouldn't *like* hurting them, even if they deserve it, and I know exactly what that makes me—not just a murderer, but a monster. And I don't want to be either of those things, but it doesn't change the fact that I *need* to be.

I suck in a breath and focus, trying to picture the faces of all the wizards I've killed. Of course, I don't know what her father looks like, but I imagine a middle-aged man with her blue eyes and the same color hair—a deep, reddish brown—and maybe the same thin nose that gets wider at the end. I saw a charcoal drawing of her mother once, and her nose didn't resemble Leora's at all. So I picture Leora's on this image I'm conjuring up of her maybe-father and search my memory for a match.

"I'm sure he wasn't one of them," I tell Leora, holding her arm steady as she climbs a couple of rock steps, slippery with mud. And I am. Pretty sure, anyway. Wouldn't I know if I'd murdered the father of the girl I love? Wouldn't I *just know* somehow?

She pauses once we're both at the top, closing her eyes and leaning toward me a little, like she's going to lean into me and let me hold her. Like she *wants* me to. And I feel warm all over and I move my arms just a little, just enough to invite her closer. But then she pulls away, and I'm left hollow and raw, wondering if I imagined the whole thing.

"You can't know that. You can't know if my father's alive or dead." She turns and stalks off toward the mausoleum.

She doesn't know that I *can* know that. She doesn't know that when I tell her I'm sure her father wasn't murdered on the street, I'm not just saying it to make her feel better. I'm saying it because I'm 90 percent certain that I didn't kill him.

Okay, 85 percent. But that's still a pretty good chance that he's alive.

"Leora, wait." I hurry to catch up with her, the light from her lantern casting exaggerated shadows across the graveyard. Her footsteps crunch against fallen pine needles, reminding me that we're not supposed to be here.

Father Moors might forgive her for trespassing, given that she's visiting her mother's ashes. But he won't forgive me for escorting her here in the middle of the night. Even if there's no way she could know that I had a hand in putting those wizards in their graves—two hands, actually, and a knife—he'd still say it was careless. But even if that was true, it wouldn't have stopped me from coming with her tonight. The mausoleum might be open to visitors during the day, but Leora wanted to visit her mother in private. Me not going with her wouldn't have stopped her, and there was no way I was letting her walk through the darkness alone.

"I shouldn't even be thinking about him," Leora says, setting the lantern down on the stone steps for a moment. "My mother died five years ago today, and he didn't even come to her funeral.

It shouldn't matter to me whether he's all right or not, because he left, and because he loved that damned *thing* more than he ever loved me."

That "thing" was some kind of experiment her father was working on. A *live* experiment, something she calls an abomination. That's all I know about it, but it's enough to know what kind of wizard he is. The kind who wouldn't want to meet me in a dark alley. "You know," I tell her, "there's one way to find out for sure. Since you're so worried."

"I'm *not* worried."

"But if you were, you could always write to *him*. Even if he's not writing to you."

She breathes out slowly through her mouth, shaking her head. Then she puts her hand on the mausoleum door, which has a heavy lock to keep us out. But a locked door can't stop Leora, not anymore.

A few months ago, the Fire—one of the two primal forces in the world—granted her the power to unlock even the most complex mechanisms.

The Fire gives everyone a gift, a magical ability, when it deems them ready. Whatever that means. Most people get theirs around fifteen or sixteen, like Leora did. Everyone except wizards, that is. Wizards have enough spells, and the Fire condemns their magic and the way they steal life from people to cast it. And if you decide to become a wizard later on, you lose whatever the Fire gave you. Forever.

Pretty much everyone I know at the church and the school has a gift from the Fire. Everyone over fourteen, anyway. I'm not sure how old I am—not exactly—but I'm old enough that it should have happened already. I'll be the only one not honored at the upcoming ceremony at the church, the one acknowledging everyone who got their ability this past year and what an important rite of passage it is. It won't just be the other acolytes from the church or the kids from the school, but anyone in Ashbury. They'll all be moving on, the whole town celebrating how much the Fire favors them. Everyone except me.

Leora closes her eyes, concentrating for just a moment before I hear the lock click. She's told me before it's like solving a maze in her mind. She eases the door open, careful not to create too much of a breeze.

The mausoleum glows with light, a stark contrast to the forsaken graveyard. A fireplace takes up one wall. The flames flicker and snap as we enter, bringing a slight gust of wind with us. One of the Fathers will be around to attend to the fire after the next bell—or maybe they'll send one of the first-year acolytes instead— to ensure that it always stays lit. The other three walls are lined with shelves of urns, made of amber-colored glass and filled with ashes. Tiny flames flicker from the votive candles that visitors have left to honor the dead.

Leora takes a new, unlit candle from a box on the floor and sets it in front of her mother's urn. "Please protect her from the darkness," she says, repeating the ritual prayer to the Fire, the force of light and warmth.

There's a muffled sizzling sound. All the flames in the room ripple, and then a spark flares up on the candle she just set down, blazing to life as the Fire acknowledges her prayer and makes a silent promise to keep her mother's soul safe within its light. To keep it safe from the chaos and violence of the Chasm.

Tears well up in Leora's eyes as she watches the light dance across the amber urn, illuminating her mother's ashes inside. "I miss you," she whispers. "I miss you *so much.*"

My throat aches, and a bitter taste fills the back of my mouth as I look away. I hate the little tendril of jealousy that slithers through my chest, painful and complicated. I can't remember my past, but sometimes I wonder why no one's ever come looking for me.

An image flashes in my head of the day Father Moors found me three years ago. My first memory. I was standing over three bodies, all in blood-soaked blue robes. Wizards. The knife was in my hands, blood sizzling as it dripped down the blade. The stink of burning flesh hung in the air. My mind reeled from the heat of the obsidian as it raced through my veins, turning my whole body hot and feverish. And I was horrified. Horrified because I couldn't remember what happened or how I got there or who those wizards were, only that they deserved it. And I was horrified because, even though some part of me knew I should feel sickened by what I'd done, I didn't. I felt *good.*

I remember how a tickle of euphoria spread through my arms, my stomach, my feet. It crept up my throat and along my jaw until a smile curled my lips, and then I was laughing.

That's how Father Moors found me. Giddy over what I'd done, but also terrified of it. The laughter only lasted for a few moments, and then I crumpled to the ground, letting go of the knife, my stomach heaving. But Father Moors reassured me that it was self-defense. He said he'd seen the whole thing and I was only protecting myself, that those wizards would have hurt me if I hadn't done what I did.

He said the Church would protect me, that they could use someone with my obsidian skills, which he believes come from the Fire and are meant to be used. So he found me a place in the Church of the Sacred Flame, and, other than writing to the High Priest about me, he's kept my secret. He knows where I go at night, though we don't talk much about it. There's not much to say, and talking can be overheard. The High Priest has sanctioned what I do for the Church, but his word isn't law, and getting caught would still mean my life. Father Moors's, too, if anyone knew he was involved.

But even if Father Moors took me in, that doesn't change the fact that I was alone when he found me. I had to have come from somewhere, and yet, I don't think anyone is out there missing me the way Leora's missing her mother. And her father, even if she won't admit it.

And if I were dead, would Leora bring a candle to my urn and cry over me, too?

I squeeze my eyes shut and don't think about it, because even though I wear the red robes of the Church, I have a feeling I won't end up in the mausoleum. The Fire has to approve these things, and it hasn't granted me a power yet . . . And I've put too many bodies in the Fire-forsaken ground to think I don't belong there myself.

I picture Leora crying over a grave. Kneeling in the dirt, hurt and betrayed and wondering how her best friend had so much darkness in him without her ever knowing. How he could have been both the person she knew and the monster she didn't, and how he could have kept so many secrets from her. I watch her now, whispering softly to her dead mother's ashes, her voice warm and loving and tinged with a raw sort of sadness. The kind that rips you apart little by little if you let it.

I want to tell her I'm ripping apart, too. That I don't know what I've lost, but I know how Father Moors found me, and that even if it really was self-defense, it shouldn't have felt so satisfying. And it wasn't self-defense all the other times since then. And I still liked it. Every minute of it.

But I can never tell her the truth, even if it's eating away at every part of me every second that I'm with her. It hurts to be apart from her, to long so much for something I can never have, and it hurts to be with her, too, to see her smiling at the innocent boy she thinks I am.

I clench my jaw, trying to banish that line of thinking, but it doesn't work and my fingers instinctively grasp the hilt of the obsidian blade at my waist. I swallow as my skin starts to burn, as the heat creeps through my hand and up my arm. Obsidian comes from volcanoes. From bright lava that pours out of a dark void in the ground. Part Fire, part Chasm, embodying the primal forces of both light and darkness, order and chaos, peace and violence. The Fathers might think my skill with obsidian means the Fire favors me, but I've got a different theory. A much darker one.

Sweat beads on my forehead and across my back. I feel like I'm standing only inches away from a roaring fire. The heat crawls over me, excruciating and euphoric at the same time. It hits my brain, making my thoughts swirl together, so that I don't have to think about the fact that Leora doesn't really know me. That she could never actually *love* me.

"Az," Leora says, her voice quiet and strained as she turns to face me.

I make myself let go of the knife, hoping she didn't see me getting my fix. My need for obsidian isn't exactly a secret—one of the few things that isn't—but she doesn't know how deep it goes. "I can't write to my father, because if I do, he won't write back. Do you think a wizard sends his daughter to a school run by the Church because he ever wants to see her again? He won't write to me, and then I still won't know if he's alive or dead, but if he is alive, it'll just be another reminder that he doesn't care. That he wants me as far away from him as possible."

How can he not care? Even if he's a wizard, how can he not care about his own daughter? About *her*?

"Leora . . ." I want to tell her to forget about him. I want to tell her that he doesn't matter because she's not alone—she'll never be alone—because she has me.

"I'm fine," she says. "It's not like this is anything new."

"He left you. He abandoned you with your sick mother, and he doesn't even check up on you, and—" I move closer, until I can feel the warmth radiating from her. My skin is still feverish from the obsidian, so that when I touch her arm, she gasps a little. "I'll never leave you, Leora." Maybe I can't tell her everything, maybe I can't admit that I'm in love with her, but I can promise her this. "Not unless you tell me to."

"I would *never* do that," she says, her voice burning, almost as if she was the one who'd touched the obsidian.

I don't say anything. I want to hold her so badly. I want to tell her how much she means to me and how much I wish I was the boy she thinks I am. But if I move at all, if I open my mouth to speak even a single word, I know it will all come pouring out. I'll spill every secret writhing inside of me, until I'm hollow and empty. Until I've taken anything good she might feel for me and poisoned it.

She shoves a new candle into my hand and smiles. "Here," she says. "You're my best friend. You're pretty much the only family I've got, so . . . Would you?" She gestures to her mother's urn on the shelf beside her.

I nod, still not trusting myself to speak. My hand shakes as I set the candle next to hers. For a moment I let myself imagine that the two of us really could be a family. We could be together. And when we died, the Fire would grant us both permission to be here, side by side, forever. I could become a normal person, the past I can't remember no longer haunting me. I could be someone worthy of her.

"Please," I whisper, repeating the same prayer. "Please protect her from the darkness."

As soon as I say it, the candles in the room waver. They don't ripple like they did for Leora—they flicker and sway angrily, as if a huge gust of wind just threatened to blow them all out. A spark singes the end of the wick, turning it black and sending an acrid wisp of smoke into the air, as if a flame really had lit and then snuffed itself out again. I blink, unwilling to believe it.

"Wow," Leora says, "some altar boy *you* are."

"This one's defective," I mutter. "We should probably get going anyway, before the next bell." But I was watching, and I know there was no flame. The spiral tattoo on my right wrist—another mystery from my past—suddenly itches, and a sense of foreboding creeps across my shoulders.

Leora nods. "Good-bye, Mom," she whispers, taking my candle back from the shelf. She holds it close to her chest and says the prayer again. For her, the Fire lights it, and a flame appears on the wick, burning just as brightly as all the others. She shoots me a look. "Defective? And you're supposed to be the professional here."

"I warmed it up for you." And it might be a coincidence that it lit for her and not for me. I might be reading too much into it. Maybe I was breathing on the candle too hard, or sucking all the air away, so it never had a chance.

But it sure feels like the Fire was sending me a message, making sure I know exactly where I stand. That there's a good reason it hasn't granted me a power like everybody else, because as far as it's concerned, I'm a monster. Irredeemable.

Condemned.

CHAPTER TWO

Three wizards drag a woman kicking and screaming out of her house in the middle of the night, while I crouch in the shadows around the corner. So close—only a few quick strides away—and yet not close enough.

I hate this part.

Because there's only one of me and three of them—and two more that slipped away inside the house—and even though I'd kill them all if I could, I'm forced to pick them off one by one. That means avoiding the soft circles of light cast by their lamps on the packed ground and lurking in the darkness like a spider, waiting for one of them to get near enough to grab.

One of the wizards holds the woman's arms. She screams as the two inside bring out her husband. He struggles, until one of them holds a green potion bottle to his wife's lips. Poison. The couple aren't wizards, so they must both have powers from the Fire. I'm guessing from the way their faces have gone pale that neither of their gifts involves any natural immunity.

They shouldn't have to worry about this. Nobody should, but especially not people who mind their own business and have nothing to do with the wizards. Until a few years ago, the wizards mostly kept to themselves. Or at least that's what I hear, since I don't exactly remember. Not that they weren't above hurting people to get what they wanted—they are wizards, after all—but their battles were with the Church, not with ordinary people.

"Shut up, both of you, or I shove it down her throat!" The wizard's voice echoes off the neighboring houses, ringing in my ears, and then the night gets eerily quiet, except for the woman's suppressed sobs. The neighbors can hear—of course they can—but no one comes rushing out to help. Smart move.

They're helpless, and there's nothing I can do. Not yet. My hands twitch, my fingers hovering over my knife hilt. But it would be stupid to make a move now. I have to keep reminding myself of that, because while killing wizards scratches an itch, spilling their blood for torturing helpless people—that's a *need*. One that's hard to fight.

One that I'd have, even if Father Moors hadn't encouraged it.

The leader of their group scratches his bearded chin and straightens his cornflower-blue robes, standing tall, his face impassive, as if he was delivering a lecture to bored colleagues, not invading someone's home. He clears his throat and reads from a small scroll, though he sounds like he's got his lines memorized, like he's done this enough times to remember. "By royal decree of King Elwise and Queen Arlissa Graves, we are authorized to search this home for stolen guild property. You are obligated, by law, to answer any questions honestly and without delay—"

"Please," the woman says, "we don't have anything like that. Nothing stolen. *Please!*"

"Any resistance on your part is considered treason to the Crown and will result in your immediate arrest and seizure of your assets. If you answer my questions and comply with our procedure, this will go much more smoothly, I assure you. Now"—he pauses, letting go of one end of the scroll so that it curls up again, then sticks the scroll inside his robes—"are there any children living at this residence?"

"Since when is it illegal to have children?" the man asks, looking the wizard in the eyes.

It isn't.

The wizard sighs. "Are there or are there not any children, including adolescents, living at this residence?"

"No," the woman says. "*No.* Only us."

"Any male children?"

"*No.*"

"Tell me," the wizard says, pulling a piece of parchment from his pocket, "do you recognize this symbol?" He shows them both the paper, watching their expressions as they squint to see it in the lamplight.

They always show them the paper. I've never seen what's on it, but as far as I can tell, no one *ever* recognizes it. And I don't know why they always ask about children. Or stolen property. It's probably just an excuse to torture people, so they can use their energy for spells and steal all their stuff.

"Mommy?"

Heads turn toward the small voice coming from the open doorway of the house. Two little girls stand there in their nightgowns, yawning, their eyes going wide as they realize something awful is going on.

"Go back inside," the woman says, her voice tight with tears. "Take your sister and go back—"

The wizard holding the potion backhands her in the face, silencing her.

The littlest of the girls shrieks and runs toward her. Before the girl takes two steps, the wizards have her and her sister.

"No children?" the lead wizard says, not sounding very surprised. Or interested. "I told you to cooperate." He turns to the other wizards. "I always tell them, and yet they always *lie*." He shoves the paper with the symbol on it into his pocket and barks orders. "Arrest them and search the house! Keep the girls—they'll prove useful during the interrogation, though send word to Maggie at the orphanage, tell her she'll have two more mouths to feed within the week."

"You can't take them!" the man shouts. His wife screams. The girls are crying.

And I can't wait for the right opportunity. This is it. There are five wizards, and there's no way I can take them all out. I only get one, and I know exactly which one I want.

My hand closes around the hilt of my knife, the familiar heat spreading through my arm and into my chest, my head. It ignites my rage, until there's only one thing I can think about. I'm already moving, emerging from the shadows at full speed. My obsidian burns in my hand, willing me to use it. Thoughts flash of how good it will feel to sink the blade into flesh—the wizards', their victims', my own. The heat makes it hard to think about anything except how much the knife *wants* me to use it.

My vision blurs. I ignore the panicked shouts coming from the wizards, dodging as one grabs for me, focusing only on my target. I slam into the lead wizard, knocking him to the ground. He gasps for breath. Sweat pours down my forehead. My hand trembles from resisting the knife's urges to sink it into the nearest person. But now that the nearest person is this wizard, I don't have to fight it anymore. I let it take over me, guiding my hand.

Somewhere behind me, a wizard shouts for me to stop. He does something to the woman, so she cries out in pain. Then the children are shrieking like mad, until there's the loud crack of a palm on skin. But it's only a lull—the hit makes them both cry harder. There's a jumble of sound as the woman sobs uncontrollably and the man shouts obscenities at the wizards. And at me.

I don't turn to look. I focus on the wizard on the ground beneath me. His eyes widen. He gasps. At first I think it's because he sees his death coming. This is it, the end of his life. But he's staring at my wrist, at the spiral tattoo just below my palm. Recognition flares in his eyes. His mouth moves. My blood pounds, the rushing of my pulse so loud in my ears, I can't tell if he makes no noise, or if I just don't hear him. But I can see the words he forms with his mouth:

Azeril. It's you.

I pull back. It's not easy to fight the knife, especially when I've already let it take over me. My hand shakes. I stumble backward, and then I feel the euphoria of knife hitting flesh. I smell burning skin and blood. My breathing turns ragged.

Then the pain hits.

I look down at my left arm and see that the knife did indeed find a target.

Me.

CHAPTER THREE

I startle awake in my bed the next morning, soaked in sweat. There's a second where I don't remember what happened last night, and then it comes back to me. The family, the wizards, the knife. The smell of blood hangs in the air, and I don't remember getting undressed, either, but I must have because my bloodstained shirt is crumpled on the floor, along with a week's worth of old laundry. Weekly room inspection is tomorrow, and I have a feeling I'm not going to pass. Again. But from the vague memories I do have of last night, I'm also pretty sure I've got bigger things to worry about than having to put in extra shifts scrubbing dishes in the mess hall.

Someone's knocking on my door. "Hey! Az! Rise and shine— we've got a visitor!" It's Rathe, one of my fellow acolytes in training.

"I'm up!" I shout back to him, before it occurs to me that maybe I should have pretended to be asleep. The rest of last night is a blur. I'm still foggy on how I ended up here and how badly I'm injured, and I don't need any company when I find out.

Rathe bursts in, frowning and wearing his most formal red robes. His short, usually messy blond hair is actually somewhat tamed today, like he just spent the last half hour running a wet comb through it. "You call that *up*? You're still in bed!"

"I'm awake, aren't I?" I move to sit up, leaning against my bad arm. There's a split second where I realize what I've just done and brace myself before the stabbing pain hits. I clench my teeth to try and hide it, my mind racing to come up with a cover story. I've had accidents before. Nothing serious, not like this, but—

The pain doesn't come. I don't feel anything. It's like it never happened. Except, when I look down at the inside of my arm, there's a thin white line where the knife went in. The wound looks like it healed months ago, not like it's only a few hours old.

"Get up," Rathe says, already pawing through my closet and throwing a dark-red robe that matches his own onto the bed. Unlike the usual robes we wear, it's got intricate, swirling flame patterns embroidered in gold thread along the cuffs of the sleeves and the edging on the hood. It's too expensive to wear on a daily basis, not to mention it's made of a stiff, scratchy wool. The Fathers only make us drag them out on really special occasions.

"Must be some visitor," I mutter, still trying to wrap my head around last night. I remember attacking that wizard and him *recognizing* me, or at least my tattoo.

Azeril. It's you.

His words replay in my mind over and over. My arm should be in excruciating pain, but it's not, and instead a heavy sense of dread seeps into me, filling in all the spaces where the pain should be. I shudder as I pull the robe over my head, not liking the idea of a wizard knowing something about me that I don't.

I remember not killing him and ending up with my obsidian in my own arm. And the waves of giddy satisfaction as it found a mark, even if it was me. And then . . .

"It's the High Priest," Rathe says.

The High Priest. I've never met him, but Father Moors had to get his approval to let me stay here. To make me an acolyte of the Church, to give me a room and an education. It was the High Priest who decided my ability with obsidian made me worth keeping. He's the one who decided I could repay their kindness in blood.

That makes him the only other person besides Father Moors who knows my secret.

"He's come all the way from the capital," Rathe goes on. "Rumor has it he's looking for an apprentice, but who knows why he'd come looking for one out here in Ashbury when he's got plenty of trainees back home? All I know is Father Moors wants us *dressed*. And, more importantly, he wants us *on time*."

I scramble to get out of bed, knowing we'll both be in trouble if we're late. My legs get tangled in my dark-green bedspread, dragging it to the floor and adding to the mess. A folded scrap of paper slips from my pillow and flutters to my feet. I don't know where it came from. Maybe it's nothing, just a random bit of paper, but a chilling wave of fear prickles across my skin. I snatch it up, hoping it's blank, but of course it's not. Inside is a note:

Azeril,
We each have something the other wants. Meet me two nights from now at the Silver Hound. Come alone.

There's no signature, just a drawing of the spiral tattoo I have on my wrist. The wizard must have written this last night. He wants to meet me tomorrow. He wants me to *willingly* seek him out.

"What's wrong?" Rathe asks. "You look like you're going to be sick. Don't you dare throw up in front of the High Priest. Father Moors will kill you. Seriously. And he'll make me clean it up."

"I'm *fine*. But . . . have you ever heard of a place called the Silver Hound?"

He wrinkles his nose like something smells bad. "That's a wizard hangout, Az. Not somewhere anyone would want to go. Not anyone *decent*. Why? Is that where you were last night?" He grins and raises an eyebrow, teasing me, because the idea of me ever getting anywhere near a wizard, let alone some place infested with them, is just that ridiculous.

"I was here last night. Asleep." I hope he can't hear my uncertainty. I have no idea where I was last night. At least, not for all of it.

"Yeah, right. You might not have been in a disgusting wizard bar, but you're not ghostly pale and lingering in bed after sunup because you were *asleep* last night. Just don't throw up on the High Priest, and everything will be crackling. I won't tell Father Moors—I swear."

I open my mouth to argue with him, but then I think better of it. It doesn't matter what Rathe thinks I was doing last night, as long as it's not the truth. Staying out all hours drinking is better than murder. Well, attempted murder. "Thanks," I say, and the relief in my voice is genuine.

"Don't thank me, just get a move on. Oh, and Az? One more thing. An order from Father Moors."

"Yeah?"

"Bring your knife."

———

All fourteen of us boys line up along the aisle in the chapel, ranging in age from ten to twenty. Everyone's in their best robes, though Tol, one of the younger acolytes, has a tear near the edge of his sleeve that he's trying to hide. Father Moors stands at the end of the line, fidgeting and muttering to himself, the flint stones around his neck clacking softly together as he moves. He's mostly bald, though he had more hair when I first met him, and his dress robes stretch tightly across his portly stomach. Father Demmett joins him in his fidgeting, and Father Gratch takes his anxiety out on us, glaring at anyone who so much as breathes too loudly.

The heavy chapel doors creak open as the Mothers enter the room, leading in the girls—who, like us, are dressed in their fanciest red robes—to stand opposite us. There are only eight of them, an unfair number as Rathe says, what with there being almost twice as many of us. He wriggles his eyebrows suggestively at Mara, who's a year younger than him, only to have Father Gratch yell out a stern, "Acolyte Marten! This is a church, not a brothel!"

Rathe's face turns bright red, though he continues to make eye contact with Mara. She shoots him a sly smile.

We should be in class right now with everyone else. I should be sitting next to Leora, writing out tedious lists of verbs and principal parts, except Church duties trump anything school related. As Father Gratch is so fond of reminding us, we don't need an education to light candles and sweep out fireplaces. Unlike the other students, who live in the dorms over at the school and whose parents pay for their tuition, we're here only at the mercy of the Church. We owe them our service.

My palms are sweating, and I want so badly to lift up my sleeve and check again to see if the scar is really there. But I don't want anyone else seeing and asking questions. I have enough of my own already.

Was that wizard from last night in my room? Did he bring me home? The thought makes me uneasy. How would he have known where I live? Unless I told him, but I can't imagine doing that. The same way I can't imagine a wizard swallowing his pride and ditching his blue robes in order to step foot on church grounds. Technically, the grounds are open to anyone. But a wizard showing up in official garb from the High Guild is like a punch in the face or a rock hurled through the window. It's an open act of aggression that wouldn't be taken lightly, and even late at night, he would have stuck out like soot on snow. *Someone* would have seen him and raised an alarm.

And I'm not an expert on wizard magic, but I've never heard of a healing spell that works that well, that fast. It shouldn't be possible. He could have turned me in, too, for trying to murder him. But he didn't.

I could have killed him, but I didn't do that, either.

I feel like I'm losing my mind.

So what else is new?

Two red-robed guys my age, with golden stars embroidered on the edges of their robes to represent the capital city of Newhaven, push open the chapel doors and hold them there. A priest and priestess come in, holding smoking censers out in front of them, making the room smell like cinnamon and herbal tea. The High

Priest follows. He's tall and pale, kind of lanky, with a mop of blond hair that falls across his face. He's got on his finest robes—or at least robes that look even more fancy and uncomfortable than ours—but other than that he doesn't really look like a high priest. Missing from around his neck is the pair of flint stones that the Fathers wear. He's also much younger than I expected. I knew he was a former pupil of Father Moors, but I didn't realize how recently that must have been. He looks a decade older than me, if that, and I can't help wondering how he got to his position so young.

His gaze runs across the acolytes, pausing on me. He must know who I am because a smile passes over his lips, just for a moment. It's so brief that I wonder if maybe I imagined it. But the feeling of dread it stirs up is real and lingers, prickling in my stomach, even after he's turned his gaze away.

"High Priest Endeil," Father Moors says, bowing his head. "Welcome back to our humble Church of the Sacred Flame."

"Welcome," the rest of the Fathers and Mothers repeat.

The High Priest purses his lips as he silently surveys the rest of the chapel. "The honor is all mine. It's good to be back."

"Please," Mother Hart says, gesturing toward the simple hearth at the end of the aisle, "grace us with your most esteemed gift. Call upon the Fire."

He nods and proceeds solemnly down the threadbare, faded red carpet, until he reaches the hearth. He kneels in front of it, saying the ritual phrase, "Let the Fire's light conquer the darkness of the Chasm once more," and then I understand why he doesn't have the flints around his neck. He doesn't need them. Flame bursts to life in his hands and in an instant spreads not just to the kindling—which one of the first-year acolytes must have been up before dawn painstakingly preparing—but to the logs underneath. It's a rare gift, one that marks him for greatness, a favorite of the Fire. I've never seen a flame take that fast. I'm a little bit in awe, at least until he turns around. There's an arrogant grin on his face, as if he's waiting for us to ooh and aah in admiration, and he's ready to eat it all up. Everyone gapes in wide-eyed amazement at the miracle he's just performed. Everyone except me, because I refuse to give him the satisfaction.

My left arm aches. I start to rub it, then realize it hurts right where my scar is.

"The Fire favors us!" the High Priest says, raising his arms toward the vaulted ceiling. It's part of the fire-lighting ritual, but the familiar words sound cheap coming from him. There couldn't have been any doubt that the flames would take. It's a lot easier to get a fire going when you're using magic. "Now, let me see how your new trainees measure up." He looks at Father Moors, who nods. Something passes between them, some kind of understanding, but I have no way of knowing what it is. "I may be in need of an apprentice, and where better to find one than at my old stomping grounds?"

He barely glances at the girls, as if he already knows he won't find what he's looking for among them, focusing on our lineup instead. He holds up a hand and lets bright flames appear in his palm, scrutinizing each one of us in their light. As if he's communing with the Fire itself to judge us.

I scratch at the scar on my arm, telling myself it's because of my robe. It's rough and itchy, especially on newly healed skin. It's not because I'm worrying about what happened last night, or about the fact that I have another missing chunk from my memory, even if it's only a few hours, not thirteen years.

And it's not because I'm debating whether or not to meet this wizard tomorrow. The answer to that is a given.

I'm going. I have to. Even if it means—

"This one looks guilty." The High Priest is peering into my eyes, the flames in his hand illuminating his face and casting shadows in all the wrong places. His eyes look sunken and his cheeks hollow, like a grinning skeleton considering which one of us to eat first. When he says one of us looks guilty, I think he's talking about himself, and then I realize he means *me*.

Of course he does.

Soft laughter echoes throughout the room as the people who think they know me express their disbelief. Except Rathe, who tries to subtly make eye contact and elbow me without the High Priest noticing.

"That's the acolyte I've been telling you about," Father Moors says, clearing his throat. "The one favored by the Fire."

A few of my fellow acolytes glare at me. As if I actually want the creepy High Priest to notice me. Or as if I actually believe for a minute that the Fire favors me.

"Ah, yes." The High Priest glances at the knife at my waist, like he's just now making the connection. But I saw the way he looked at me when he first came in. He *knew* who I was and the secret I keep. "Tell me," he says, "do you have anything to confess? A guilty conscience, perhaps?" There's an edge to his voice, and every muscle in my body goes tense. A smug smile slides across his face, reminding me of a cat with a mouse in its clutches, watching it panic as it knows it's caught. That it will never break free.

He's toying with me. As if my life is a game to him. My insides squirm, and I feel the overwhelming urge to *run*. But I don't.

"High Priest Endeil—" Father Moors starts, but the High Priest interrupts him.

"Let the boy speak."

And suddenly it feels like the whole room is holding its breath, even though only a moment ago everyone was laughing at the idea of me being anything but a saint. If he's come to expose me, he's not wasting any time, and I wonder if he'll really do it.

I grit my teeth and tell myself he *won't*. He just wants me to know that he could. Or at least that's the hope I cling to as I stand in my finest, itchiest robes, under the whole church's scrutiny.

I look the High Priest right in the eyes as I answer him. "I serve the Fire and the Church of the Sacred Flame. I have nothing to feel guilty for."

I've killed only wizards, and each of them deserved it.

Understanding flashes in High Priest Endeil's eyes. A pleased smile replaces the sinister one, and I find myself equally proud and sickened that I've done anything to gain his approval.

"Good," he says, and then, just like that, he moves on to the next in line.

CHAPTER FOUR

I'm in the middle of getting changed when my door flings open and Leora storms in. "Az, did you hear? It's all over, everyone's talking about it, and—" She blinks, suddenly noticing I'm only in my underwear. "Whoa. Az, what are you *doing*?!"

"Me? What am *I* doing? I'm trying to get dressed!" I'm not wearing my formal robes any longer than I have to. Father Moors might have wanted me to dress up for the High Priest this morning, but he didn't say anything about what I had to wear after that.

"Yeah, but here? Now?"

"This is my room!"

"You knew I was coming over after my morning classes, remember?"

"And *you* knew I wasn't there, on account of the High Priest's visit." News of him coming here must be all over the church and the school by now. "It's not my fault Father Moors made us dress up. Not that I should have to apologize for changing my clothes in my own room."

It dawns on her that she's gaping at me, and she bites her lip and looks down. Then she seems to think better of where she's looking and glances away, her whole face turning red enough to match the robes I'm not wearing.

The door opens, just missing hitting Leora, and Rathe steps in. He's still got his dress robes on, though his hair is back to normal: messy and all over the place. "Az, I—" He stops when he sees me standing there in my underwear, with Leora in the room. "Er, are you two finally . . . *you know*?"

"Rathe!" A little late, I grab my dress robes off the floor and hold them in front of me.

"Sorry, Az. Didn't mean to interrupt."

"It's not what you think," Leora tells him.

"Riiight. I was just going to ask if you had any clean robes I could borrow. Letton got gravy on my last good set. But I can see I've come to the wrong place if I want anything that's not *dirty*."

Fire take me. "Will you shut up and get out of here?" I grab my pillow off the bed and throw it at him.

He moves to the side just in time to not get hit in the face. "All right, all right! I'm going." He laughs. Then, from behind Leora so she can't see, he mouths, *We'll talk later*, before slipping out the door.

"Sorry," I mutter, because I'm not sure what else to say. "He's . . . He was just kidding."

Leora smooths down the sides of her ash-gray skirt, like she doesn't know what to do with her hands. "Just hurry up and get your clothes on. I have to tell you what I heard. It's *horrible*."

"You can tell me while I get dressed. Just . . . you know. Look over there or something." I gesture toward the bookshelf in the far corner. It's short, hardly taller than my nightstand, and doesn't hold that much, so that I had to start piling more volumes on top of it. I only have one bookend—an ugly rock with sparkling purple crystals inside it—and it doesn't do much to keep the books from toppling down to the floor. That's going to be even more demerits during room inspection.

"Okay, well," Leora says, "everyone's talking about it. It's an outrage."

"What is?"

"This new royal decree! The king and queen have officially sided with the wizards. To do this to the Church . . . it's beyond insulting!"

Like I said before, the Fire doesn't grant powers to wizards. They have to steal their magic from the life forces around them, sucking them dry. Something the Fire doesn't approve of. And the king and queen are ordinary people with gifts from the Fire— they're no wizards—so them siding with those blue-robed bastards feels like a betrayal. Especially since the wizards aren't known for their kind treatment of people they see as beneath them, which would be pretty much everyone.

"I can't believe them," Leora says. "Now they're fully backing the High Guild and giving them more seats in court."

"Great. That's *exactly* what the wizards need—more power over everyone."

"They've got the majority now—it's overwhelming. And that's not the worst of it. They're giving them authority over the Church! They have permission to search Church grounds at any time. Not just the chapel, but the school, too. Can you believe that, Az?!" She turns toward me, forgetting she's not supposed to look.

"Leora!"

"Oops. Sorry. I just got carried away."

"And what do you mean they can search Church grounds? What do they think they're going to find?" I remember the wizards asking about stolen guild property. They can't think they're going to find it stashed away in some church, can they? It's bad enough that the king and queen gave them permission to search people's homes. If they're letting them into the church, too, then they're pretty much giving the wizards free rein. As if they don't care what happens to the citizens they're supposed to protect. I wonder how much of the stolen property the wizards confiscate ends up in the royal coffers.

"Oh, you didn't even hear the worst part yet. And what's taking you so long, anyway? You put a robe over your head and you're done."

"I have to find it first." My blankets are still tangled up on the floor, and there are dirty clothes everywhere. I don't have any clean robes to put on—Rathe would have been out of luck even if he hadn't walked in on us—and somewhere in this mess is my usual, more comfortable set. But what I'm really looking for is my bloody shirt from last night, so I can hide it before she notices and starts asking questions I can't answer.

"Well, anyway, the wizards are saying it's the Church." Her voice gets a little quiet, more serious. "You know how someone's been . . . How the wizards have been— *Oh.*" She gasps, putting a hand over her mouth. Her jaw trembles, and then she marches over to me and grabs my left arm. "What is *this*?!"

"*Nothing.* I thought you were going to give me some privacy?!"

"Why? So I wouldn't see the horrible scar on your arm?!" She stares at the white line on my forearm, one hand gripping my wrist, like she's afraid I might flee at any moment.

And I might. I want to. Even though it's *her*, and my skin tingles where she's touching me, and part of me wants her to never let go. But my heart is pounding, and the back of my neck prickles with sweat, and I don't care if she sees me naked—I just don't want her to see this.

"It's not so bad," I mutter. "It's hardly even there."

She's shaking her head. "Fire take you, it's over a vein. There would have been a lot of blood. So much, and . . . This wound matches the shape of your *knife*, Az. And I've never seen it before."

"You don't know about all my scars."

"Oh, yeah? You have one on your ankle from that time you fell two years ago, when you were climbing that apple tree behind the school."

"When you *dared me*, you mean."

"And then there's all the ones from before I knew you, like the one on your shoulder. And the little lines that run across your stomach. And then there are the scars on your wrists."

"No. There aren't any on my wrists. You know about all the ones under my clothes, but my wrists? You get those wrong? I know where *your* mind has been."

Concern fills her eyes. "Maybe they're not normal scars, but the tops of your wrists . . . they're darker, like . . . like from a rug burn that never quite healed."

I shake my head. "I don't know what you're talking about."

"Don't tell me you never noticed." She tightens her grip on my arm, digging her fingers into me, and it's all I can do not to jerk away from her.

"Because there's nothing *to* notice. There isn't. It's my body. I would know."

"Az, look at them. Look at them and tell me you don't see it!"

"I *don't*."

"You're not even looking!" She pulls my arm up, holding it out and making me look, so I can't *not* see the slightly darkened band that mars my skin. She's right—it looks like a rug burn, like it got really roughed up and then never healed all the way. I'm not sure what scares me the most, the fact that it's there or that it never registered before.

I don't say anything—I just gape at my own arm in horror. I hate the way my head is spinning, and the way my insides feel jumbled, as if I'm falling. As if someone pulled the ground out from under me.

"It could be anything," I tell her, and even to my own ears I sound desperate, panicked. "A birthmark or something. It's just *like that*. It always has been." It's barely there, the darkness. I never noticed it because it's nothing. It doesn't mean anything.

But if it doesn't mean anything, then why does looking at it make me want to throw up?

"So, how do you explain the identical mark on your other arm?" Leora asks. "And your ankles. You have the same thing around your ankles."

I have to close my eyes, so I don't see. So I don't look down at my feet and see that she's right about that, too.

"You didn't not know, Az. *I* knew. There's no way you didn't." There's a waver in Leora's voice, a tremor of fear that mirrors my own. "This whole time I've known you, I thought you just didn't want to talk about it. Chasm take you, how could you not have seen?"

"I saw," I lie. "Of course I saw."

But I can tell that neither of us believes it.

Leora's quiet for a while, and then she says, "What about the scar on your arm? I *know* you, and that wasn't always there. Something awful happened, and you kept it from me. I thought we told each other everything."

"It was nothing. Just an accident. I didn't want you to worry about me."

"Yeah, right."

"It looks worse than it was. I mean, seriously, Leora. If I'd hurt myself *that* badly, do you think I could have hidden it from you?"

She sucks in a deep breath, thinking that over, then lets it out slowly. "You're right—you're a terrible liar. And you're kind of a baby when you get hurt. Like when you fell from that tree, I could tell you were crying."

"I was not." But I grin at her, glad that she's teasing me instead of getting mad.

"Whatever." She rolls her eyes and punches me in the shoulder. "And get dressed already. You think I like seeing you in your underwear?"

I can hope.

But I keep that thought to myself. Instead I sigh and scan the floor, catching sight of a scrap of red peeking out from under the bed. I grab my robe and pull it on, then reach for my belt. I hesitate before buckling it, considering leaving the knife behind. But of course I'm bringing it. My hands are already shaking, wanting to touch it so badly. To feel its fire in my head and to forget about the scars on my wrists and my ankles, and the fact that I never noticed them. That even thinking about them fills me with a raw, primal terror I've never felt before.

I don't want to think about them or how I got the scar on my arm.

And I especially don't want to think about Leora seeing me almost naked and not caring. Or saying she doesn't.

Because she might have been right about the scars, but she was wrong about one thing. We don't tell each other *everything*.

One of us is a murderer in love with his best friend.

One of us has secrets to keep.

———

There's a trapdoor in a closet behind the chapel that leads down to the basement. The Fathers and Mothers keep it locked, and no one is supposed to open it. Ever. But a locked door can't stop Leora, and ever since the Fire deemed her worthy and granted her its gift, exploring forbidden places has become our favorite hobby.

It's dark down here in the church basement, the only light the single candle I'm holding. My heart races from the thrill of trespassing on forbidden ground. Of digging up other people's secrets instead of worrying about my own.

"And over to your left you'll see a, um, thing. That they used to do stuff with." Leora waves her arm toward what looks like an old iron stove, her voice echoing throughout the mostly empty room.

"Some tour guide you are."

"If someone would hold the candle better, then maybe I could *see*. This used to be a dungeon, you know."

"In the church?" I glance around, holding out my candle to try and peer into the dark corners of the room. It looks more like a storage cellar to me. There's the dusty stove off to the left that probably hasn't been used in ages, and then there are some shelves along one wall. Nothing looks particularly sinister.

"The Church is apparently full of surprises." She lowers her voice to a whisper, even though no one could possibly hear us. "Like I started to tell you earlier, the king and queen are all pro-wizard now, supposedly because of some scandal. But it's not true. It *can't* be."

"What can't be true? And look, there's a door over there."

"That one must lead to the dungeon." She grins at me and crosses over to it, waiting for me to bring the candle before putting her hand on the knob. She licks her lips and concentrates, and a second later I hear the click of the door unlocking. She makes a big deal of dusting her hands off. "You know how we were talking about wizards and how they've been . . . disappearing?"

Cold air blows through the door as she pushes it open.

"Wizards. Disappearing." *Never heard of it.*

"Come on, don't just stand there. Unless you're afraid?" She locks her arm with mine and pulls me through the doorway. Her fingers graze the scar on my left arm, which aches a little from the wet and the cold.

There's a hallway. Dark and empty, with a dank, musty smell. Our footsteps echo off the stone walls. The light from the candle doesn't reach nearly far enough to see what's at the end of the hall.

"Great," Leora says. "This is just a boring old basement." But she presses closer to me, clinging to my arm and jumping at the slightest noise.

"This is a church, Leora. What did you expect? They don't torture people—what would they have needed a dungeon for?"

"The least they could do is have something *interesting* down here. And I know they don't torture people. They don't murder them, either, but that's what the wizards are saying. That . . ." She pauses and shuts her eyes for a moment, and I know she must be thinking of her father and what might have happened to him. "That members of the Church have been killing them. In cold blood."

I suck in my next breath the wrong way, so that I'm suddenly coughing and choking on my own saliva. "That's crazy." My voice sounds too high-pitched. She's right about me being a terrible liar. But she said *members*, plural. Not one acolyte, not one altar boy with a knife. They don't know it's me.

"Agreed. It sounds more like what wizards would do, not the Church." She moves toward the end of the hall, her footsteps slow and cautious.

"We could turn back," I tell her. "If you want. It's just a regular basement, after all. They probably only keep it locked so couples don't come down here to . . ." I trail off, my face getting warm. "You know." What Rathe thought we were doing earlier.

"Oh, yeah, it's *so* romantic. All this dust and these spiderwebs that keep touching my hair really set the mood. And I'm not turning back—not on your life—so keep walking, Altar Boy."

My tongue feels heavy and too thick, so that it's hard to say the words, but I make myself do it anyway. "So you think the Church is responsible for murdering wizards."

"That's what the wizards are saying. But I can't believe it. I won't."

"Do they know who it is? I mean, who *they* are? Supposedly?"

My stomach twists into a thousand knots. Of course they don't know it's me, because if they did, she wouldn't be down here in this basement with me. She wouldn't be walking arm in arm with a murderer.

"No, because it's not true. And the fact that the wizards are making this claim and they don't even have a suspect makes it all sound even stupider, and—" Leora jumps as there's a skittering sound. "By the Fire, what was *that*? Something just ran across my foot!" She grabs my arm extra tight and presses against me, like I can save her from whatever's lurking in the darkness.

And okay, maybe I can see why couples would come down here. "Probably a rat."

"A *rat*?!"

"Yeah, well, what kind of dungeon doesn't have rats? You're getting the full experience."

She loosens her grip on me. "I think we've established this is just an ordinary, rat-infested basement. The church doesn't have a dungeon, and they're not responsible for killing wizards. That's just . . . It's crazy."

"And if it was true? Ow!" She pinches me, hard, on the arm.

"Why would you even say that? I just go to school here, but *you*, you're wearing red robes and lighting candles every morning. This is your life. If the Church was responsible for murdering wizards, it would mean it was corrupt. So corrupt that the king and queen would be right for . . . By the Fire, they'd actually be right for siding with the wizards, of all people. And we couldn't stay here. Neither of us could be part of something like that."

"Right. Of course not."

"It's a just a cheap ploy by those blue-robed bastards to get the Monarchy on their side."

"The Monarchy was already on their side—they just made it official. The wizards are out there torturing people every night, and I don't see the king and queen doing anything about *that*." I guess if you pay enough taxes, you can get away with anything. The Monarchy must know how the wizards are abusing their authority. Maybe that's the point. Let the wizards keep ordinary, Fire-gifted citizens in a state of perpetual fear and just look the other way. But just because the wizards are hurting people with the king and queen's silent permission doesn't make it right.

We finally reach the end of the hall. There's a door. A wooden door half rotted away.

Leora coughs and covers her nose to block the musty smell. "I opened all the others. It's your turn."

"Oh, I see. You might finally have found your dungeon and you're too scared to open it."

"Only one of us ever mentioned turning back this whole trip, and it wasn't me. You're the one who's scared."

"I didn't say I wanted to turn back. I was offering *you* the chance, since you, you know, seemed kind of terrified."

"You shut up this instant, Altar Boy. I'm not afraid of *anything*."

"Great. Then open the door." I step back, gesturing for her to have at it.

She glares at me, the candlelight flickering across her face. A rat squeaks somewhere behind us. The dust that's settled on my skin starts to itch, and cold air rustles across the stone floor.

Leora might have said she's not afraid of anything, but I watch her steel herself for this. She presses forward, cringing as she puts her hand against the rotting door and pushes it open.

And that's when I run my finger down her spine, and she jumps and screams bloody murder. "Az!" she shouts, whipping around to yell at me as I try not to laugh and fail miserably.

"I thought you weren't scared of anything?"

"Right now *you* should be scared of *me*." She smacks me in the arm a couple times, and I'm laughing so hard I end up dropping the candle.

It rolls past the doorway, into the room, but miraculously doesn't go out. I rush after the candle to save it—it might not be much light, but it's better than having to find our way back in the dark—and as soon as I bend down to grab it, a draft makes the flame flicker, then die.

And in that moment, as I'm plunged into complete and utter darkness, I feel like I'm in another place and another time. I don't know where I am, but I'm not at the church. And despite the fact that there's no light, I see a chair in the middle of the darkened room. A thick, heavy stone chair with straps on the arms and on the base. The kind of straps meant to hold down a person, to capture his hands and feet and keep him there forever.

The scent of blood fills the air, so strong I can taste it. Old, decaying blood that makes bile rise up in my throat. A wave of overwhelming, suffocating fear fills my lungs, replacing the air.

Not just in me, but in the whole room. I want to scream, but I can't. I can't make a sound—I can't even breathe.

Then the candle's flame flickers back to life. I'm on my knees, in an empty room in the church basement. There is no chair. Rat droppings litter the floor, but otherwise, there's nothing here.

I suck in air like I'll never get another chance, and I pick up the candle, careful—so, so careful—not to let it flicker out again.

My other hand goes for the obsidian at my waist. Its fire flows through my veins, purging away all the terror. I let its heat rage inside me, spreading to my head, burning away the image of the chair with its straps. And the thoughts that lurk just beneath the surface—thoughts of the scars on my wrists that I never let myself see before today.

"Az . . . ?" Leora's voice is barely more than a breath, and still it sounds loud and startling. "What just happened?"

She tries to put her hand on my shoulder, but I flinch and feel my stomach twist in on itself at the threat of anyone touching me. I'm on my feet in an instant, and I see her eyes widen at the sight of the knife. *"Don't."* The word is out there, hanging in the air before I can stop myself. It doesn't sound like me. More like a scared, desperate kid. Someone who might totally lose it at any moment.

"Okay," Leora says, taking a step back, her hands out in front of her. "But, Az, you're scaring me."

I laugh. A low, menacing kind of laugh. "I thought you weren't afraid of *anything*?"

A whimpering sound escapes the back of her throat.

I realize I've moved closer to her, forcing her back against the dank and dirty wall, the knife burning so hot in my palm and in my brain that I'm hardly aware of what I'm doing.

I swear under my breath and throw the knife to the ground. My hand starts to shake and I clench my fist hard to keep from reaching for it again. "Fire take me, Leora, I'm sorry. I didn't . . . I would *never* . . ." I move toward her, one hand clutching the candle, the other reaching out to her.

Some of the horror on her face drains away, but she still keeps her distance from me as she scrambles from the wall, not letting me touch her.

My wrists suddenly itch like crazy. I scratch at them, drawing blood, tearing at the skin, but unable to make it stop.

Leora puts her hands to her mouth, watching me with tears in her eyes. Watching me like she's seeing me for the very first time. "Az," she says, one of the tears sliding down her cheek, "what happened to you? When you went into that room . . . ?"

"I saw something. In the dark." I make myself stop scratching, even though the itching hasn't stopped and it's driving me mad. I bend down and grab the knife, hurrying to sheathe it before I can give in to its fire. Even if I want to so very badly. Even if it's the only thing I want, except . . . Except for her. More than anything I want her to stop looking at me like I'm a wild animal. I want to comfort her and tell her everything's all right, even if it isn't.

"You saw something," she says.

"All this dungeon talk must have gotten to me, that's all. Come on." I notice how far down the candle's burned and silently pray to the Fire to keep it lit. Not that it will listen—not to *me*—but I do it anyway, out of habit. "We should get out of here."

"Yeah, sure. This place is giving me the creeps." She hugs herself, rubbing her arms, and walks beside me. Not pressed against me like before, but close enough that our fingers occasionally brush against each other. "But I still want to know what you saw that scared you so much."

I stop and turn toward her, our shadows flickering together in the candlelight, blending so well that it's hard to tell where one of us stops and the other begins. Sharing the same darkness. And in that moment I could tell her. I could hand over a piece of myself and tell her exactly what happened, except . . .

Except how can I, when *I* don't even know?

"It was nothing," I tell her, letting my fingers brush up against hers and linger there. But if it was nothing, I wouldn't have needed the knife. I wouldn't be reliving the shock of horror I felt when I looked into that pitch-black room and saw that chair.

If it was really nothing, it wouldn't be burning me from the inside out, haunting me with every heartbeat. Burrowing into all of my thoughts, lacing them with dread and the sense that something terrible happened.

That it's all going to happen again, and that there's nothing I can do to escape it.

CHAPTER FIVE

That evening, the High Priest approaches me in the chapel while I'm sweeping out the fireplace. We're the only people in the room, so when he says, "I know all about you," I know he's talking to me. Even if I wish he wasn't.

He's been here a day, and I already wish he'd never come at all.

I keep sweeping up the ashes, watching dust particles swirl in the air and pretending I didn't hear him. I remember the hungry way he looked at me, when he accused me of having a guilty conscience. In front of everyone. I don't want to be anywhere near him, least of all *alone* with him.

"I know how Father Moors found you, and I know all about the skill the Fire's given you," he says.

As if he didn't make that perfectly clear before. "I'm trying to do my chores." I scratch the side of my face, then catch a glimpse of how much soot is on my hands.

"You mean 'I'm trying to do my chores, *High Priest Endeil.*' And those are first-year chores, boy. You're not in your first year. I *know*—I remember when Father Moors found you."

Sweeping out the fireplaces is a job usually reserved for new acolytes, but I needed something to take my mind off what happened in the basement. And the fact that I have no idea what happened last night, but I'm supposed to go meet a wizard tomorrow who knows who I am. Who I *really* am.

My worst enemy knows more about me than I do. It was either sweeping up ashes or touching the knife. Getting my obsidian fix is inevitable, but after what happened with Leora, I'm trying to resist. At least for another hour or two. When all the fireplaces are clean, and I have to go back to my room and be alone with my thoughts, then I know I'll give in. I'll choose the darkness, just like that. Just like it's chosen me.

But that's none of High Priest Endeil's business.

"It was three years ago, and I've been keeping up with you ever since. After all, someone with such skill with obsidian gets my attention. So does someone with no memory of where this skill came from."

I don't know what he's getting at, but whatever it is, I don't like it. He's used to getting his way, and he wants something from me. "I have other fireplaces to attend to."

I move to leave, but he grabs my arm, not letting me take another step. Every nerve in my body comes alive, and it doesn't escape me that it's my right arm he's holding, so I can't reach for my obsidian. Not without putting up an obvious struggle.

"It's a tough subject, I'm sure," he says, moving his hand to my shoulder, as if he was just trying to comfort me, not control me.

But my stomach twists in disgust, and I don't believe that for a second. "It is," I say. "And I'd rather not talk about it. High Priest Endeil."

Concern flickers across his face. "You see, Azeril, I would like very much to talk about it. The two of us have a lot in common. The Fire's granted us both very interesting powers. Powers that raise us up above everyone else. The Fire bestows minor gifts on the common person. Farmers, acolytes, the Fathers . . . even the royal family. Those traitors who've sided with the enemy. They have only a hint of the kind of power we have. That has to tell you something. Believe me, Azeril, when I say you're meant for much better things than sweeping out fireplaces."

My shoulder itches where he's touching it. I hate that he used my name, like he knows me. He doesn't. No matter what Father Moors has told him, he doesn't know the first thing about me. "You're wrong. The Fire *didn't* grant me a power—so I guess we don't have anything in common."

"Father Moors told me you'll be sitting out at the ceremony next week. That you think the Fire has ignored you. But I think the reason it hasn't granted you a power is because you already have one. One it must have given you in your past, in the years you can't remember."

I shrug him off and scratch my shoulder. Father Moors told me pretty much the same thing. He believes my ability to control obsidian means the Fire favors me, giving me the power to bring order to the Chasm's chaos. Maybe there's something to that, but . . . I've never been convinced before, and I'm not convinced now. "What's that got to do with anything?"

"You and I both have powers that link us directly with the Fire. It chose us. The ability to wield obsidian without hurting yourself or others is a rare and special gift not to be taken lightly."

I rub my left arm self-consciously, reminding myself that there's no way he could know about my injury.

"You might not remember how you got this ability, but there's only one place it could have come from, and that means the Fire has far from ignored you. In short, we share a common bond. And I want to help you."

"Help me?"

"I can help you with your memory. I can help you get it *back*."

I bite my lip. He's lying. He has to be. "What makes you think I want it?"

"You're missing over a dozen years of your life. *You want it back.* The Fire obviously favors you, and you can't tell me you're not the least bit curious about how that happened."

"Maybe the Fire made me forget. Maybe it's for my own good." The image of the chair flashes through my head.

"I can get your memories back, Azeril. With your cooperation."

I hate that he used my name again. And I can't help it—I take the bait. "How?"

"With the Fire's help, of course." Flame comes to life in his palm, light flickering over his face. His green eyes shine feverishly bright. "The flames can reach the innermost corners of your mind, if you'll let them. If you'll let me. It won't be easy."

He smiles as he says that last part. It's a smile that says whatever he's got in mind is going to *hurt*, and he's going to enjoy every second of it. Maybe he saves this smile just for me, or maybe it's something no one else would notice. But I notice. One monster recognizes another.

"Why?" I ask. My throat feels dry, and my voice comes out a croak. "You don't really know me. Why would you want to . . ." I pause, trying to come up with the right word. I was going to say "Why would you want to *help* me?" but that's not right. I don't believe that he intends to do anything to help. I clear my throat and look him in the eyes, daring him to tell me the truth. Wondering, just for a moment, what it would be like to have my memories back and who it would make me. "Why would you want to do this for me?"

"I know what you're thinking. You already owe me everything—if not for me, you'd be out on the streets, or in prison, if not dead—so how could I possibly have more to give?"

I swallow. That's not what I was thinking at all.

"Even now I could snap my fingers and order you out." He shrugs, as if it would be no big deal.

But it would be a big deal. Of course it would. "There was something in it for you then, just like there must be now."

He touches his fingertips together one by one, pleased with my assessment. "Smart boy. I'd be lying if I said I wasn't dying to know what's inside your head. We could benefit each other. We're both chosen by the Fire, destined for great things, and believe me when I say no one will ever understand you the way I do. But there are more practical reasons. If you're to be my apprentice—"

"I'm not looking for an apprenticeship."

He gestures at the chapel walls surrounding us. "Oh? And what do you think you're doing *here*?"

"I'm cleaning out the fireplace."

High Priest Endeil moves closer and leans in, keeping his voice low, though there's no one else around to hear. "You're better than this. You could be doing so much more than lowly chores that don't even belong to you. You shouldn't be here, covered in soot. I know what you've done in the fight against the wizards. All the secret victories you've accomplished, the body count as you pick off our enemies one by one. You're waging battles, and I'm talking about winning a *war*. The two of us together could be unstoppable. That's why you should be in Newhaven, with me, taking advantage of the gift the Fire has bestowed upon you to its full potential. Something I believe can only be achieved by restoring your memories."

"That's great that you think that, but—"

"You could change the world."

"I don't want to change the world." *Just myself.*

His eyes narrow and his shoulders stiffen. "That choice isn't up to you. Not when you have such a powerful gift. One that could prove very *useful* for my plans."

I could have the knife in my hand and at his throat before he'd have time to react. He'd smell his own skin burning before he'd even know what had happened. I could show him firsthand how useful I am.

And I think about it. About killing the High Priest. My fingers twitch, and something in my gut tells me the world would be a much better place without him in it.

But I grip the broom handle tighter and don't reach for my obsidian. Because if I killed him, it's not like it would stay a secret. Leora would find out what I'd done. And Rathe, who thinks my worst crime is staying out all night, and Tol, who always looks up at me with such wide, innocent eyes. They would all know who I really am then, and that would change the world way too much for me.

High Priest Endeil studies my face. "There's no point in thinking it over. You have no choice."

For a moment, I think he can read my thoughts. He's actually telling me to kill him, before it's too late.

"When I said you'd be my apprentice, I wasn't *asking*. Because you really do owe me everything. And I'm not afraid to collect."

"You're threatening the wrong altar boy."

"The wrong murderer, you mean? You and I may see your actions as justified, but I wonder if anyone else would see it that way. Your friends must think they know you so well. And that girl Father Moors says you're always with—"

"You leave Leora out of this." My hand shakes with the effort of keeping my fingers off the knife. "If you touch her, I'll kill you."

"And somehow I think *my* death wouldn't go unnoticed in the eyes of the Church. You'd be caught. Tell me, do you think she'd still care about you if she knew the truth? Do you think she could ever *love* you?"

"I don't have anything you want. I can use obsidian and that's it. I'm no chosen one."

"There's only one way to find out, now, isn't there? You have twenty-four hours to make your *choice*. I suggest you make the right one, if you know what's good for you."

"You can't bully me into being your apprentice."

"Well." A grin lights up his face. "There's only one way to find that out, too."

CHAPTER SIX

Leora sits next to me at the edge of the pond and studies her reflection. The pond is on the far side of the church, meaning it's well away from the school, where we're supposed to be right now, learning about how wizard magic is unholy and evil. In case any students were thinking about defecting, now that the High Guild ranks above the Church.

But it's not like either me or Leora needs reminding how awful wizards are. Skipping one class won't hurt. And the pond is secluded enough, hidden by a willow tree, that we're not likely to get caught.

Leora smirks and sticks her tongue out, watching her reflection do the same.

I look at myself in the water. A dark-haired boy in red robes with green eyes. I stick my tongue out, too, copying Leora, but my heart's not in it. I can't stop thinking about what the High Priest said to me last night. "You know, Leora, if . . . if something *happens* to me . . . I mean, if something ever happened and I had to . . . I want you to know how important you've been to me. Are, I mean."

She picks a blade of grass and tears it into strips. "Where did that come from? By the Fire, you make it sound like you're about to keel over."

"You know, you invoke the Fire an awful lot for someone going to a school run by the Church."

"Chasm take you, you can't just confess something like that and then change the subject!"

"So now you're calling on the Chasm? And it wasn't meant to be a confession. I mean, you should know that I . . ." My ears are starting to burn, and I wish she'd stop staring at me, making this more difficult than it already is. "It's always been me and you, since I first got here. Nobody else would even talk to me back then, but you came right up to me and told me we were going to be friends. I don't know who I'd be without you." Except I do. Because without her I wouldn't have the version of me that she sees. I wouldn't even know that person exists. Then I'd only be the murderer, the wizard killer, the Church's secret attack dog.

"Az." Leora grabs my hands, digging her thumbs hard into my palms. "Is this about yesterday? About what happened in the basement? Because I know something bad must have happened to you, before I met you. I mean, there are all those scars, and then . . . But all of that's in the past, whatever it was. You don't even *remember*, so don't talk about it like it's not over, like something else is going to happen."

"But if it did. I wouldn't want to go without telling you how much I—"

"*Go? Go where?*"

"Nowhere. I just meant—"

"If you're not going anywhere, then why does this sound like a good-bye? Are *you* dying? Because you're making it sound as if . . . Damn it, Az! There can't be something wrong with you. You can't be dying. Because if you are, I'll kill you."

"I'm not dying! I swear."

"Good. But something's up. Otherwise you wouldn't have said that. Come on, spill it. You can tell me."

"I was just thinking about when I first came here. How easily I could have ended up on the street and never met you. I could still end up there, if the Church decided to kick me out. And now the High Priest wants me to be his apprentice. He wants me to go back to Newhaven with him."

"Wow." Leora blinks. Her mouth slips open, and she just stares at me. "That's . . . great." Her shoulders slump, and she tears up some more grass, any remnants of her good mood going sour. "So you *are* leaving."

"I didn't say that."

"Who am I supposed to talk to when you're gone?"

"I'm not going. And anyway, it's not like you don't have other friends."

"Not like you. Not that I can *talk* to. Everyone knows my father's a wizard. It was bad enough before, but now that the High Guild has free rein . . . I've seen the way everyone looks at me, like I don't belong here. And I get it—I really do. My father's a wizard, but I go to school *here*, of all places, and he pays for it? Because we both want to be as distanced from each other as possible? It's not your average situation. And it's obvious he hates me—"

"Leora—"

"—and I hate him. But it still hurts when he doesn't write."

"He can't hate you. He doesn't have to pay for you to be here. He could have said no."

"So maybe he felt guilty for abandoning me with my mother. For not even coming to her funeral. But that isn't the same as caring about me." She pauses. "I had friends before, you know. Lina and Mel. Years ago, when I first started going here, but we were close. Then they found out about my father. Things got weird after that. They didn't trust me anymore—they didn't *get* me. But you do, Az. You know what he is and where I come from. You hate wizards more than anyone I know, but you didn't hesitate to become my friend. And you get how I can hate him and still worry about him. Everybody leaves—my dad, my mom, my friends, and now you—but it doesn't mean I stop caring about them."

"I'm not going anywhere, Leora. I promise."

She shakes her head. "The High Priest wants you to be his apprentice. That's huge. You can't turn that down."

"I don't *want* to be his apprentice." But I don't want to be out on the streets, either, and the High Priest could make that happen if I don't do what he says.

"But you're talking like you're not going to be around anymore. So you're considering it." She gets to her feet, like she's heard enough.

I get up, too, not wanting her to go. "Maybe, but not because I want to. Only because—" I want to tell her this wasn't my idea, that it's the last thing I want to do. That the High Priest creeps me out and I'd rather be an altar boy for the rest of my life than ever sign up with him. But telling her that might lead to more questions. And I don't want Leora thinking I'd ever choose to leave her, but letting her believe that is better than telling her the truth.

Maybe Endeil is right. Maybe she could never love me. How could she? You have to know someone to love them, and she can never find out who I *really* am.

"You can admit it," she says. "If you want to go. I'll understand." But the way her mouth turns down and the way she kicks a rock into the pond say otherwise.

I should lie and tell her I want to go, that this is some wonderful opportunity for me. I *should*, but I can't. "I don't want to go, Leora. I don't want to leave you, and— I might have to, anyway. I'm a ward of the Church, so it's their call." Not a lie exactly. It's the truth. I just left out all the interesting parts. "But it's my life. They can't *make* me go."

"And what? You're going to give up everything and get kicked out over this? I'd never see you either way. I don't know what I'd do if I lost you, Az."

"You won't. Maybe everyone else left, but not me."

"Don't do anything stupid. I'd rather you moved to the capital than see you end up on the streets."

"I won't let him take me away from you. I won't let his stupid offer tear us apart."

She moves in close, studying my face. There's a heat between us that I know I'm not imagining. Her lips part just a little, and I think we're going to kiss. I tilt my head, slowly closing the gap between us. My insides squirm with anticipation and fear and everything in between. I don't know how long I've waited for this. I don't know how long there's been this hollow ache in my chest whenever we're apart, and now—

Now Leora shoves me, and I stumble backward. There's a confused moment where I don't know what's happening. And then there's the splash and the overwhelming shock of cold as I hit the water. I break the surface and sputter, flailing my arms and kicking my legs.

"What was *that* for?!"

The heaviness of our conversation still hangs in the air, but now she has a playful smile on her lips. "That's for thinking anything could *ever* tear us apart."

CHAPTER SEVEN

I consider not going to the Silver Hound that night. I change out of my red robes—I'd never even get through the door dressed as an altar boy, never mind make it home again—and into plain black clothes and a long, dark leather jacket that hides the obsidian at my waist. Even then, I have to take a deep breath and steel myself. For the thousandth time, I think about not going. There's no guarantee I'll find any answers tonight. And maybe answers are overrated. But a wizard knows my name. He knows who I am, and I have to find out why.

Even if it means going alone into wizard territory. I can't take anyone with me, and I can't even tell anyone I'm going. Not even Father Moors. What would he say if he knew I was meeting a wizard tonight? One who knows who I am, or at least who I was? Father Moors would get that line between his eyebrows, the one that means he disapproves, and then I'd remember all the reasons why this is a bad idea.

The Silver Hound is across town, and Rathe is right—it's not somewhere anyone decent would ever go. I'm not exactly what most people would call a decent person. But still, I don't make a habit of visiting seedy taverns crawling with wizards, and even now, after coming all this way, I hesitate before going in. The windows are steamed, and the light is dim, giving the place an eerie glow. But even through the haze, I can make out the blurry shapes of blue robes everywhere. From the looks of it, there's hardly room for one more person to squeeze through the door.

Not for the first time, I consider that this might be a trap. I have no idea what I'm walking into.

A tall iron gas lamp lights the cobbled street, and I instinctively step out of the circle of light and into the darkness. My palms start to sweat, and my fingers twitch, already slipping inside my coat, reaching for my knife. But I stop myself. I need a clear head for this. And if I'm going to panic this early in the game, I might as well turn around and go home.

The stink of wizards hits me as I open the door—dried herbs and sour sweat. I force myself not to gag.

Several wizards turn to look at me, their gazes scrutinizing. I remind myself they don't know who or what I am—they can't—other than that it's obvious I don't belong.

Some of them sneer and go back to their drinks, and some continue to stare as I make my way through the packed room, scanning for the wizard who called me here. I worry for a second that I won't be able to recognize him. They all look the same, all wearing the same shade of medium blue. The same blue that would stick out like a sore thumb in the church, and here there's a sea of it. But then I spot him—balding, with short reddish-brown hair and a well-trimmed beard—at a little round table in the corner, in the shadows, and I realize there's no way I wouldn't have known him.

The image of him mouthing my name, with recognition sparking in his eyes, is burned into my memory.

He scowls at me as I sit down. "You couldn't have covered that up?"

At first I think he means my knife, which I *did* cover up, but his eyes are on the tattoo at my wrist, not quite hidden by my sleeve. It's hot in here, and I'm already sweating, but I have no intentions of taking off my jacket. I place my palm on the table. My fingers curl into a fist. "No one will see."

He looks skeptical, but he picks up his half-finished drink and doesn't argue with me. I look him over, noting the five symbols sewn in gold along the collar of his robe. They're a mixture of dots and half circles, all tilted different directions. They must mean something, but I have no idea what.

I jump as someone accidentally backs into me, their beer sloshing to the floor. Every nerve in my body flares to life, my muscles tense. This place is so busy, even the corner table isn't secluded. My back is to the rest of the room, and I feel like I'm out in the open. Vulnerable. Maybe they don't know it, but everyone here should want to kill me. I glance at the wizard and nod at his seat. "Trade me places."

"Some things never change," he mutters, but he gets up and switches with me.

I feel better with my back to the wall. Not a lot, but enough.

"I suppose I shouldn't complain," he says, so quietly I almost don't catch it. "It's my fault, after all."

"What?"

"Nothing." He shakes his head. "You know, Azeril, for what it's worth, it's good to see you again." He sighs. "Despite everything that's happened between us, you could have come to me, you know. I realize I'm probably the last person you'd think that of, but I would have taken care of you."

He doesn't know that I don't remember anything. I swallow and try to look like I know what he's talking about. "Like you did the other night?" I hold up my left arm. Something bubbles up inside of me, a feeling of actual gratitude, for a *wizard*. Father Moors would flay me alive if he knew and tell me how foolish it was for me to come here tonight. How I'm risking both of our necks. "Thanks," I say, not looking at him and not liking the sincerity in my voice.

The wizard frowns at me, his forehead wrinkling in an unasked question. I get the impression that this was the wrong thing to say, but I don't know why, and I can't ask without raising his suspicions even more.

"You should have come to me, instead of taking it upon yourself to . . ." He lets his words trail off, remembering where we are.

I fidget with the edge of my sleeve, peering at the tattoo on my wrist. I said I'd keep it covered, but I can't help tracing the spiral shape with my finger. "And what would you have done if I had?" I sound nervous. Great killer, terrible liar, that's me. I feel like I have the words "doesn't know anything" scrawled across my forehead.

But if it's obvious I'm fishing for information, he doesn't notice. Yet. "What would I have *done*?" He clenches his fist, slamming it on the table. "For one thing," he growls, "I would have kept you from acting like an idiot. You think I don't know what you've been up to? That you've been parading yourself around town, practically begging to get caught? You *did* get caught, and if it had been anyone else—*anyone else* besides me—where in the Chasm do you think you'd be right now?!" His voice rises and his face reddens. I've never seen someone so angry—at least, not with me. "*Well?!* Answer me!"

My mouth slips open, not expecting this. Sweat drips down my back, soaking into my shirt. It's too hot in here, way too hot, and I don't know what I'm supposed to say. "I had to do something. People were getting hurt."

Rage flares in his eyes, but it's the silent calm that comes over him—the fact that he stops yelling and sits unmoving, his nostrils flaring in and out—that unnerves me. I feel small, like the time Father Gratch said I cheated on a test and told me I was going to get kicked out and be back on the street. I didn't cheat. It was a history test, and I knew the answers—they just came to me, like the way I knew my name even when I didn't know anything else about myself. I was new. I had no idea that wasn't how it was supposed to work. Father Moors convinced him I didn't know any better and not to say anything to the Academic Council. But Father Moors still believed I'd cheated, even if he thought I didn't know better, and that made me feel like my insides were shriveling.

The way this wizard looks at me now, like I've done something unimaginably *wrong*, I feel like that again.

"Don't lie to me," he says, leaning across the table, keeping his voice low. "You liked killing them. You knew they were looking for you, and you knew what would happen if they found you, but you *liked* watching their faces twist in horror as you ended their lives. And don't look at me like that, like you're surprised. I *know* you, Azeril. So don't sit there and lie to me."

My stomach plummets. They were looking for me. All those wizards I killed, all those people they hurt . . .

The wizards were searching for *me*. And I realize that paper he wrote the note to me on . . . it was the same paper he showed those people, asking if they recognized the symbol. The same symbol I have on my wrist.

I'm no one. A boy without a past who's good with a knife. But wizards don't need knives. That's what spells are for. So why would they have cared about me? All this time, I thought no one was looking for me.

I was dead wrong.

But why drag people out of their homes? Why the interrogations? They always asked them about stolen property. Maybe that's their way of saying kidnapped.

I think of my first memory, of the wizards lying dead around me, the knife bloody and burning in my hand. Father Moors said it was self-defense. I remember the fear I felt, the overwhelming terror over what I'd done, and I'd wanted to believe him. But I remember the giddy satisfaction over killing them, too, and that doesn't exactly scream innocence.

My arms start shaking. I sit on my hands, trying to keep still, or at least to keep the wizard from seeing. This wizard who knows my darkest secret—that I kill people. That I like it.

This was a bad idea.

I think about bolting and getting out of here. But I glare at him instead. "You don't know *anything* about me."

"Oh, please," the wizard says, rolling his eyes. "It's only been three years. Did you really think I wouldn't remember? Who do you think *made* you? I might be getting older, but I'm not senile."

Made me? "You brought me home the other night. If you were really searching for me, why did you let me go?" If he knows I'm a monster, if he knows who I am inside, why am I still here?

"My dear boy, I did *not* bring you home. Though," he adds, giving me a stern look, "perhaps I should have. Perhaps it was foolish of me to leave you on your own. But you insisted, and the bleeding had stopped, so I slipped you that note and left."

There's an edge of concern buried under his sarcasm. "You healed me, and then you let me go . . ."

He scowls. "Who do you think I am?"

I have no idea.

"I'm no miracle worker." He snorts, shaking his head. "And I didn't invite you here to be mocked."

So he didn't heal me. But if he didn't, then who did? "But you let me go. And then what, you told the wizards that the Church is responsible for killing them? You didn't tell them my name. You could have, but—"

"That wasn't me." He clears his throat, his lip curling a little as he says, "I didn't even know you were with the Church. But I suppose I should have. After everything that's happened . . . Of course that's where you were. If any one of us stepped foot on the grounds, they'd raise the alarm. It must have seemed like the safer of two evils."

I ignore that last remark. I pull my hands out from under me, too fidgety to keep still. "If it wasn't you who told, then who was it?"

"I didn't see the message myself—it arrived while I was here—but an anonymous letter showed up at headquarters in Newhaven. Anonymous, but sealed with the Church's very own insignia." He pauses, leaving his silent implication hanging in the air. *It was an inside job.*

Someone betrayed us.

I don't know if I should believe him. Even if he didn't turn me in, that doesn't mean I trust him. And he just said he didn't even see this supposed letter sealed with the Church insignia. It could have been a fake. It might not exist at all—just something the wizards made up to discredit the Church even more. And why would anyone in red robes sell out our order to the wizards? And to do it anonymously, without even asking for anything in return? It doesn't add up.

But I believe it wasn't him, so I let it go. "If you were looking for me, why didn't you . . . ?"

"Why didn't I what? Capture you? Turn you in to *them*?" Hurt flashes across his face. "Maybe for the same reason you didn't kill me. You swore once that you would, but you didn't. Not then and not now."

"Maybe next time."

He smirks, a grim smile tugging on one side of his mouth. "She would like you, I think."

"Who?"

"No one."

"My mother?"

"For the Fire's sake . . ." He leans forward, peering into my eyes. "Well, your pupils aren't dilated." He glances down at the table, like he can't remember what I was drinking. He seems surprised to find that the only glass there is his.

"I'm not *on* anything."

"You could have fooled me. Your *mother*. Honestly."

My mouth feels dry. I lick my lips, terrified to ask my next question. "Knowing who I am—who I *really* am—how could you let me go?"

"Ah." He picks up his glass, even though it was empty a long time ago, and drains the last few drops. He holds it over his mouth, waiting for them to fall. It takes impossibly long.

"While I'm around . . . people are in danger." It hurts to say the words, and yet I'm relieved to finally admit it.

"Yes, well. Call it arrogance. Call it sentimentality."

"I don't understand."

"We grow attached to our creations, our projects, our legacies. Especially as we get older. Maybe someday that will make sense to you."

Creations. Projects. Legacies. Which one am I? "I'm dangerous." I trace a knothole in the wood with my finger, pretending to be fascinated by it so I don't have to look at him. "I hurt people, and you know I like it."

"But that was always the *point*, wasn't it?" He says it like he's talking to someone else, someone who's not in the room. He rubs his forehead. Then his eyes flick to mine. "It's my fault. It's my fault you turned out how you did, and who would I be if I condemned you for it? How could I, when I'm the one who made you that way?"

I could have been normal. Innocent. Who knows who I was before he . . . before he did whatever he did. "Who was I before that?" The questions burn in my throat, as if my body, my flesh, is telling me not to ask them. "Who was I before I was a killer?"

He laughs. The most serious question I've ever asked anyone, and he laughs in my face. "You were *no one*."

My insides feel like they're being torn apart. He thinks this is some kind of joke. "Being a killer makes me *someone*, is that it?" I spit the words out, the edges of my fingernails digging into my palms.

"We both know it's what you live for."

That's it. I'm out of here. I can't process this—all I can do is escape. I push away from the table. My chair tips over and clatters to the floor, and then I'm pushing through the crowd, searching for an easy way out. There isn't one. This place is packed.

"Azeril, wait!" the wizard calls out. He sounds desperate, pleading.

I barely hear him. The room spins, full of wizards. Laughing, talking, plotting. I feel like I'm drowning, like there isn't any air in here and I'm going to suffocate if I don't get out.

My elbow collides with someone to my right, and I hear a waitress cry out in surprise and then the crash and slosh of full glasses hitting the floor. The smell of spilled alcohol fills the room, adding to the salty stench of so many bodies in one place. I keep my arms in front of me, shoving people out of the way, because it's the only thing I can do to keep my hands off the knife.

A tall wizard grabs my wrist, wrenching me from my path to the door. "Watch it, kid! You think you can push me around?"

"Don't. Touch. Me." My voice shakes from the effort of holding still, of not reaching for my obsidian. If I do, he'll be dead, but in a room full of wizards, so will I. And yet it's like I can't stop. Fear floods my veins and fights all my rational thoughts. Fear and addiction and something else, urging me to strike.

The tall wizard tightens his grip, his fingers pressing into my wrist so hard, there's going to be a bruise. His thumb digs into my tattoo, the one no one here is supposed to see.

"You think you're something, don't you? Coming in here, where you don't belong." He wrenches my arm and shoves me in the chest with his other hand. "Don't touch you?" A cruel grin creeps across his face. *"Make me."*

Something inside me snaps. My mind flashes to the image of that dark room. I'm in the chair this time. Leather straps bite into my ankles and my wrists, holding me down. Breaking me. I'm screaming, my throat raw and torn, but no one cares. I'm drowning in waves of fear, in a horror so strong, it stabs through my chest, threatening to stop my heart. I blink and the image is gone, but the mind-numbing terror isn't. I can't fight it, I'm going to kill him.

Words I don't know come out of my mouth. They sound like wizard words, like a spell. I'm suddenly aware of everyone in the room, of all these bright sources of energy I could draw from. And I don't know what any of it means or where it's coming from, but I know without a doubt that the tall wizard with his hand on my wrist is going to *hurt*. He's going to be desiccated from the inside out, the water evaporating from his vital organs first, then the rest of him, until he doesn't know anything except pain. Until he's nothing but a dried-up husk.

Then a hand clamps over my mouth. The wizard who brought me here, who knows too much about me. He pushes the other wizard away, breaking our contact and startling me into silence. He lets his hand slide down to grip my shoulder. "He's with me," he says to the tall wizard, his voice icy and not expecting any argument. He tugs on his collar, emphasizing the gold symbols sewn there.

And they must mean something, because the tall wizard's eyes go wide and he takes a step back. "I—I didn't know, sir. I wouldn't have—"

The other wizard holds up a hand, silencing him, and drags me outside.

As soon as we're out the door I suck in air as fast as I can, like I've never breathed before, like I might never get to again. I twist away from the wizard who just saved me, not caring that I knock him back a step.

I fall to my knees on the cobblestones. My eyes water, maybe from gasping for air, maybe from something else.

I feel a hand on my back. Just for a second, and then he pulls it away again. "I'm sorry," the wizard says, sighing. It's a wistful sigh, full of layers of deep regret.

Hadrin. That's his name. It floats to the surface of my mind, instantly familiar, like I've heard it a thousand times. "Hadrin," I whisper, my throat raw, as if I really was screaming.

In a dark room, screaming. Terrified. Losing myself to them.

"I'm here," he says, confirming what I already know.

"You saved my life."

"Yes, well, like last time, I had my reasons."

Last time?

He takes a step back, giving me room to get to my feet, and smooths a few wrinkles from his robes. "Never trust anyone who wants something from you."

"I don't."

"Smart, but I was actually hoping you'd make an exception. Just this once."

"Who do you think you are to me?" I ask, looking him in the eyes and hoping his answer will tell me what I need to know, what I can't ask without giving too much away.

"Someone who desperately needs your help," he says. "Even if he doesn't deserve it."

My fingertips graze the knife.

Heat sparks against my skin and races through my veins. Fire burns my palm as I grab the hilt. It shoots up my arm and spreads through my shoulders, turning my blood to liquid embers. A euphoric fever consumes all my thoughts, turning them to ash and letting them fall away, and for the first time tonight I feel like I'm finally thinking clearly. I didn't come here to kill him. I didn't. But I didn't come here for any of the things that happened tonight.

Hadrin's eyes dart down to the knife, then back up to meet mine. Otherwise he stands perfectly still. This is something he's seen before. Enough to know to be afraid. "Azeril . . ."

The obsidian burns so bad, but it's the best feeling in the world. My thoughts flick to High Priest Endeil and his offer. Maybe I should let him use the Fire on me. Would it be so different?

"There are people here," Hadrin whispers, his voice much calmer than I would have thought possible. "If you use that, someone will see."

"If I kill you, you mean."

"If you use that, they'll know everything about you. You'll go back—"

"*No.*" I cross the distance between us in one quick step. I don't know where "back" is, but I know it involves the dark room and the chair and the straps. Terror eats at my chest like acid, and I know I'll *never* go back there. Not alive. "You want my help. Tell me why you don't deserve it."

He can't look me in the eyes. He tries, but he flinches and has to glance away, and I don't know if it's because of what I've asked him, or because of the heat from the obsidian coursing through my veins, making me look crazed.

"Please," he whispers. "You know why. Don't make me say it."

The door to the Silver Hound opens, and a small group of wizards stumbles into the night. Out of habit, I take a silent step back into the shadows. Hadrin has his chance. He could call to them. He could join them and walk away. But he doesn't. Something holds him back, and I don't know if it's guilt or fear, but I have my suspicions. He doesn't seem like the type to give in to fear.

I wait until we're alone again, the wizards' voices soft, unintelligible echoes down the street, before I bring the blade up to Hadrin's throat. I want to use it so badly—it's all I can think about. I pull the knife back and touch the flat edge to the back of his neck, taking pleasure in the way he winces and cries out. Not enough to alert anyone inside, just enough to expose his terror and pain. Sweat beads on my forehead and slips into my eyes.

"My hand is shaking," I whisper into his ear. "You have seconds to tell me. They'll never hear your scream. And even if they do, I'll be gone by the time anyone comes to check."

"You know my sins." His voice wavers. He sounds like he's on the verge of tears. A grown man, a *wizard*, reduced to this.

I grin. "I want to hear you say them. Confession is the path to deliverance." My arm muscles strain, and my hand twitches, the effort of fighting against the knife's desires almost unbearable. It's not just the knife. Some part of me, deep inside, wants to kill him. The same part that remembered his name, but offers no other hints about who he is. Or who I was.

Am.

"You sound like one of those damned priests."

The knife slips. I can't help it. It's all I can do to keep from slicing his throat open. The edge catches the side of his neck. Not enough to drain him, just enough to draw blood. To smell the burning stench of human flesh. The sight of the blood brings me to my senses, just for a moment. Just long enough that I push him away from me and stumble backward.

He turns toward me, and I'm right, there are tears in his eyes. "It's my fault," he says, holding his hands out, palm up. Seeking forgiveness I already know I can never give. "It's my fault, what they did to you."

"In that dark room, you mean. With the chair and the straps and the pain." With the broken boy who exists in me, somewhere deep inside.

He nods, and the tears streak down his face. "You were mine, my responsibility, and I . . ." He shuts his eyes, drawing in a shuddering breath. "I let them hurt you. Worse than that, I ordered them to. Even afterward, I should have stopped it. I could have, and I didn't. But that was the point of the whole project. The whole damned thing! And I was so . . . I thought my work was all that mattered."

He goes silent, leaving me to take all that in. I don't know what any of it means. I drop the knife to the ground, to break its hold, because I don't have the willpower to sheathe it yet.

"I have confessed," he says, his voice choked. "Am I delivered from my sins?" He laughs, already knowing the answer. "We were going to change the world, and all it would have cost was one innocent boy. One who was made to . . . It wasn't supposed to matter. *You* weren't supposed to matter. I wasn't supposed to *care!*"

All the heat drains from my body. Ice water trickles through my veins. The sudden change leaves me colder than it should, making me shiver. "Now you want something from me. Is that why you were searching? Is that why you tortured innocent people?!"

"When I— When the Guild thought you were stolen from us, we couldn't just let that go. Not with something so valuable. So dangerous. But I won't let them take you again, Azeril." He puts his hand over his chest, where his heart is. And yes, wizards have hearts. I'd be skeptical, except that I've seen enough of them, red and raw and bleeding.

"I don't need you protecting me. I don't need you for anything, so why should I help you?"

"Because the Church isn't the sanctuary you think it is. And because I need a weapon."

I reach down and pick up the knife. I hold it out to him, hilt forward. "You want to borrow mine?"

"Very funny. But you know as well as I do what our best weapon always was."

"You didn't come to borrow this." I sheathe the knife, flickers of regret running through me, and I have to force myself to peel my fingers away from it.

"No, Azeril, I didn't. I came to borrow *you.*"

CHAPTER EIGHT

It's later that night and I'm lying next to Leora, in her bed. It's not what it sounds like.

I wish it was, but it's not.

She was just falling asleep when I arrived. I'm not supposed to be here, at least according to the school and the Church, but if they really cared about stopping late-night visits, they shouldn't have put in windows. And anyway, I don't care what anyone else wants. Not the school, not the Church, and not Hadrin. Leora was glad to see me, and that's all that matters.

We just lie there for a while, her fingers intertwined with mine, neither of us saying anything. There's only the sound of our breathing. I think she's asleep when she startles me, saying, "So, are you ever going to tell me why you're here?"

Because I couldn't be alone. Not with that dark room inside my head. All I got was a flash of it, a scrap of memory brought on by terror, by a *wizard* putting his hands on me, and now I can't stop reliving it. It's a horror lurking in the dark parts of my mind, waiting for me whenever I close my eyes.

It turns out the dark parts are better left unseen. And High Priest Endeil wants to shine a light on them . . .

"Do I have to have a reason?"

She squeezes my hand. "Is this about earlier? Don't tell me he's already making you go."

Her room is dark, except for the fat pillar candle with three wicks on her nightstand. Its light wavers back and forth against the wall. I turn my face away from her. "That's not it."

"So then why did you come here if . . ." Her fingers dig into my shoulder. "Az," she whispers. "Just tell me what's wrong already."

"Nothing. *Ow!*" She pinches my earlobe. I wince and sit up, wriggling out of her grip.

"Don't lie to me. Something was wrong earlier and something's wrong now. And it's not just the High Priest wanting you to be his apprentice. I *know* you."

Not as well as she thinks. Hadrin said almost the same thing, and it turns out he really does know me. Better than Leora does, and I hate him for that. And I hate myself, for the things I can never tell her. I draw my knees toward my chest, wrapping my arms around them. "I can't sleep. That's all. So I'm here, hoping I can stay."

She studies my face, chewing her bottom lip. I can tell she doesn't believe me, but she doesn't say no, either. "You can't be here in the morning, when the dorm mistress makes the rounds for wake-up call."

"But before that?" Now is all that matters. Because right now, I can't handle who I am without her. When I'm with her, I see myself through her eyes. A person, not a monster. Not a weapon. Someone worth caring about.

She nods. Both of us fall silent. And I feel the heat between us again and am suddenly overly aware that we're in her bed together. And I've got her permission to stay. To spend the night with her, and even if it doesn't mean *that*, it does mean something.

The candlelight whispers across her face, caressing the shape of her cheekbone. The end of her nose. Her lips. I can't help reaching out to touch her, to trace the path of the light. My fingertips brush against her skin, heat sparking to life all over me.

She sighs softly. Her hand meets mine and covers it, pressing it to her cheek. "Is this what you came here for?" she asks. "Because it's okay if you did. I thought you never would."

Heat seeps into my chest, the warm ache there spreading through the rest of me, and all I know is I need to be closer to her. Closer than we could ever possibly get.

"Is it?" she repeats.

I drop my head. "I couldn't be alone tonight. I saw something again. A memory, maybe."

"That's . . ." There's a touch of embarrassment in her voice, but mostly disappointment, like she was hoping I'd secretly shown up just for her. "What was it?"

"I don't know. Not yet. I might not be who you think I am." I'm already not. I never was.

"You're my best friend." Her eyes flick away from mine. "More than that."

"I don't know who I was. I could have been someone you wouldn't like." Someone who was no one until he was a killer.

"No. I know you, Az. *You* know you. You could never be someone like that. You just couldn't."

But I remember how she looked at me in the church basement, when I had the knife in my hand. And Hadrin said I was a weapon. The best weapon the wizards had, whatever that means. I didn't stick around to hear more about it, but I remember the way Father Moors found me, with blood on my hands and dead bodies surrounding me.

My skin feels feverishly hot. I lean toward her. "I see it every time I shut my eyes. That dark room and the—" My throat closes in on itself, refusing to speak the words. *And the straps, the pain, the horror.*

The broken boy in the chair.

She smooths my hair away from my face, questions burning in her eyes. "What do you mean, the—" She swallows the words back, maybe knowing I won't answer—that I *can't*—or maybe not wanting to know. "Don't think about it. I don't care who you were, Az. I *don't*. Neither should you."

"I don't want to be alone."

"Then don't be. Stay with me."

She thinks I mean tonight. I do, but I also mean so much more than that.

I take a deep breath, looking her over, at the way her silky pink nightgown clings to her. Only a thin layer of fabric separates me from her, teasing me with the curves of her body—her shoulders, her breasts, her hips—and all the forbidden places a friend isn't allowed to touch. "Maybe I shouldn't."

"Az." She looks me right in the eyes. "I'm going to say it nice and simple. Stay. With. Me."

"But—"

"Don't make me say it any plainer than that. You don't want to be alone tonight. Maybe I don't, either."

I smile. It feels like the first time in ages, though I know that's not true. Tonight's events have skewed my sense of time, creating a chasm that stretches out between now and before. Before I met Hadrin, before I got a glimpse of who I was. Leora smiles back at me, and in that moment there is no darkness. There is only light, exposing everything about me. Making the dark parts of me disappear. And I'm not a monster—I'm just a boy alone with a girl, and I don't have anything to hide.

Could a monster ever love anyone this much? Hadrin was wrong. I was no one before *this*.

She watches me, her eyes warm and inviting. I lean in close to kiss her. Finally, after waiting a lifetime. My lips almost touch hers. *Almost*, but then I hold back.

Because these are the same lips that would have killed that wizard at the bar tonight with their words. I didn't know where the words came from, but I knew exactly what they would have done. How much pain they would have caused. The realization hits me like a stone, jarring me out of whatever illusion I was under. These are the same lips that uttered a spell dark and cruel, meant not just to kill, but to torture. And I would have enjoyed it. Even now, I'm a little disappointed that Hadrin stopped me. And Leora doesn't know. She can *never* know.

I pull away from her, shrinking back into the darkness. I scramble off the bed. I don't know what I was thinking. Even in her light, my shadows still lurk. And without the darkness to hide them, she might see the truth. She might finally see who I really am.

"Az, wait— What's wrong?"

"I didn't come here for this. I shouldn't—I can't—"

"Stay. Please, just stay." She's on her feet, her hand on my arm. Not letting me go. "We don't have to . . . Nothing you don't want. Just stay."

"I'm not what you think I am."

"Yes, you are. Because you're mine." She takes my hand. She kisses the spiral tattoo on my wrist. The first time she's kissed me, and it has to be there. I don't know what the tattoo means, but I do know it ties me to a wizard. Would she still press her lips to it if she knew that? "That's what you are," she says. "You can't tell me you're not."

No, I can't. I'm hers. I always have been. For as long as I can remember, which is the only time that counts. "I love you," I tell her, the secret tearing itself from my chest, leaving me raw inside. Red and raw and bleeding. But it's a relief to say something so normal, so honest. It's one secret I don't have to keep hidden anymore.

Something sparks in her eyes. Something warm and beautiful. Her shoulders relax, as if she'd been waiting forever for me to say those words.

I make myself look away. Because the boy she feels that way about, the one she thinks she knows so well . . . He isn't me. At least, not all of me. "You're the most important person in the world to me," I add, "but I shouldn't stay here tonight. Or any night."

Her hands squeeze my wrists tight, sending a shock of fear through my nerves. "Az, *please*, don't—"

I twist out of her grasp, and my hand is already on the doorknob. I'm in the hallway before she can even finish her sentence. Fleeing the scene of the crime, like a thief in the night. A thief who isn't quite sure what he's stolen, only that it was valuable, and that his steps are heavier leaving than when he came in.

"Az, please! I love you! So don't go. Chasm take you, *don't go!*"

But I do. I keep walking, even though it tears me apart. Even though the heartbreak is excruciating. So much so that it might even block out the screams of the broken boy in the chair.

So maybe I got what I came here for, after all.

CHAPTER NINE

Rathe gapes at me as I stumble into class the next morning. I haven't slept—maybe a few minutes here and there, but otherwise, nothing. I have a pounding headache and my eyes sting.

I motion for him to scoot over and then slump down next to him at the long wooden study table in the back row.

"What in the Chasm happened to *you*?" he whispers. "Man, your eyes are bloodshot."

Mother Hart is at the chalkboard in the front, writing out a sentence for us to diagram.

The king and queen were lied to by those insidious wizards.

"I couldn't sleep."

"You missed candle service this morning. Father Moors is going to have your hide if Father Gratch doesn't get to you first. Your room didn't pass inspection again—big surprise there—and you've been missing chores lately. One more offense and Father Gratch says the Council is going to have to do some 'reevaluating' around here."

I clench my fists under the table. I so don't need this right now. It's bad enough the High Priest is trying to bully me into becoming his apprentice—though it's been more than twenty-four hours, and he hasn't made good on his threats, unless this reevaluation was his idea. But I doubt it. Father Gratch has had it in for me since the day I got here.

My chest feels heavy, regret over what happened last night still clawing at me. I glance around the room, taking in the scattered acolytes in red robes like me and Rathe, and the regular students, here purely for school, in their crisp ash-gray uniforms. I look for Leora's dark-reddish-brown hair . . . but I don't see her.

"She's not here," Rathe whispers.

"Where is she?"

He wrinkles his forehead. "You're asking *me*? I thought you were the expert on that."

So she didn't show up for class. I can't blame her—I almost didn't, either. But I dragged myself here because I wanted to see her, even if I was pretty sure she wouldn't want to see me. Or talk to me ever again.

Is that why she's not here? So she doesn't have to be in the same room with me?

"Cheer up," Rathe says, clapping me on the back. "She'll get over it."

"You don't even know what it was." I swallow back a bitter taste in my mouth. I should have stayed with her. I tore a secret from my chest and instead of handing it to her on a silver platter, I threw it at her and ran.

I love you.

"Well, she'll *probably* get over it. Is that better?"

My eyes are bleary. I rub my palms against my face and wish I'd gotten some sleep. But then again, maybe it's better I stayed awake. I can't imagine my dreams would have been anything but nightmares.

Last night flashes through my mind. She *loves* me. She wanted me. To spend the night, to sleep in her bed, to . . . to stay with her. I picture the warmth in her eyes when she looked into mine. I should have kissed her. I don't know what's wrong with me.

Except I do. Because as soon as I imagine her loving me back, I remember that shock of horror. The moment when the monster almost kisses the girl, and she has no idea who he really is. He looks into her eyes and falls for the image he sees of himself. Of the way she sees him. But it isn't the truth. There's something evil and broken inside of me, and her loving me doesn't change that.

The classroom door opens, and for a second I perk up. She's just late, not avoiding me. I picture her walking in, glancing over at me, angry but worried. Hurt but forgiving.

But it's not her. Just Bran, a fellow acolyte playing messenger. He bows his head, greeting Mother Hart, who pauses in the middle of writing her next sentence: *Given recent events, it's clear that the king and queen both have their heads up their—*

"I'm here for Azeril," he says. "Father Moors needs to see him in his office right away."

Great.

Mother Hart sighs at me, as if she's been expecting this. "Go," she says, waving me toward the door.

I exchange a look with Rathe, who mouths, *Nice knowing you.*

Bran waits until we're in the hall and the door is closed before saying, "Father Moors is so pissed at you." He sounds happy about that, like it's the most exciting thing that's going to happen all day.

It probably is, but I still glare at him. It turns into a yawn, and I wonder if anyone would notice if I didn't come back to class. If, after Father Moors is done chewing me out for missing candle service, I could just slip back to my room and sleep.

"He's going to tear you apart."

"Wonderful. *Thanks.*"

"I'm just preparing you for what's coming. I'm not the bad guy here. I'm trying to do you a favor."

"Well, don't."

"All right," he says, leading the way down the hall. "I won't. But if I was—"

"You're not."

"—I'd tell you that this isn't just about you missing some chores or whatever. He didn't *say* what it was, but I could tell it was big."

I squeeze my eyes shut and rub my temples. I wonder if Father Moors is mad about the wizards accusing the Church of murder. Does he think it was my fault? And if he does, why didn't he call me in yesterday or the day before?

I mull that over as we make our way out of the school, across the grounds, and over to the church. When we get to Father Moors's office, Bran knocks on the door and waits until he hears a "Come in" before turning the knob and making a big show of gesturing me inside. As if I haven't been here a thousand times before.

It smells like old soup and woodsmoke in here, just like it always does. The room is small and cramped, the walls lined with dusty books. The fireplace is lit, but it's burned down to coals. Just a few glowing embers clinging to the last traces of life.

Father Moors is pacing in front of the fire, and when the door opens, he turns and glares at me, like I've committed an unforgivable crime. Which of course I have, but he's never had any complaints about it before.

"Leave us," he tells Bran.

Bran smirks at me and then dashes out the door.

"Sit," Father Moors growls, pointing to the chair in front of his desk.

I don't move. I'm so tired of people telling me what to do. "If it's all the same to you, Father—"

"It's not. Sit. *Down.*"

I look at the chair waiting for me. My palms sweat, and a wave of fear prickles in my chest and claws its way down my back. I pretend like I didn't hear him and slouch against the wall. Instinctively choosing a spot where I can see both him and the door.

He frowns, muttering something to himself. I don't catch the words, only that he sounds upset. "This isn't going to be easy," he mumbles at the wall, and I can't tell if he's talking to me or to himself.

Maybe Father Gratch has already convinced the Council to do their reevaluation of me. It seems awfully fast, but . . .

You have twenty-four hours.

Father Gratch couldn't have called a Council meeting this fast, but the High Priest could have. I stare down at the dark-green rug in front of the fireplace, counting where sparks from the fire have burnt little holes in it over the years. There are five of them. I don't look at Father Moors's face, afraid that if I do, I'll see it in his eyes.

The Council's decided I'm out of here, and they've made it his job to tell me.

I don't want to leave. If I was out on the streets, if I wasn't part of the Church, or near Leora, then . . . then it feels like I'd only be one step away from ending up in that chair again. But if this is the High Priest's way of forcing me to become his apprentice, he underestimated me. Because if it comes down to leaving the Church or letting him put his hands on me, I'll take my chances on the streets any day.

Even so, my voice shakes, already pleading for Father Moors to tell me this isn't happening. And he hasn't even given me the bad news yet. "I—I don't want to go. Whatever case Father Gratch made . . . I'll do extra chores! I'll make up what I missed, I promise, just—"

"This isn't about what you missed. And no amount of chores could ever make up for it."

A horror that sits heavy in his words passes from him to me, sliding across my skin. Coating me like oil. "I was careful. I don't know how the High Guild found out about the Church's involvement, but it *wasn't me.*"

He shakes his head. "I know you were out late last night. Well after curfew. And you were seen leaving the girls' dorms over at the school."

Words stick in my throat. I have too many things to say, and none of them make it out.

"I see you don't deny it," Father Moors says, the anger and frustration draining from his voice so that he just sounds tired. And disappointed. "You paid a visit to Leora last night, didn't you?"

Of all the things I've done, *this* is what they're going to use against me? Spending the night with a girl—the one crime I *should* have committed, but didn't? "It's not what you think. I didn't . . . We didn't . . . Nothing happened." Something could have, if I'd stayed. "I know I broke curfew, and I know I was in Leora's room when I shouldn't have been. But I swear, nothing happened."

"But something *did.*" Father Moors crosses over to me. He grabs my shoulders, making me look at him. "Something monstrous happened! And you were *there.* Tell me you didn't . . . By the Fire, I knew when I took you in that this might happen. I keep telling myself it couldn't have been you, despite the evidence. Because if it was, I've failed you. So tell me you didn't."

I feel sick. Like there are stones settling at the bottom of my stomach. "Didn't what?"

"She's covered in burns, Azeril. Burns shaped like a knife. And the worst of it . . . the charred stab wound in her chest . . . It looks like the work of *obsidian.* And *you* were seen leaving the dorms last night."

The room suddenly feels ten times smaller and about a hundred times larger, all at the same time. His words swim in my head, separate from each other, not making any sense. *Burns. Knife. Her.* Acid burns the back of my throat. My head feels too light. This isn't really happening. "No. *No.* You're lying. You're making that up!" I sound hysterical. My voice is too high, too unstable. "Leora wasn't—"

Stabbed in the chest. My own personal brand of vengeance. Of murder.

I tear away from him, twisting out of his grip so hard, my shoulders hurt. I bang my head back against the wall, where it hits with a jarring thud.

"You didn't know . . ." Father Moors lets out a deep sigh. Both relieved and burdened. Relieved that it wasn't me, that his attack dog stayed on the leash, and burdened now with the task of giving me the worst news of my life. "I'm sorry, Azeril. I'm so sorry."

"It's not her. Because if it was, there's no way you could ask me that. It's someone else. Some other girl." My jaw trembles, my teeth chattering. She can't be dead.

I left. Why did I leave? By the Fire, why did I leave her?!

This is why she wasn't in class. It had nothing to do with me. Nothing and everything.

But it's not her. So it's okay. Because it can't be her. I can't exist in a world where something that awful could happen to her, and I'm still here.

Father Moors hesitates. "I'm sorry," he says again, but the words have no meaning. I wish he'd stop saying them. "I know you were close to her."

I laugh. I can't help it. I can't comprehend any of this. "And you think what? That I *hurt* her? That I—" My throat closes up, unable to say it out loud. Hot tears sting my eyes and streak down my face. I hardly feel them. I can't breathe. The world is suffocating me. If she's gone, then so is all the air.

"No," he says, but I know part of him wasn't sure. "You could never— You wouldn't. Not to someone who didn't deserve it."

I press the back of my arm against my eyes. He still hasn't said her name. Not directly. It could be someone else. It could.

But I know it's not.

Every part of me feels raw. Each breath feels like sucking broken glass into my lungs. Maybe existing always hurt this much, and I just never noticed. I've been living in some kind of dream. Some kind of haze where being alive isn't excruciating. This pain—this is the reality.

I force myself to choke out the words. Because I have to say them. I have to, at least once. "I didn't kill her."

"Azeril, I never said—"

"I know what you think! I know what it looks like!" I didn't do it, but I know who would have. Who would have hurt her to get to me. My hand falls on the knife hilt, the obsidian's heat igniting my blood. I'll give myself to it completely this time. I won't hold any part of myself back.

I am the knife. We are one and the same.

Unbreakable.

Father Moors takes a step back, fear washing across his face. "Azeril, I didn't say—"

"I'll kill him. It'll be slow. High Priest Endeil will find out what it's like to *burn*. He can conjure fire, but he's met his match this time because that won't stop me."

"Azeril!" Father Moors shouts, as if I'm not standing two feet in front of him. As if I'm very, very far away. Perhaps it's too much, seeing his trained dog in action. Apart from that first time, when he found me, he's never watched.

"You can't stop me. And if you try—"

"Azeril, please, listen to me! I never said she was dead!"

Time stops. My thoughts shatter into a million pieces. She's alive.

I blink, fighting the heat of the knife. I'd already resigned myself to giving in to it. To not holding back. Now I have to struggle to think clearly. "Leora's still alive," I say tentatively, testing out the words.

Father Moors nods. "Barely, but . . . the knife missed her heart."

And there it is. Proof that I didn't do it.

I would never have missed.

CHAPTER TEN

Her room in the infirmary is dark, except for the light of one dim candle. Just enough light to throw shadows across her face. Black drapes already hang over the walls, waiting to fit her for her burial shroud. Because the physicians are so sure she's going to die. They told Father Moors it's only a matter of time. A very short time. She's the one lurking in the shadows now.

I creep into the dark room. A broken boy, even without the chair. The scent of her blood hangs heavy and metallic in the air— even though the wound has been tended to and bandaged, the burns treated with a pungent salve that stings my nose when I get close. I kneel next to her bed, tears springing to my eyes. But I hold them back. She's still there, hanging on somewhere between the darkness and the shallow rise and fall of her breathing, and letting myself cry here would be like admitting this is her deathbed. That this is the final time I will ever see her.

I find her hand, lifeless and cold, and hold it with both of mine, pressing it to my forehead. There isn't anything I can say that won't sound like a good-bye, so for a while I say nothing at all.

Endeil did this to her. Because I defied him. He took a knife and lit it on fire with his hands. It wasn't obsidian. If it was, there wouldn't be so many burn marks on her. There'd be only one, right where it counted, and she would be dead. The knife likes flesh. It doesn't play around.

I bring her hand to my lips. I kiss her knuckles. My chest feels like it's folding in on itself. Maybe I'm a monster, but I'm *her* monster, and I would have done anything to protect her. I still would.

Leora's breathing becomes more ragged, her struggling more obvious. There are a few endless moments where I stay perfectly still, afraid that if I move I won't be able to hear if her next breath is her last. I hold my own breath, as if I can give her my air. My lungs. If she can't breathe, then neither can I.

I don't know how much time passes before the fit stops. But when it does, her breathing isn't as steady as it was.

Tears fill my eyes again, and I can't stop them this time. If she dies, I'll die with her. Her death is my death. She'll become one of the dark shadows haunting my mind. And then she'll see all my secrets, all the things I've done, and then what was the point of fleeing last night?

A choking sob wracks my body. I let go of her hand, covering my face. Trying to stay silent, to pretend this isn't the end and that I'm not totally losing it.

But there's no pretending, not anymore. And there's no holding back. I cry at her bedside, until my breathing sounds almost as ragged and strained as hers.

A whimper escapes her throat. She stirs, just a little, and even that's a struggle for her. "Az," she murmurs, though her eyes are closed and I can't tell if she's awake. She moves her arm, as if to reach for me, but it flops down at her side.

There are voices outside her room, physicians discussing her fate in hushed tones. Telling one of the nurses to expect her bed to be free by tomorrow morning.

They can't know that. They *can't*.

No one asked me if she was allowed to die.

Leora's arm slips off the edge of the bed, her fingers grazing the inside of my left arm. There's a twinge in my chest, a raw, hollow ache, remembering how worried she was when she saw my scar. *She* was worried about *me*, and now here we are. Another painful sob escapes me, threatening to rip me apart, to turn me completely inside out, and I press my face into the side of her bed to stifle it.

By the Fire, *it's not fair*. I stupidly slice my own arm open with obsidian and wake up the next morning with hardly a scratch on me. She's never done anything to anyone. She's never even held a weapon, and yet the High Priest sticks an ordinary knife in her chest and takes her away from me.

She's not dead yet. It's not too late. The thought breaks through the cloud of pain, and I'm so numb, already feeling like I'm dying along with her, that at first it doesn't mean anything.

But maybe whatever saved me the other night could save her, too. If I knew who did it or what it was.

Hadrin might not have been the one to heal me, but he knows exactly what happened that night.

He'll tell me, at a cost. If I agree to be a weapon for him. I thought crawling back to him was the last thing I'd ever do, but it turns out it's not. Not if it will save her.

I get to my feet. I rub my eyes dry with the back of my hand. My knees are sore from kneeling too long, and I pretend that's why I feel so shaky. Not because I have to face a wizard who knows all my deep, dark secrets. Not because I'll owe him everything for this.

Leora's hand twitches. "Az," she mutters, her voice barely there. She reaches out for me and tries to speak, to tell me something, but it comes out a moan. Her mouth moves but can't form the words.

I wince. Her weak hand finds mine, trying to squeeze it. And I don't need to hear her words to know she doesn't want me to leave. It's last night all over again, the same mistake repeated.

But no. This is different.

"I'm coming back, Leora." I won't let her die. And Chasm take me, I won't let her die alone.

I hesitate, holding on to her hand a moment longer, pressing her palm to my heart. "Please watch over her," I whisper, praying to the Fire. Maybe the Fire favors me, maybe it condemns me for my sins, but it can't have anything against her. "Please keep her safe."

Protect her from all the monsters.

Because I'm going to be back as soon as possible. I'm going to save her life.

I just have to sell my soul first.

———

Endeil's waiting for me in the hallway outside the infirmary. He stands in my way, arms folded. "I thought I might find you here." He says it so casually, as if he found me lighting candles over the altar. As if he's someone I would ever want to run into.

But today, it's the other way around. He's the one who should be avoiding *me*.

My hand hovers over my obsidian. It's killing me not to touch it, but if I do, if even one finger grazes the hilt, I know I'll kill him. I won't be able to stop myself.

And I *will* kill him, one way or another, but not here and not now. Not when I could still save her.

"*Move.*"

"And let you flee from your crimes? It looks to me like I've caught a murderer. And don't look so surprised. I warned you."

"And I told you I'll never be your apprentice."

"You'd better change your mind very quickly."

I laugh. "You've already taken her away from me. You think I care about *anything else*?!"

"Yes." He's maddeningly calm. Deadly serious but calm. "You think you have nothing left to lose, but if you don't agree to become my apprentice, if you don't let me restore your memories, you're going to be imprisoned for the one crime you didn't commit. You'll be hanged for murdering the girl you loved. Everyone will know you're a killer, except they'll think you're a worse one than you already are. Maybe some of them would see making wizards disappear as justified. Illegal but justified. But creeping into her bedroom in the middle of the night, doing who knows what to her, and leaving with her life—"

"I know it was you who stabbed her, and if you *touched* her—"

"What kind of monster do you think I am?" He holds a hand over his heart in shock.

"The kind who's going to get out of my way."

"Gladly. Pledge to be my apprentice, and you can go. Otherwise, I call the guards. It's your call, but, personally, I'd prefer if you picked the first option."

It would feel so good to plunge the knife into his chest. To slice him open, bit by bit, sharing the obsidian's pleasure as its heat burns away any other thought, any other feeling, except the ecstasy of making him *hurt*.

My thoughts must be obvious, because the blood drains from Endeil's face. He takes a step away from me.

"You're lucky she's not dead," I tell him, "because you don't want to see who I am without her. You asked what kind of monster I thought you were. You should be more concerned with what kind of monster *I* am."

"If you were going to kill me, you would have done it by now." But he doesn't look so sure about that. His eyes dart to the knife, and flames spread over his hands, like ethereal gloves. "The school's borrowed a few city guards to make the students feel safe. To keep their parents from withdrawing their tuition, more like. But I happen to know that the guards are just over in the mess hall. You have three seconds before I call for them."

I can't let him do that. If they take me away, then there's no chance of me saving Leora. And there will be chains. Restraints around my hands and my feet, covering the old scars and driving me insane.

"One."

And if I become his apprentice, he'll own me. He'll send his fire into my head and shine lights into all the dark places that are best left forgotten. He'll dredge every dark memory up to the surface, and while I don't know what he hopes to find, I know with absolute certainty that it will shatter me.

But for Leora, I would do it. I would let him break me if it would mean she lives.

"Two."

I wrap my arms around myself, already anticipating having to hold myself together. The image of the chair flashes in my mind. There's a reason I don't remember anything, a reason why it should stay that way.

"Three. Time's up." He sucks in a breath, getting ready to shout for the guards.

"No, wait. *Wait.*"

"You'll be my apprentice?" He taps his long fingers together, practically giddy with anticipation.

"I . . ." Sweat drips down my back. My mouth moves so slowly, not wanting to say the words. I can't let the guards take me, and I can't let him mess with my head. "I'll . . ."

"Yes?" He cups a hand to his ear.

And then it hits me. What Hadrin said last night, about the wizards getting tipped off by someone from the Church. I might be completely wrong, but . . . only two people besides me knew the Church was behind the murders, and one of them is standing right in front of me. "I'm not going to be your apprentice, and you're not going to call the guards. Because if you do, I'm going to tell everyone what you did."

He snorts. "She has burn marks all over her, made from a knife. I'm the High Priest and you're a street-urchin-turned-altar-boy Father Moors dragged in. Who do you think the Church is going to believe?" His smile says it all—he thinks he has me right where he wants me.

But that's where he's wrong. "I think they'll believe me when I tell them it was *you* who informed the wizards that the Church is behind their disappearances."

"I don't know what you're talking about."

But I see the surprise flicker across his face, and I don't think I'm so far off. "Let me go, or I'll tell everyone exactly how you betrayed your order."

"And why would they believe something so far-fetched? And from a murderer?"

"They wouldn't. Not at first. But the king and queen would when the High Guild handed over the letter you sent. The one with the Church's own seal on it and your handwriting all over it." He could have dictated the letter, but that would mean letting someone else in on his secret.

"How do you—" He hesitates, and when he speaks again, the slightest tremor creeps into his voice. "You're lying."

"Am I? You want me to call the guards and test that theory?"

"You don't understand."

"You're right. I don't. And neither will the rest of the Church when they find out their high priest sold them out to their enemies."

"It was for the greater good. I'm the High Priest—I know what's best for them, and how dare you accuse me of anything less."

"Let me go. *Now.*"

"You're not going to tell anyone, because if you do, I'll turn you in. You'll hang for your crimes."

"And you'll be cast out of the Church. Excommunicated. The only person who's ever meant anything to me is in that room, dying, because of you. And if I can't save her, then I've got nothing left to lose. But you, you've still got everything. So what's it going to be? You have three seconds before *I* call the guards—"

He steps aside, giving me room to pass. "It's not what you think."

"What I think is that I'm never going to work for you. I'm *never* going to be your apprentice or let you put your filthy hands on me to try and see inside my head."

"You say that now, but when you change your mind—"

"I *won't*."

"But when you do, when you realize I'm working toward something bigger than both of us, you know where to find me."

CHAPTER ELEVEN

I pound on the door to Hadrin's room at the inn next to the Silver Hound. He said to come here if I changed my mind. I swore I wouldn't. I swore nothing could ever make me go near him again.

He must have believed me, because his eyebrows jump up and his forehead wrinkles when he opens the door. *"Azeril?"*

I hold up my left arm, pointing to my scar. "Who did this to me?"

"You did. You know that perfectly well. What are you . . ." He peers at my face. He must notice I've been crying, because he glances away, as if he's just seen something he shouldn't have.

"I know I did it," I tell him. I remember the sweet euphoria of the knife sinking into flesh. The excruciating pain of every nerve alive and on fire. "I need to know who healed it."

He frowns. He looks back and forth down the hallway, then beckons for me to come inside. There's a split second when I consider not following. But I do. Of course I do.

His room is plain but comfortable. There's a large soft-looking bed, a desk with papers and books piled all over it, a white couch that takes up half of one wall, and a little wooden table. Flames crackle in the fireplace, giving the room a cozy feel.

"What happened to you?" he asks, and I can't tell if he means today or over the past three years.

"I'll do anything you want. Please, just tell me who healed me." He gestures to the couch. I shake my head. Hadrin sighs and pours two cups of tea, not bothering to ask if I want one. He's ignoring my question, as if time doesn't matter. As if each second that ticks by isn't slicing through him like a knife.

Must just be me.

He tries to offer me a cup. I shake my head again, but he shoves it into my hands anyway. I can't hold it steady, and the cup clatters against the saucer.

"Nothing was ever solved with hysteria," he says.

Like I'm going to drink anything he gives me.

He pulls a chair closer and sits down, leaving me the couch, but I keep standing. "You don't remember who healed you." It's not a question, more like a tentative statement, offering me the chance to correct him.

"You said it wasn't you. Just tell me who did it, because I don't have time for this. I promise, I'll come back. As soon as she's all right, I'll be back. And . . . I'll do whatever you want."

"So there's a she," he mutters. "Of course there is. You've grown up."

"Do you not understand what I'm saying to you?" A couple drops of scalding hot tea splash against my hand, it's shaking so hard. "I'll be your weapon, or whatever it is you want from me." Whoever he wants me to kill. I'll be the monster. Even if I can never tell Leora, even if I can never be with her. As long as I can save her.

"It was you," he says. "You healed yourself."

He's joking. He has to be. Except he's not smiling. If anything, he looks upset. "I didn't. It's impossible."

"One of us remembers that night and one of us doesn't. I have nothing to gain by lying to you. You used a spell and you healed your arm. You rinsed the blood off in a fountain, and you told me you were fine. That you could get home on your own and that if I even thought about following you, you would stick the knife down my throat and slit me from the inside out." He says it calmly, then takes a sip of his tea. As if he'd just described something as mundane as making his bed in the morning.

"Sounds like something I'd say, but it doesn't ring any bells."

"I assure you, you did. And you cast that spell, not me. I'm afraid you don't need my help, after all."

"But . . ." I sink down onto the couch. I stare into my cup, watching bits of leaves swirl around, mimicking my thoughts.

Last night, I almost cast something on that wizard who threatened me. "You're telling me I cast a spell. A wizard spell?"

"You really don't remember?"

"There are a lot of things I don't remember. I don't suppose you memorized it?"

He laughs. "You're joking."

"I've never been more serious in my life." I glare at him. "The girl I love is *dying*." It feels strange to admit something so personal. But he knows everything else. And of all the secrets I have, it's the only one I'm not ashamed of.

"You're in love. Or you think you are." He scoffs a little, like he finds that amusing and hard to believe.

I start to get up. "If you're not going to help me—"

"Then what? You'll find someone else?"

"I don't see you doing anything."

"And what exactly am I supposed to *do*? Wave my hand and magically make everything better?" He pauses. "How could you have forgotten? It's only been two days. And . . . it's impossible."

"I—I don't remember anything. Not since I came here three years ago. Sometimes there are bits and pieces, little flashes, just not . . . not spells."

His eyes widen. There's a crash as his cup and saucer drop from his hands onto the hardwood floor. A chunk of the cup handle breaks off and skitters to my feet. What's left of his tea escapes across the floorboards. Hadrin gets up, turning away from me, holding a hand over his mouth like he can't believe what I've just said. Like he might be sick.

"*Nothing?*" he hisses. Then his voice rises to a shout. "You're telling me you remember *nothing*?! You useless, *useless* boy!" He tears at his hair. He stomps across the room, getting as far away from me as possible without actually leaving. He covers his face with his hands and takes a long, shuddering breath. When he speaks again, he's no longer shouting. "But you remembered a spell last night. And two nights before that."

Both times, I was in danger. And there were wizards.

A dark room. A broken boy in a chair. Screaming.

I set my cup on the end table and get up from the couch, moving to stand in front of Hadrin. Unable to believe what I'm about to do. "There might be a way you can help." I spread my arms out, making myself open, vulnerable. Leora's dying. I have no choice. There's no other way I would ever do this. "You can hurt me."

His mouth twists in disgust as he realizes I mean it. His pupils dilate so wide, his light-blue irises almost disappear. "Absolutely not."

I ball up my hands and expose my wrists, offering them to him. "Please. Whatever it takes."

"No." He's shaking, and he can't look at me.

"Tie me to the chair." The words scrape my throat. Even as I say them, my hand twitches, wanting to reach for the knife. I grab it from its sheath and drop it to the floor, kicking it away. I force him to make eye contact with me. "You've done it before, haven't you? You think I'm the one who likes causing pain, but you're no better than I am. You used to hurt me. I know you did. You—"

"No!" He shoves me away from him.

I stumble back a step. It's not enough. A wizard cowering in fear was only ever good for one thing, and I've already dropped the knife.

He stares at his hands, horrified that he pushed me. "I didn't," he says, shaking his head. "I told them what to do, but I . . . It was a mistake, all of it. I swore I'd never hurt you again!"

"And I swore I'd kill you. Sometimes we break our promises."

"I can't. Not this. Ask me to do anything but this."

"She's dying! She's dying and she doesn't have much time, and you're the only one who can help! I need to remember that spell, so I'm telling you—I don't care how you do it. *Just hurt me.*"

He raises his arm, as if to strike me. As if to slap me across the face. But he wavers. His arm hovers in the air, unmoving. And then he crumples to the floor. "Leave," he says, his voice cold and hard. "Get out of here!"

"Please. Please—"

"I won't listen to this. I won't listen to you begging me to hurt you!"

"It has to be a wizard." And there's no way I could ever let another one put his hands on me. "It has to be you. It can't be anyone else."

He squeezes his eyes shut. Then he opens them, getting to his feet. "Get out."

"Make me."

His nostrils flare. "I can't be a part of this. I won't."

"It's life or death. You think I'd ask you to do this if it wasn't? If I had *any other choice*?!"

"No," he says. "But I hope you understand *I* don't have any other choice." He moves past me, toward the door, and storms out of his own room.

He abandons me. Just like that.

I don't remember any spells, but I do remember this. It feels so familiar, him leaving me alone with my fears.

After all, there's a reason I swore I'd kill him. There's a reason he deserves it.

But now isn't the time to think about it. Not with Leora lying in a dark room of her own. If Hadrin won't make me remember, then . . .

Then I have to go crawling back to the one person who will.

CHAPTER TWELVE

I'm sitting in the pews in the chapel with Endeil, side by side. Alone. It's creepy and dark in here, only a few candles in the corner casting any light. "I'll be your apprentice," I tell him, the words hot in my throat, cutting me like knives.

"Yes. You will."

"Nothing's changed. I don't believe what you believe, about some stupid destiny. I just need to know what's in my head. I can bring her back if you . . . Just get my memories back and let me save her, and then I'll do whatever you want. That's the deal."

"You don't believe you have a greater destiny, but you believe you can bring the girl you love back from the very brink of death?"

"Do we have a deal or not?"

"Oh, we most certainly have a deal." Endeil clasps his hands together, the edges of his mouth curling into a grin. He doesn't have to say "I've got you right where I want you" or "I said you'd be back."

"Don't look at me like that," I say, my voice echoing off the walls. "Don't you *dare* look at me like that. Not after what you did to her."

"And how am I looking at you? Like you threw my offer in my face and then came to me only hours later, desperate for me to take you back? Whatever I did to her, I did *for* you. The way I sent our enemies that letter. The wizards have been dragging people from their homes and making them disappear into the night for years. They torture them, for what purpose I don't know, and they seize their property. And as long as the Guild pays their taxes and keeps the royal coffers full, the Monarchy turns a blind eye. Everyone knows, and nobody says a thing. Nobody stands up to them. You know that better than anyone. And now I sent them that letter and everyone is up in arms. Every acolyte, every priest, and every student of the Sacred Flame is talking about it. They're outraged about the lies they think the wizards told to put themselves in power. They're watching the wizards' every move now, questioning what it's all for and wondering why exactly the Monarchy would side with them. And what did we lose? A few measly seats in court that no one was taking seriously. Everyone knows those positions are filled by old men, by ancient priests who want to sleep through law discussions and collect their pensions. Never arguing, never even *listening* to what's going on! No one was ever going to see the truth. They were just going to keep their heads down and never think about the world around them."

"You gave the wizards power over us, over *everyone*, just to piss people off."

"You're missing the point. And here I thought you were smart. But you weren't smart enough to listen to me when I told you that you were going to be my apprentice. You think I wanted to hurt her?"

"Yes." He's a monster, just like me. But unlike me, he doesn't care who he hurts or whether they deserve it.

"You needed motivation. Believe what you want, but we *will* change the world, and for the better. The Fire has put me on the noblest of paths, and I will stop at nothing to see it to the end."

Maybe he really believes that, but I can't believe the Fire would want him to hurt someone like Leora. Even if the Fire does favor him, the idea that his ends justify his means is all in his head.

A slight draft makes the candlelight waver across the walls. I could kill him, like I told Father Moors. Two swift movements, one to grab the knife, the other to stab it through his heart, and this would be over. The world would be safe from him and his great destiny. But then Leora would die.

And anyway, I didn't just say I'd kill him, I said it would be slow. I said I'd make him *burn*.

"The next time you think about crossing me, just remember that if you'd decided to become my apprentice when I first asked you, we wouldn't be here right now. She wouldn't be lying on her deathbed, and you wouldn't have had to come crawling to me for forgiveness." He licks his lips, savoring his words. "But, then again, I kind of liked that part."

Anger boils my blood, emanating heat. I realize my fingertips are on the knife, just grazing it. Just enough to burn. I force myself to let go. I put my hands between my knees, squeezing them together. It's several seconds before the rage subsides enough for me to speak. "Whatever I did, I'm not the one who put that knife in her."

"That's odd," he says, "because I don't know who else could have done it. Who else could have used obsidian that way?"

"Maybe you should find him and make *him* your apprentice."

He grins. "But I've already asked you."

To anyone who might walk into the chapel, our hushed conversation might sound like just a young acolyte conversing with the High Priest while he's in town, maybe hoping to win his favor. Maybe hoping to become his apprentice. They'd see the boy, the simple acolyte, and have no idea his knees are shaking from the effort of not killing the man next to him.

We both know it wasn't obsidian. But it doesn't matter. "Can you get my memories back or not?"

"Such a quick change of heart. I thought you didn't want them. I thought you were *never* going to let me put my filthy hands on you."

I unsheathe the knife and set it on the pew before getting to my feet. "Let's get this over with." He's right, I don't want my memories back. But I need one of them more than I've ever needed anything else. And if getting that one memory back means dredging up everything that made me how I am, then so be it. "How quickly can you do it?"

"My, we're in a hurry, aren't we? Maybe we shouldn't rush this. Maybe you should come back tomorrow."

"I asked you a question."

He takes a breath, staring down at his knees, thinking it over. "It's not like I've done this before, you understand. I suppose I could try to make the process quick, but it'll cost you. In pain."

He's the one who hurt her, and yet I'm the one paying for it. I'm the one begging him to let me sacrifice myself. Playing right into his hands. My chest feels tight with the terror of what I'm about to do. When I said I'd sell my soul, I thought it would be to Hadrin. That was bad enough. But there won't be any coming back from this.

"Come with me," Endeil says, sliding past me into the aisle, hurrying toward the altar.

There's an arch of candles behind it. He touches them, one by one, flames springing to life on each wick until the arch glows. It casts a soft halo of light around him, creating long shadows. He looms over the altar, waiting for me.

My footsteps are heavy, my whole body sick with shame. Dread squirms inside me, and I can't shake the image of a lamb being led to the slaughter.

This is wrong. It's a trap. He's not going to help me.

"Kneel. And lay your head right here."

I do what he asks. I shut my eyes. The hard stone floor digs into my knees. The wood of the altar is cold and smooth against my cheek. I half expect him to draw a knife. To butcher me right here, as if that's what he'd intended all along.

My heart leaps in my chest, uncontrollable fear making it beat faster and faster.

High Priest Endeil presses his palm against the side of my head. "This is going to hurt."

And I hear the smile. The one that says he knows he's got me, that he's won.

Flame rushes to my brain. A heat so intense it melts my thoughts and makes my skull feel like it's going to split apart. It reaches into the darkest recesses of my mind with long, probing fingers. I thought Leora's light would chase away my darkness, but here I am with the High Priest, and it's his fire that invades every part of me. Searing all of me away, until my very essence—whatever makes me *me*—cracks open, oozing and raw.

White-hot pain spreads through my head, through my arms, my legs. It blocks out everything else, except the sound of my screaming. And the sound of Endeil laughing.

A memory flashes through my head.

Alone in a dark room. Strapped to the chair.

Hadrin, barking orders in the background. "Don't tell me you couldn't make him do it! Don't come to me complaining of his screaming. You knew what this was when you signed up. If he's not screaming, you're not doing it right! Now get back over there and become his worst nightmare. Unless you need me to show you how it's done?"

I shudder, knowing what's coming. The shuddering is uncontrollable, like I could shake myself apart. My wrists itch. I could kill every one of these wizards if it wasn't for the straps.

Hadrin appears before me. He's holding a rag, blue like his robes. He grabs my face and forces my jaw open, shoving the rag into my mouth. "If you can't handle the screaming . . ."

I gag. Choking. I manage to spit it out, just for a moment. A spell twitches on my lips, something that will hurt.

I only get a few words out before he slaps me, hard, across the face. My tongue stings and I taste blood.

He stuffs the gag in before I can stop him this time. "We talked about this," he says. "You know that won't work on me. Not while I have this." Hadrin slides back the sleeve of his robe, revealing a spiral tattoo on his forearm.

The same tattoo I have on my wrist.

"*Now,*" *he says, sounding exasperated,* "*let's get back to work, shall we?*"

The images fade, leaving me hollow. Exposed. I'm breathing heavily, sweat drenching my face, soaking the altar. Endeil takes his hand off of me. The fire stops. I feel so cold that my teeth chatter. I stand up, my legs unsteady. My eyes sting and so does my tongue, like I really did bite it.

I look up at Endeil, who's staring at his hands like he's never seen them before.

"It didn't work," I tell him. I don't remember anything. Nothing useful anyway. No spells, nothing that will save Leora. Only darkness, and . . . Hadrin.

"I saw everything," Endeil breathes. And he's still staring at his hands, as if they hold the key to the universe.

It kills me, but I have to ask. Because if there's even a chance . . . "Did you see anything that could save her? Any . . . spells?"

"Filthy wizard spells, you mean. Your head is full of that rot. I saw something much better than spells. A source of pure power. And the source itself reached out to me, so dark and raw, so *divine.*" He tilts his head back and shuts his eyes for a moment, a single tear spilling down his cheek. "I was touched by greatness once, when the Fire bestowed its gift on me, and now I've been touched by greatness again. You say it didn't work?" He holds out his hands. A golden-green fire flares in his palms, rising higher and higher. Turning blue, pink, purple.

Black.

"Oh, but it *did.*"

———

I crumple on the cold chapel floor. It was for nothing. *Nothing.*

I let Endeil do what I said I wouldn't. I let him touch the darkest parts of my mind. Now his hands blaze black, and I don't know what that means, only that it can't be good. It came from whatever he saw inside me, and that makes it worse. So much worse.

I hate him for doing this to me. And I hate Hadrin for everything he's done, and for not helping me. For making me come back here.

And even after all this, I still can't save her. Leora's going to die because of me, and somewhere in my head there's the magic that could stop her from leaving, the one bright spot in all my shadows, and I can't touch it.

My stomach cramps. I feel sick and disgusted, but also empty and starving, and I can't remember the last time I ate.

It dawns on me that I was never going to be able to save her. Tears fill my eyes and suddenly I'm crying for her and for me, for all the lost things that will never be all right again.

I'd ask what I ever did to deserve this, but it's not exactly a secret.

"Azeril." Endeil's voice echoes softly through the chapel.

I'd almost forgotten he was here.

He crouches down beside me. "I told you I didn't want to hurt her, and I meant it. It was a necessary evil, to make you listen to me. Like I need you to listen to me now."

He sounds so calm, so rational, even as he spews out more of his insanity. "Chasm take you, leave me *alone.*"

"I can save her." He holds out his hands, the flames in his palms so dark that they seem to suck in all the light from the room. "I can do what you couldn't."

I blink back tears, trying to see him clearly, to see if he's tell-ing the truth. Because I haven't been betrayed enough times today. "You can't, so just—"

"I *can*. I can feel it. And I'll do it, but you have to do something for me first."

He already has everything. I don't know what else he could possibly want from me. And yet I know that whatever he asks me to do, no matter how twisted it is, I'll give in. If there's even the slightest chance that he can save her. "Anything," I whisper.

Endeil closes his eyes as he savors the word. I see him mouth-ing it silently to himself. *Anything.* "You have to beg me. Kneel before my altar and *pray to me* to save her."

"*What?*"

All the candles in the room flicker and go dim. Endeil gets to his feet and looms over me, his robes swishing against the floor. "Pray for your miracle, and I will deliver it to you."

"*Please.*"

"Is that how you beg? Is that all she means to you? One measly 'please'?"

"She means everything to me. *Everything.* I'm begging you, if you can save her—"

"*If?*" He scowls and raises an eyebrow.

"You *can* save her. You . . . you alone can deliver her from darkness."

He holds out a hand, beckoning me toward him. "Closer."

I move to stand, but he motions for me to stay on the ground. I crawl to him, on my hands and knees, the stone floor cold and unforgiving beneath me. "She's dying. Every second that we spend here, she's slipping away, because of what you—"

Anger flashes in his eyes. He opens his mouth to correct me, but I beat him to it.

"—because of what *I* did. Because of me."

"Again."

"It happened because of me!"

"Because you didn't believe in me. Your faith faltered, and she paid the price. It was your fault."

"It was my fault," I repeat, squeezing my eyes shut, not wanting to think about the truth of that statement. He's the one who put the knife in her. It *wasn't* me, but I could have stopped it. There were so many things I could have done differently.

"You were faithless. You were *nothing*. I had to make you see that."

I nod. I press my forehead to the ground in supplication, dirt from the floor sticking to the tears on my face. "I . . . I believe in you."

"One word from me and you'd be out on the streets. Or arrested for murder. With one finger I could reach inside your head and show you your nightmares. I could make you feel them so vividly, you'd believe you never left that dark room. Oh yes, I know *all about* that dark room and your time at the wizards' guild. And with that same touch I could save the girl you love. Or I could send her to her death."

"No!"

"Then you believe in me?"

"Didn't you hear me?!" I scream.

"I said, *do you believe in me*?!"

"Yes! Yes, I believe in you!"

"Tell me, Azeril, do you deserve mercy? After all your sins?"

"I—" The lie sticks in my throat. I shake my head. "No. I don't. But Leora does."

Endeil smiles. The light in the room seems brighter. Or maybe I only imagined that it ever went dim. His eyes glint with mischief, not madness, so that I'm left wondering if this was just a game. I can't tell if he's really that insane, or if he was only toying with me.

He offers me a hand, pulling me to my feet. "See?" he says. "That was all you had to say."

CHAPTER THIRTEEN

Leora sits next to me in the first row of pews late the next evening. Flames crackle in the fireplace, but other than that, we're alone, almost mimicking when I was here last night with Endeil. Before she was healed and before I landed on that altar. Only she doesn't know about that part.

She turns toward me and sighs. "Will you stop that already?"

"Stop what?"

"*Staring* at me. And you can sit closer. I'm not going to break."

It's not that I think she's going to break. More like that if I touch her, she might turn out to not be real. I watched Endeil heal her—I watched him put his hands on her and do what I couldn't—and I saw as the color returned to her face and her breathing strengthened. And still it feels like it was all a dream. Like I'm going to wake up any moment to find her gone and have my heart broken all over again.

I slide a few inches closer to her.

She closes the gap between us, grabbing my hand and squeezing it tight. "I'm *fine*. You could have gone to class today. You didn't have to miss your duties this morning, either. I know you're on probation. You could have—"

"No, I couldn't."

Leora watches my face for a minute. Her eyes have a sort of haunted look to them. "You could have at least got some rest. I hate to break this to you, but you look *terrible*. Like you haven't slept in days."

I laugh. "How do you expect me to look? The girl I love was dy—"

She puts her hand to my mouth, not letting me finish. "Don't say it. They put all those black drapes up, but I don't know what for. It's not like . . . it's not like I was really going to *die*." But the way a tremor of fear hangs in her voice, I know she doesn't believe that.

"I wouldn't have let you," I whisper, sliding my hand over hers. "Trust me, Leora, I would have done *anything* to keep you here."

She bites her lip, suddenly pulling away and studying my face again, like she knows there's something I haven't told her. "Az, what did you—"

"I shouldn't have left. That night . . . I shouldn't have run off like that."

"Are you saying that because I got hurt?"

"You didn't just get hurt, you got *attacked*."

"The wizards make up that stuff about the Church, and then look what happens. A wizard's daughter gets—" She chokes up. "I don't know who to trust anymore. It could have been anyone. At first I thought it was you, coming back to tell me what an idiot you'd been for leaving. And then . . ." She winces at the memory. "His face was covered. I couldn't see who he was."

She doesn't know that the High Priest who healed her is the same man who put a knife in her chest. She doesn't know this wasn't a hate crime but cold, calculated blackmail. And I should tell her the truth, except . . . except then I'd have to explain why I'm now the apprentice of the man who tried to kill her. How he hurt her because I defied him, and how I let him look into the darkest parts of me, the parts I could never let her see.

"I don't remember much after that," she says, "but I knew instantly it wasn't you. I would know you anywhere, even in the dark. The sound of your footsteps, your breathing . . . I would know."

"And if I had been there—" I swallow and get to my feet, pacing in front of the fireplace, clenching and unclenching my fists. I stop pacing and face her, my eyes meeting hers and my voice dead serious. "I would have killed him, Leora." *And I would have enjoyed it.* "He would have been the one with a knife to the heart. I would never let anyone hurt you."

She gets up, storming over to me, putting a hand to her chest where her wound was. "But *you* hurt me, Az. You *left.* You tell me you love me, and then what? You walk out?!"

One of the logs in the fireplace pops. A spark lands on the hearthstones, just missing my foot. The heat from the flames makes sweat prickle on my forehead. That and Leora demanding to know why I betrayed her.

"I shouldn't have left—I know that—and not just because of what happened after. But I'm here now." I take her hand, pressing it between both of mine. "I'm here and I'm not going anywhere. I love you, Leora. I've always loved you, since the first day we met."

"Then *why* did you leave? You're the one person who's supposed to stay."

"I hurt people," I tell her, looking away. Another crackle in the fireplace sends the logs shifting, as if in agreement. "It's what I do."

"Don't be dramatic, just tell me the truth."

She doesn't know I mean it literally. "I wanted to stay. But I . . ." I remember the darkness. The dark room and the chair. Broken, shaking, screaming. Hadrin hitting me across the face to shut me up.

I push the memory away, fighting the urge to kick the wall.

"I panicked." I thought she'd get hurt if I stayed. I thought *I'd* get hurt. Instead she almost died because I left. "I made a mistake, but this time I *won't* leave. I promise I won't." Even if being close to her means someday she'll find out the truth about me. Even if it means someday she'll hate me.

I pull her close to me, wrapping my arms around her. If we could just stay like this forever, maybe everything would be okay. Maybe it really wouldn't matter that I'm a monster. No one would ever hurt her again. We wouldn't have to worry about people like Endeil and Hadrin. And I would be here, with her, not out killing wizards.

Just a normal person.

She presses the side of her face against mine. "Do you mean it this time?"

"I always meant it."

The heat from the hearth adds to the fever already burning my skin from being so close to her. I'm not going anywhere. This is real.

I kiss her, slow and deep. Fire surges through me. She could be made of obsidian. We both could be. Her breathing becomes my breathing. We fade into each other, my darkness and her light, and for a moment I feel whole. Like there was always a piece of me that was missing. Like when our lips meet I'm no longer broken.

"Ow!" Leora jerks back, breaking away from me. She holds up her finger, watching blood well up on its surface. She plucks out a sewing pin from her school vest, where she had to repair the pocket the other day, and tosses it into the fire.

I try to put my arm around her, but right then a log explodes with a startling CRACK that makes me jump. It's so loud, so jarring, that for a moment I can't tell if it happened in the fireplace, or if something inside me just split open.

The flames rage, blindingly bright, getting higher and higher until they lick the flue. A cloud of sparks leaps out toward me, a couple of them landing on my arm, lighting my nerves on fire before I can bat them away. I feel restless, like all I want to do is get out of here. Like if I don't, something terrible is going to happen.

Just as suddenly as they leaped up, the flames die down to ash and ember. To coals that burn an angry red that pulses into orange, then red again. I can feel my own pulse in my ears, matching the shift in color. Red. Orange. Red. Orange. Like the fire has a heartbeat of its own. Like it matches mine.

Leora sucks the blood from her finger. I can't shake the feeling that someone's watching us. *Judging.* And that's when I realize my finger's bleeding, too. It doesn't hurt, and there's no wound, but a few drops of blood have welled up in the same place they did on Leora. I wipe them off on the sleeve of my robe before she sees.

The Fire thinks I'm a monster.

No, it knows *I am.*

It's all just a coincidence. None of this means anything. Not the fire crackling and splitting us apart. Not the blood on my finger when it was Leora who scratched herself on that pin.

"Come on," Leora says. "Let's get out of here. I don't know about you, Altar Boy, but this place is giving me the creeps."

I couldn't agree more, but as I glance into the fireplace one last time, at the dead ash and the glowing embers with their angry red light, I feel naked and cold. Like the coals can see everything about me, looking right through my clothes, my skin, down to where it matters.

Like the Fire itself can see straight into my heart.

And then there's a burning feeling in my head. And an image of Leora, drenched in blood. Sobbing into her hands. It's more than just an image—it feels like a vision. A vision hot and searing in my brain, like the Fire itself put it there.

I blink and they're gone, both the burning feeling and the image. And I know it wasn't a memory this time. No.

It was a warning.

CHAPTER FOURTEEN

Leora takes me to her room. We could have gone to mine—it was closer, in the church dorms, instead of all the way across the grounds at the school—but she brings me here. A second chance at the other night, a chance to accept what's offered to me and not run from it. I won't get caught leaving the girls' dorms tonight, because I'm not going anywhere.

She lights the three-wicked candle on her nightstand with one of the torches from the hall.

"We don't need light," I murmur, moving her hair out of the way to kiss her ear and then her cheek. If the light isn't strong enough to chase away my shadows, I'll hide them in darkness.

I feel her smile, the muscles in her face twitching beneath my lips. She lights more candles and places the stolen torch on a sconce in her wall, ignoring me. "I've spent enough time in the dark," she says, and I know she's remembering the black drapes hanging from the walls, waiting to bury her. "I want to feel *alive*."

I see the image of her drenched in blood. It lasts for the space of one pounding heartbeat, and then I push it away. I don't care about the Fire's warning. I would never hurt her.

"You don't have to stay here, where it happened," I tell her. "We can go to my room."

"No. I'm okay. I'm okay while you're here."

Because I'm a monster dark enough to scare away all the others. But no. I look into her eyes, and I see only trust and warmth and love. If she feels safe with me, it's not because I can protect her. It's because I'm another candle, adding light and heat to chase away the dark and the cold. The warmth of the Fire conquering the darkness of the Chasm. And I know there's no way I could ever leave her.

She leans into me. I can feel her heart beating against my chest, her breath soft and warm on my neck. She smells faintly of lavender. It conjures up memories of the summers we've spent together. Lying in fresh grass, eating strawberries hot from the sun. The sweetness of the apples from the tree I climbed.

She remembers the scar on my ankle from when I fell. I remember the way her fingertips brushed against my leg, inspecting my injury. I did have tears in my eyes, because it stung so bad and I was trying so hard to act like it didn't, so she wouldn't take her hand away.

Now I press my lips to her neck, kissing her softly. She sighs with pleasure, sending thrills all through me that start in my stomach and race to the tips of my fingers and down to my toes. I can't believe I came so close to losing her, to never looking over during morning candle service again and seeing her in the lines of students, making faces at me, trying to get me to laugh when we're supposed to be quiet and solemn.

I came so close to missing out on ever being with her. Of feeling her heart beating warm and alive against mine. Maybe we were never two separate people to begin with, and that's why it hurts so much to be away from her, and why it feels like no matter how close we get, it will never be enough.

She kisses me, slowly at first, and then it's like all our years of holding back catch up to us, and our kissing becomes urgent, frantic, as if we might never get the chance to be so close to each other again. I feel like I'm drowning, like I might die if we stop, and yet I've never felt more alive.

She slides her hands down my sides and traces the edge of my belt with her fingertips, avoiding my obsidian. Her hand brushes against my stomach through the fabric of my robes and thrills race all along my nerves again. Then she starts to undo my belt buckle.

I pull away, panting, before I can stop myself.

"What's wrong?" she asks, her face flushed, searching mine for an explanation. "I thought you wanted—"

"I *do*." *More than anything*. But going any further means getting rid of my obsidian. It means being weaponless and vulnerable—just a normal person. A boy alone with a girl. A *boy*, not a monster, and that's what I want, so why do I have this wild, panicky feeling?

"You're sure about this?" I ask her, slipping my arms around her and pulling her close, aching to kiss her again. To tear her clothes off. Or maybe to undress her, agonizingly slowly, until neither of us can take it anymore. "I mean, you're sure you don't care who I was?"

"Az, there's nothing that could make me change my mind about you. I *love* you. I . . . I always have. I always will."

She reaches for my belt again, and this time I let her unbuckle it. I let it and my knife fall to the floor, forcing away the panicky feeling that doesn't belong here.

My hands shake as I fumble with the buttons on her gray school vest. Hands that have killed people without ever wavering, now clumsy and practically useless. And I don't know if it's desperation or nerves that makes them tremble—probably both—but I only get two of the buttons undone before she gets impatient and undoes the other two herself, tossing the vest away.

She presses against me and my mouth finds hers and we're kissing again. Drinking each other in. Burning alive. I reach around and undo the laces on the back of her shirt. A quick pull on a knot is all that separates me from the bare skin underneath. And yet it's more complicated than that. The barrier between us—separating the closeness of friends from the closeness of *this*—has never been just a string. Now suddenly it is. Just threads and fabric rustling as I take off her shirt. As we break apart long enough for her to pull my robes over my head.

My hands slip down to her hips, tugging at her skirt. Wanting to just rip it off of her.

She steps out of it, still in her underwear. Not quite naked, but so, so close. Then she takes those off, too, and climbs onto the bed. I do the same and follow her, lying down beside her. Both of us completely naked. I watch the glow of the candlelight play across her shoulder and down her breasts. Part of me can't believe we're really here, that this is really happening. And part of me feels like this was always going to happen, that it was inevitable, because the two of us have always belonged to each other.

She studies my bare skin, running a hand over my chest and down across my stomach. Her face looks so intense, I wonder if it's not only my skin that's exposed, but all my secrets, as if they were written all over me, as plain as my scars.

But then she sighs and kisses me, wrapping her arms around my neck and drawing me closer to her. I'm feverish and burning, my mouth desperate against hers, my hands taking in the softness of her skin. Tracing the shapes of her body, memorizing every inch of her. I've waited so long to tell her I love her. To kiss her. To be *here*, with her, in her bed. Not as her friend but as someone more. Someone who can forget himself, who can be whole, unbroken.

She doesn't care who I was. Maybe I don't, either.

There's a knock on the door. A pounding fist, shattering the moment and the illusion that it was just us in the world, that nothing else ever mattered.

The door opens. Leora screams. I'm torn between shielding her from whatever threat just walked in and reaching to the floor for my knife. But reaching for the knife means leaving her alone, even just for a moment, and so I hesitate.

"I came as soon as I heard— Oh, Chasm take me!" I can't quite see his face, the light's too dim in the doorway, but his voice is familiar. He shields his eyes and turns away, and I almost don't recognize him without his blue robes. He's changed clothes to come onto the church grounds. He'd have to. But I still recognize him.

And I could never forget that voice. The same one that ordered another wizard to torture me and swore he'd never hurt me again.

Hadrin.

Leora grabs a blanket to cover herself, sitting up and glaring at him. "What are you *doing* here?"

Any fear is gone from her voice, replaced with anger. I slide off the bed and slip on my robes, feeling around on the cold floor for my belt and the knife.

"What am I doing here?!" he shouts. "I came because I got an urgent letter that said my *daughter* was *dying!*"

His daughter.

Leora's father's a wizard. But I knew that already. I just didn't know his name.

He waves his arms around like a madman, not focusing on me yet, too busy yelling at her. "And now I find you perfectly fine, and . . . and in bed with some . . ." He can't even finish his sentence, he's so angry.

"I'm *not* perfectly fine! But I'm healed, I'm not dead, and you don't have to sound so disappointed about it!"

"You're obviously all right if you're all right enough for *this*." His lip curls in disgust. "Get dressed. And you—" He turns his attention to me.

Our eyes lock. I see the exact second recognition hits.

"No. *No*." He presses his hands to his forehead in disbelief. In revulsion. Then he storms over to me and grabs my wrist.

I jerk it away. "Don't touch me!"

"You stay away from her!"

"Leave him alone," Leora says. "You have no right to come in here like this. We haven't spoken in years, and now you think you can just—"

"You didn't tell me it was for *her*! To save *her*!"

"You would have been willing to hurt me if you knew? You would have broken your promise? I know what you did to me! When I was in that chair and you *wanted* me to be afraid! I know what you—"

He hits me across the mouth. To shut me up, like he did in my memory. It's not anger on his face this time, but fear. Pure terror of what I might reveal to his daughter, of what he might have to remember.

I taste blood. Just like in my memory.

Leora puts her hand to her mouth and gapes, horrified, as her fingers come away bloody. She makes a strangled yelp in the back of her throat.

"What have you done to her?" Hadrin asks, his voice shaking. "You said you were with the Church, but I didn't . . . I didn't make the connection with the school. You were never supposed to meet. You were never supposed to *touch* her!"

I shut my eyes. I think of the blood on my finger when it was Leora who'd pricked hers. It started when I kissed her. But was that really so wrong? How could kissing the girl I love be *wrong*?

I see the image of her drenched in blood.

Hadrin looks me over, at the blood on my lips from where he hit me, and winces. He tries to put a hand on my arm, lightly, but I step out of his reach.

"You broke your promise," I tell him. "Be careful or I'll keep mine."

"Az," Leora says, "what's going on?"

Her father was working on an experiment. A *live* one, an . . . abomination. Whatever that means. Her father, Hadrin. The wizard who haunts my memories.

"Your father and I have met before," I tell her. "I don't remember when exactly, but the experiment he was working on, the one you—" The one she hated so much. "I didn't know, but now I do, and . . . it was me, wasn't it?" I look to Hadrin for confirmation, but he just bows his head in shame.

Leora's face crumples, her mouth making movements like she's going to speak, but her jaw is shaking too hard. Like she's frozen and shivering. Like all the warmth just got sucked out of the room. She bursts into tears. Into heart-wrenching sobs. I recognize the sound from when I was crying at her deathbed. It's the sound of having someone's life so closely bound with yours, and then having them ripped away. And I feel the pain all over again, the pain of the world tearing her from me, leaving me hollow and raw. Only there's no one left to sell my soul to this time. There's no way to fix this.

She said my past didn't matter, but it turns out it does. She said who I was could never change how she felt, but if that were true, would she be crying her eyes out right now? Would she sound like someone just told her the boy she loves is dead, like he never existed in the first place?

All I want to do is comfort her, but there's nothing I can say. It's obvious she doesn't want me here right now. And so I do the one thing I said I wouldn't.

I turn away and I leave.

———

Hadrin follows me, catching up to me in the empty stairwell at the end of the hall. "Azeril, wait."

I don't stop. "I'm not supposed to be here." Not in the girls' dorms, not in the church, not . . . not anywhere.

"I'm sorry."

"Sorry for what?" I spin around to face him. "Sorry for hitting me? Sorry that you made me a monster? Or are you sorry that you didn't do what I asked, because you didn't know it was for her?" He would have sacrificed me for her. I get it. I do. But it still hurts.

"I don't know what I would have done."

"You had no problem breaking your promise just now." I fold my arms, tucking them around myself. Keeping all the broken pieces from falling away. "Tell me one thing. Am I . . . Tell me Leora and I aren't related." I can't bring myself to ask if he's my father.

"You really don't remember, do you?"

"Just tell me."

He sighs and shakes his head. "No. But there are other reasons why I can't approve of this. Why you have to stay away from her."

"Because of the blood."

"I made a mistake once."

"*Once?*" I laugh, bitter and mocking, wanting to hurt him like he's hurt me.

"I cast a spell I shouldn't have, though I didn't realize it at the time, not until . . . I needed the hair of a young maiden, and I used hers, thinking nothing of it. I didn't know it mattered, that you'd be linked. Not until I came home that night to find my ten-year-old daughter, my little girl, covered in blood." There's a hitch in his voice when he says it. A note of true regret.

"Let me guess. The wounds she bled from matched all the horrible things you'd done to me."

"Yes," he says, and at least he has the decency to sound ashamed. My hands ball into fists. It's not fair. None of it. He cared that she was bleeding, but I was the one he'd hurt. And yet . . . it's Leora we're talking about. And I can't begrudge her own father regretting that he'd done something awful to her. Even if he couldn't have cared less about what he did to me.

"So I cast a second spell. One to keep her safe. One that it appears *you've* now broken."

"The damage is done then. I don't see how me staying away from her helps anyone but you."

"And if it were to get worse? If the bleeding is just the beginning? The two of you are linked in a way no two people ever should be."

"Cast the spell again."

"Why? So you can break it?" He waves that thought away. "It doesn't matter. I no longer have the right energy to draw from, now that her mother is . . . You don't know what it cost before. She was never the same after."

"Leora?"

"No. You don't know the price that was paid, and now here you are, ruining the work I've done to protect my daughter, all so you can weasel your way into her bed."

"That's not—" I swallow back the words. He's got it all wrong, but I don't have to explain myself to him. "I would *never* hurt her. You have to know that."

"And yet you already have." He tilts his head, challenging me to think about that.

"I saved her, didn't I? No thanks to you."

"You did, and . . . I'm sorry, for what happened in there." He gestures in the direction of Leora's room. "For what I did to you. I know you don't believe me, but I am. I didn't want my daughter to know what a horrible person her father has been, but showing her was not the answer. You didn't deserve that."

She doesn't know what a horrible person I've been, either. I guess we have that in common. "I'm not going to forgive you."

"No, I expect you're not. I expect you'd rather not see me again, in fact. But you're forgetting. I still need your help."

All I want is for him to go away. I want to go back in time to before he walked in on us. To have her all to myself, for her not to be sobbing because the boy she loves isn't who or what she thought he was.

"You want me to be a weapon. You already know my answer. You had your chance, and you threw it away. Now you really expect me to help you?"

"It's not me who needs your help. Not *just* me. The Church isn't the sanctuary you think it is. And the High Priest—"

"Is crazy."

"He's planning something. Our greatest augurs have read the signs—I've read them myself—and something terrible is about to happen. Something we won't be able to stop without your help."

I give him an incredulous look. "You want *me* to help the *wizards*? You're just as deluded as Endeil."

"And you're not nearly as powerful as you could be if you had your memories back."

"Good thing for you I don't have them then."

"And if there was a way you could? Azeril, there's a war coming. You don't need to cast divination spells or read the bones to know that. And I'm telling you that you're our only hope to stop the High Priest. If you had your memories back, *you* would decide who won the war."

He means it. A war between the wizards and the Church. And he expects me to side with the wizards? To help them win, so they can do what, exactly? Destroy the Church and keep everyone as powerless as possible, living in a state of constant fear? So they can steal everyone's energy for their spells? The High Priest might be crazy, but I'm not. "And if I got my memories back, who would that make me? There's more than spells buried in my head. You know that better than anyone, so how can you even ask me?"

"Because I also know you, and I know what you want most in the world."

"Oh, yeah? And what's that?"

"Redemption. If you did this, Azeril, it would be a sacrifice, yes. But it would also redeem you from your sins."

I stand there, taking that in. I do want redemption—he's right about that, at least—even if I've killed only wizards, only people who deserved it.

But I liked killing them. I'm a murderer and a monster. I was never who Leora thought I was, but maybe I could be. If it's possible for a monster to be redeemed. For sinners to be made innocent again.

"If you don't do this," Hadrin goes on, "a lot of people are going to get hurt. A lot of them will die."

"Is that a threat?"

"No. Stay away from my daughter or I'll send you back to the chair. *That's* a threat. This? This is the truth. A war will have many casualties on both sides, and a lot of innocents will die in the middle of it. I know what you think of us, and why you *should* think that. But whatever the High Priest is planning, it's an evil that will destroy us all. Wizards and the Church alike."

"I'm his apprentice, you know. You refused to help me when I needed it, and now I'm his Fire-forsaken apprentice. Where were you and your hope of getting my memories back then? Or are you planning to hurt me again? Because that was a onetime offer."

A grim smile tugs on his mouth. "I'm not as cruel as you think I am."

"You're right—today you proved you're worse than that. You've taken everything from me. Even the girl I love." And the one perfect moment I was going to have with her. "If I got my memories back, it would change me. How could it not? So you're here asking me to sacrifice who I am, and for what? For you?"

"No," he says. "Not for me. For all the people who are going to get hurt if you don't. And, most importantly, for yourself. Because I think we both know that you're more than just a killer."

"I'm a monster. And what I've done can't be erased."

"I know, but I have to believe that even a monster can find redemption. It's the only way I can fall asleep at night and get up in the morning, knowing what I've done. And in a way, my sins are worse than yours. You were made to be this way. It wasn't your choice. But I'm the one who made you."

"You know I can't join the wizards. No matter what you say."

"And you know I can't let you be with my daughter. I suppose that makes us even."

"No. It doesn't." And I don't need his permission to be with Leora. Just hers.

He turns to leave, his gaze lingering on the blood on my mouth. "If you change your mind about what I'm asking you—if you need me for anything—I'll be in town another week or so. You know where to find me."

He leaves, with no idea that his words echoed the High Priest's, the man he wants me to help defeat. The two of them are more similar than he realizes, though that isn't exactly a surprise. After all, none of us is innocent. We're all monsters here.

CHAPTER FIFTEEN

The Fire-Gifting Ceremony takes place two days later, honoring everyone in Ashbury who got their ability from the Fire this year. That's *everyone*, not just those of us who are with the Church or going to the school. Their families show up, too. It's such a huge event that it doesn't take place only inside the church, but across the grounds, spreading from the churchyard over to the school. It feels like the whole world is here. Like this is the most important event that will ever happen, and I'm not a part of it.

Except that all of the acolytes have to be present during the formal ceremony, which takes place inside the church. The Fathers and Mothers call out the names of everyone the Fire deemed worthy this year and hand them a lighted candle. Those of us not being honored in the ceremony have to stand to the side of the altar. On the right side are all the acolytes who got their gifts in previous years. And to the left are those of us still waiting.

The girls stand separate from the boys, making my group even smaller. Last year there were five of us on this side, including me and Rathe and Bran. Now they're both being honored, and it's just me and Tol, who's only ten, and Karl, who's twelve. Making me stand out as the oldest. And even in the girls' group, there are only four of them, and all of them younger than me.

None of them are murderers condemned by the Fire. None of them are a wizard's experiment, an abomination. None of them have wizard spells lurking in the depths of their memories. Any of those is reason enough for the Fire to ignore me, to leave me standing off to the side while everyone I know moves on.

My feet hurt from standing here for so long. I shift uncomfortably, aware of some of the other acolytes staring at me from across the aisle. At the gold star now pinned to my collar, marking me as the High Priest's apprentice, something he formally announced yesterday morning. Letton in particular sneers at me, like he can't figure out how I got the job.

You don't want to know.

The worst part of the ceremony isn't the standing there for two hours—the time it takes for them to call out over a hundred names and hand out just as many candles—though I can't say I enjoy it. And it's not seeing Rathe or any of the other acolytes going through a rite of passage I'm pretty certain I'll never be a part of. In fact, Rathe even grins at me as he takes his candle from Father Moors and uses his ability—the power to shape wax at the touch of his hand—to form it into an apple and then pretends to take a bite out of it. He gets a quick smile out of me that's gone again a moment later.

The worst part of the ceremony is when Leora walks down the aisle. Instead of her school uniform, she's wearing a purple dress with matching flowers in her hair. Because this is a special occasion. I watch her as she moves down the faded red carpet and then stands with the Fathers and Mothers. My eyes are on her the whole time, when they call her name and when they light a candle and hand it to her, signifying the Fire giving her its gift. And not once does she ever look over at me. She *knows* I'm here and where I'm standing—the same place as last year—but she never even glances my way. I'm her best friend, or at least I was, and now she doesn't want to have anything to do with me.

There's a big celebration after the ceremony's finally over, out on the grounds. There's a band playing and some tables set out, covered in fruit and roasted meats. It's dark by now, and there's a big bonfire in the middle of everything. I hear bursts of laughter in the dark, the sounds of people enjoying themselves. Eating, drinking, dancing.

I stand there in the churchyard, watching for a moment, and I don't think I've ever felt so alone in my life. Not since Father Moors found me standing over those dead wizards, the knife bloody in my hand. But that was different. He took me in. And back then I didn't know what I was missing.

My hand twitches, wanting to reach for the knife. But I don't let myself. Not in front of all these people, even if they're not looking. Even if I feel like I'm invisible.

I didn't get a power from the Fire. And I don't have a family waiting to greet me. I thought Leora was my family now, but if that was true, she wouldn't have stopped talking to me, or having anything to do with me, now that she knows what I am. And there's no way Hadrin would come here for this, so I know she's alone tonight, too. And still she doesn't come and find me.

My duties for the night are over, and I'm free to do whatever I want, but all I want to do is go back to my room. Maybe I'll feel less alone, without all these people around to remind me of what I don't have. Or with the knife's fire to make me not care.

I hesitate, searching the crowd one more time for her before giving up. Then I turn to go.

"Hey, Az!" Rathe calls. He's out of breath as he comes running toward me. "Where do you think you're going?"

"Bed."

He rolls his eyes at me and grabs my arm, not letting me leave. "Don't give me that. This is a *party*. You should be having fun."

"No, *you* should. I'm not part of this and you know it."

"Why? Because you haven't gotten your ability yet? Maybe the Fire doesn't think you're ready because you act like a pile of wet leaves every time something goes wrong."

"I'm not . . . A pile of wet leaves?" That doesn't really sound like me, does it?

Rathe nods. "*Everyone* gets a power sooner or later. Well, except wizards. You just have to be patient, right?"

"Sure." Not at all. "But I didn't get it this year. I don't belong, and I . . . Can't I just go to my room?"

"And sulk? What kind of a friend would I be if I let you do that? Look, I don't know what happened between you and her—and yes, I *know* something happened, everyone does—but just because you finally got together and things didn't work out doesn't mean you can't enjoy yourself. And if you seriously insist on sulking in your room all night, then I'm going with you."

"But *you're* actually part of this."

He shrugs. "Not if you aren't."

"And you think I'm going to let you do that? Give all this up to hang out with me?"

"Or you can come with me and join in the party. Either way, I'm not letting you go off alone."

"You would do that for me?"

"You remember last year? When I sprained my ankle and was so slow on those crutches, but you walked to candle service with me every morning, even though we were always late? You got written up for it, but you kept doing it anyway. Everybody else passed me by, but you made sure I didn't get left behind. You remember that, don't you?"

"Of course."

"And the time the girls stole all my robes in the night, so I couldn't leave my room? You were the one who loaned me yours until I got them back."

"They were dirty," I remind him. "And it wasn't a big deal."

"It was to me. And this is a big deal to you." He gestures to the festival going on without us. "And I'm not leaving you behind. So, what do you say? Let's go eat one of everything and maybe find the girls and put ice chips down their backs."

"You know, there's a *reason* they stole all your clothes."

He grins. "I'm not hearing a no."

"Fine," I say, grinning back at him. "We'll make the rounds. And then . . ."

"And then if you want to sulk in your room, we can do that, too. But for now, let's go have some fun."

CHAPTER SIXTEEN

"Forget her," High Priest Endeil says, adjusting a painting on the wall in his temporary office. It's an image of a volcanic crack in the earth, of bright magma filling in the darkness, representing the Fire conquering the Chasm. The primal force of warmth and life triumphing over violence and death. "I can practically hear your heart breaking with every dramatic sigh. So, whatever she's done to you—"

"It's none of your business."

"Ah, but my new apprentice has been moping around here for days. That makes it my business. And I know how you feel about her—don't forget, I've seen inside your head." He holds up a hand, wriggling his fingers.

As if I could ever forget. I turn away. It's been five days now since I last spoke to Leora. And it's not because I care about Hadrin's wishes. She's been avoiding me. First there was the Fire-Gifting Ceremony, where she completely ignored me. And the last few days she's been looking into my eyes in class like she wants to say something important, and then running from me the second we have a chance to talk.

I wish I could talk to her about Hadrin's offer. About me joining the wizards to fight the Church. She'd think it's as crazy as I do. But even if Leora was talking to me, I couldn't ask her. Because admitting I'm not sure I made the right choice, that I really do want redemption for all my sins, means owning up to all the things I don't want her to know about me.

Hadrin believes in redemption. Or he wants to, at least. I'm not sure if I can.

"You gave up everything for her," Endeil goes on, interrupting my thoughts, "and now look how she treats you." He steps back from the painting, eyeing it to see if it's level. "I'm telling you, you're better off without her. You're my apprentice now. You're going places. You don't have time to be"—he pauses, struggling to think of the word—"*wasting* your talents."

"Do you need me for anything today or not?"

"You must be dying to use that obsidian of yours. A skill like that, and you have so few chances to make use of it, especially now that the wizards are suspicious of us." He pauses to admire his handiwork with the painting and dusts his hands off, then whirls around to face me. "You'll be pleased to know that you'll be using it today."

I'm anything but pleased. And I'm not dying to use it, because I've been using it plenty. Holding on to it every chance I get, even if I'm not killing anyone. Its fire is the only thing that can drown out my thoughts. About her. About Hadrin.

But even though I've been getting my obsidian fix every night, still my fingers twitch just thinking about it. About all the things I wish I could block out forever.

I force my hand away from the knife, not wanting to give him the satisfaction.

But it's clear from the smile twisting his mouth that he already noticed me reaching for it. "There's a reason you know how to use obsidian. A very *interesting* reason. Would you like to know what it is? I saw it, you know. When I—"

"*No.*" I never need to know anything that happened in my past again.

"It seems our guest is here anyway."

Rathe knocks on the half-open door and pokes his head in. "I'm— Oh, hey, Az. Are you here for this, too?"

I glance from him to Endeil, a sense of unease sliding over me. "Here for what?"

"Azeril's going to be assisting me with this . . . experiment," High Priest Endeil says, hesitating on the last word. He must know what a loaded word it's become for me. He must know what I am.

Even if I don't.

"Please," Endeil says, offering Rathe a chair. "Sit down."

He does. He seems perfectly calm, like he has no idea what he's getting himself into. I don't, either, but it can't be anything good. I crouch down next to him while Endeil's back is turned.

"You shouldn't be here," I whisper.

"Don't be jealous, Az. I know how you feel about not getting your ability, but think what this will mean."

"What? I don't know what you're talking about."

"You'll get yours, too. You're his apprentice. I'm just the test subject."

"But what does that—"

"Now," Endeil says, clapping his hands together and interrupting our conversation—one I'm sure he could hear, despite our whispering—"let's get started with the procedure. It won't take long, though it might pinch. Just a bit. Get comfortable there, Rathe, while I speak to my apprentice." He slings his arm around my shoulders and steers me toward the hall, stepping just outside of the door.

I shrug him off. "Whatever's going on in there, whatever he *thinks* is going on, I'm not—"

"Oh, but you are. You *agreed to be my apprentice*, remember? And everything that entails. Or have you forgotten your promise so quickly? And you're going to like this. I saw it in a dream." He lights a fire in his palm and stares into it, as if he's reliving the dream right now. "I've been having so many dreams lately, since I looked into your mind. Since I stared into the darkness and was touched by a higher power. I told you we're going to change the world, Azeril, and it starts with a gift for your friend in there and a gift for you."

"I don't need anything from you. Neither does Rathe."

"Don't you?" He tilts his head, the flames in his hand turning a sickly shade of green. "I saw inside your head. I know exactly what you need." He reaches up and touches his hand to my temple before I can step away.

The flames burn inside my brain, just for an instant, and then my hand is on the knife. My blood blazes white hot, fighting against him, but it's not enough to drown out his fire.

He moves his hand away, leaving an image burned into my mind. Him with his hands pressed to either side of Rathe's head. Me, stabbing the knife into Rathe's palm. Loving that moment as the knife touches flesh, watching Rathe gasp in pain as blood wells up on his skin and drips onto the floor.

I let go of the knife. I think about what Hadrin said, about stopping Endeil. About me being the only one who can.

"It will feel good," Endeil says, "to have someone else in the chair for a change. To be the one causing his pain. Won't it?"

I look away, but I can't bring myself to deny it. "He's my *friend*. I'm not going to do that."

"He's here by choice. As I said, this is a gift for both of you. He will have compensation, and it will be worth it to him. Trust me on that. I saw this in my dream. I saw what I can give to people and how you can help them. It starts here, with one volunteer, and with one apprentice in desperate need of healing."

Whatever we're about to do, it doesn't sound like healing. "And if I refuse?"

He laughs and picks a speck of dirt out from under his fingernail. "You won't. You already made your choice, back in the chapel, when you were on your knees and said you would do anything. But if you want to play that game, let me remind you that I know where to find her."

"If you *ever* touch Leora again—"

"The last time I touched her, I believe I healed her of those terrible wounds. But for the record, I wasn't planning to have any physical contact with her. I was thinking she ought to know about some of the awful things I've seen in your head. Things that you've done that I suspect you haven't told her and that you would never want her to know."

"She'd never believe you." A lie. She *wouldn't* have, before she knew what I was.

"Well, it's a good thing I won't need to test that theory, isn't it? As I said, this is a gift." He leans in close, whispering. "A gift I believe you'll be more than happy to accept."

I think about the knife hitting flesh. About how good it would feel for it to taste blood. Even if it's blood from my friend, not from a wizard, not from anyone who deserves it. Maybe I've been getting my fix every night, but I've been denying the knife the one thing it wants most. I've been missing out on the euphoria that goes along with it. The joy of causing pain.

My hand shakes, and a painful longing twists inside me, so that for a moment I know I would do anything to give the knife what it wants. To fill a need that's become more than just the knife's, that's become my own. I don't remember the last time I denied it for this long.

But I can't. I shouldn't. "Get someone else. I'm your apprentice, not your slave." The words come out uncertain. I'm already reaching for the knife, even as I tell myself I won't do it.

Endeil puts a hand on my shoulder and looks me in the eyes. "I need you for this, Azeril. I think you know that. You're the only one who can do this without killing him."

"He's my friend."

"Not much of a friend if you'd let him die. I could get someone else to help me, but it has to be obsidian for this to work. It has to be your specialty and mine. And you know what would happen if someone less skilled with the knife lost control. Think of all the blood that would be spilled. The life draining out of him. You can't deny that it's a strong possibility."

"He doesn't have to do this."

"He's already made up his mind. He's going through with it. The question is, *are you*?"

———

Rathe sits in the chair with his back to me. I still don't know what he thinks he's getting as compensation for all this, what could possibly make him want to go through with it, only that there's still time to back out. I should be leaving. I should be turning around and walking away.

This isn't like hunting wizards. Cutting into him means never looking him in the eyes again. He's my friend, the same one who made me join in the festivities the other night, who wouldn't leave me behind, but after this he won't be. He *can't* be.

I wanted redemption, and this is the exact opposite. But I don't walk away. Just like Endeil knew I wouldn't. Just like I knew.

Maybe Hadrin's wrong about me. Maybe I'm not better than this, after all.

Endeil stands behind the chair. He puts his hands on Rathe's temples, mimicking the vision he showed me. "Hold out your right hand," he tells Rathe.

Rathe's breathing hard, his face pale, a bead of sweat sliding down his forehead. Whatever's going on here, it's hardly even started, and he's already terrified. But he nods and holds his trembling hand out, like Endeil wants. "I'm ready," he says, even if the tremor in his voice says otherwise.

Sparks fly along my nerves, and I'm not even touching the knife yet. I want to leave. But more than that I want to stay. "What's going to happen?" I ask, my voice quiet, matching the eerie feeling in the room.

"A miracle." Endeil sounds so serious, so certain, that I can't help but wonder if it's true. And then fire blazes in his hands, and he presses them to the sides of Rathe's head. Rathe screams like he's on fire, and I expect the familiar scent of burnt flesh and hair, but it doesn't come. Whatever's burning is inside his head—not out. He kicks at the chair and twists his torso, trying to get away.

"Now!" Endeil says.

I just stand there, my chest prickling with fear.

Don't come to me complaining of his screaming. If he's not screaming, you're not doing it right!

"Azeril, now!" Endeil shouts.

I blink, suddenly aware of what I'm supposed to do. I unsheathe the knife and grab Rathe's wrist with my other hand. His skin burns. So does mine, but not because the High Priest's got his hands on me. I struggle against the obsidian's desire to cut into him, to rip him apart. The cut has to be precise. Calculated.

Time slows as I press the tip of the knife into his palm, right in the center. Rathe's eyes meet mine, his look almost vacant, and I wonder if he's even aware of what's going on right now. I hope he won't remember this, that he doesn't know I'm here. But then he *sees* me. He sees me and the knife and the blood spilling from his hand.

He must see the smile on my face. The pleasure of the knife tasting flesh. But I'm the only one who can do this. The only one who won't kill him. And it's too late to stop either way.

Then fear flashes in his eyes, and in that moment I'm human again, a stab of guilt jarring my resolve. *What would Leora think?* runs through my head, unwelcome, but still there.

I falter, losing my precision, the knife overpowering me in our struggle. The blade slices deeper and burns hotter than I ever meant it to. And through the burning of the knife, I feel its power collide with Endeil's. My skin crawls all over, nausea suddenly twisting my stomach like a punch to the gut.

Rathe cries out and jerks his hand away, cutting an even longer gash across his palm. He presses his other hand to the wound, blood spilling over both of them.

The fire in Endeil's palms blazes bright red, matching the blood. And then the fire turns dark, and I know whatever Endeil's doing is *wrong*. He thinks the Fire touched him, but he said he saw darkness, and whatever power this is, it doesn't feel like the Fire's magic. It feels cold and empty.

Like it came straight from the Chasm.

The nausea hits me again, and I put a hand to my stomach, my knees bending. I think I might actually be sick, and then, in an instant, the flames disappear. Endeil lets go of Rathe. The ceremony's over.

"It worked," Endeil breathes. "I know it worked."

"Heal him."

But Endeil signals for me to be quiet. "Do you feel different?" he asks Rathe.

How can he *not* feel different? After all the dark magic that flowed from Endeil into him . . . I felt it, just for a moment, and it sickened me. Rathe got a real dose of it.

Rathe bites his lip, fighting the pain in his hand. His face is red all over, his breathing strained. "No. Yes. I—" He holds out his right hand, blood dripping from his palm and pooling on the floor. He points to a dead beetle lying upside down on the stones. It looks like no more than a husk—like the slightest breeze could blow it away. But Rathe reaches his outstretched finger toward it, as if some unseen force is compelling him, moving his hand for him.

When he touches the beetle, its shell turns from a washed-out gray to bright blue. Its little black legs wriggle and twitch. The beetle flails around until it tips itself over and scuttles across the floor, swerving to avoid the pool of blood.

Rathe's already pale face goes ashen. He slumps back in the chair. "What just happened?"

"A miracle," Endeil says. "You have two powers now. I *did* that. *We* did that," he adds, nodding at me.

But I don't want credit for the disgusting thing I've just done, the magic we've just worked, even if it's too late to take back my part in it.

We gave Rathe another power. It's one thing to melt and shape wax, but bringing creatures back from the dead is something else, and nothing about it seems natural to me.

Rathe looks to Endeil, then at the beetle rubbing its feet together in the corner. "This changes everything." He stares at his bloody hands, his face lighting up as he realizes what he's just done. But there are shadows on his face where there didn't used to be, and I hardly recognize him. Maybe it's the pain and the blood loss taking their toll, but he doesn't look right. Gone is Rathe's smile, the one I've seen a million times—the one that's always bright and sincere—replaced by something hollow and empty and not him at all.

And I can't help thinking, if I'd said yes to Hadrin, if I'd listened to him, would I have been here today? Would I still have hurt my friend? And would there be those dark shadows on his face and that grim, hollow smile?

I take a step back. I have to get out of here.

My movement catches Rathe's attention. His eyes meet mine, his blond eyebrows coming together in a scowl. And there's a darkness that wasn't there before. A raw anger burning inside him. He doesn't say a word, but he doesn't need to. His expression says it all.

I know what you did to me. That you liked *it.*

There's no air here. I scramble for the door, fumbling with the knob like it's covered in oil. Finally it turns and I run. I run down the long, twisting hallways, until I reach the main doors. I burst outside, into the sunlight, and sink to the ground.

Out here, the world seems normal. Springy blades of grass press against my hand. The sun shines above me in a blue sky with white, puffy clouds. I can hear some kids playing and laughing in the field next to the school.

What just happened in Endeil's office seems far away. But it isn't. Rathe has two powers now, because of me, and one of them is anything but miraculous.

CHAPTER SEVENTEEN

I'm sitting on Leora's bed when she comes in after dinner. She gasps and puts a hand to her chest.

I admit, sneaking into her room might not have been the best move to win back her trust, but how else am I supposed to talk to her? It kind of stings to think that's what I'm doing—winning back her trust. I shouldn't have lost it in the first place. But whatever she thinks about me, it isn't the truth. Not the whole truth, anyway.

"Az," she says, her eyes darting toward me, then away again. "The door was locked."

"And the window was open. Besides, a locked door wouldn't stop you. Why should it stop me?" I grin, just a little, remembering all the times she let herself into my room.

She steps back, like she's going to bolt.

"Leora, wait." Less than a week ago, we were lying in this bed together, taking each other's clothes off. Now she acts like it's a crime for me to come anywhere near her. "I need to talk to you."

She hesitates, thinking that over. Then she shuts the door, though she doesn't come any closer to me. "So you break into my room and scare me half to death?"

"What was I supposed to do? You won't talk to me. You've been avoiding me, and—" I get up and take a step toward her, but her eyes go wide in fear. I sit back down and hold my hands up in surrender. I wonder if she notices I came here unarmed. I left the knife in my room. Partly to make myself seem less dangerous, but mostly so I wouldn't be tempted to touch it. Because right now, with her looking at me like I'm a rabid dog that's got her cornered, I can't help wishing for the knife's fire. Just to take the sting away.

"Did you know?" she says. "Did you *know* what you were?"

"Of course not. By the Fire, Leora—"

"Don't. Don't invoke the Fire, Az. You might be dressed like one, but you're no altar boy."

"Fine. I don't know what I am. But I know *who* I am, and I'm still *me*. You know me."

"I thought I did. But that was before I knew you were my father's project." She crosses her arms over her chest, staring at the floor. "You took him from me. He loved you more than he ever loved me."

I laugh. It sounds so out of place right now, but I can't help it. "He doesn't love me. He *never* loved me."

"He was obsessed with you."

"If that's what this is about—"

"It's not." She edges toward me, then sits down on the bed. Not exactly next to me, but not as far away as she could be, either. "I mean, it is, but there's more to it than that. You're . . . I don't know what's real anymore."

"*I'm* real. I'm flesh and blood. And I love you."

"You can't say that. You don't know what you are."

"So tell me."

"Az, you don't—"

"You said whoever I was in my past didn't matter, but that's obviously not true. So *tell me*. What's so horrible that it could turn you against me?"

"I'm not against you." Her voice goes quiet. Full of regret, but not apologizing.

"I'm an . . . experiment." *An abomination.*

"I was so young. I don't remember very much. It's not like my father came home every night and told me what went on at the guild. But I picked up bits of information, here and there."

"Hadrin said I was a weapon. Is that it?"

A short laugh escapes her lips. "*It?* Is that *it*? You say that so calmly."

I'm good with the knife, and I've killed my fair share of wizards. Finding out I'm a weapon isn't exactly a shock. But she doesn't know that. "It explains the obsidian," I mutter, my fingers flexing over where the hilt should be. "And, I mean . . . So what if he wants me to be a weapon? It doesn't mean I am."

Her forehead wrinkles a little. "Not just some weapon. You were created to be a *super* weapon." *Created.* I don't like that word, either. "Worse than all the wizards put together."

"Great. Is that all?"

"It's not funny. They put all these spells into you."

"How?"

"I don't know. He never told me what they did to you."

I laugh. "No, I'll bet he didn't."

"What does *that* mean?"

"Nothing. And it's not like I remember these spells. So . . . I'm still me. You're still you. Nothing's changed."

"But just because you don't remember doesn't mean they're not still there, somewhere inside you. You told me yourself you remembered something the other day. Your memories, they could all come back."

It seems like everyone wants me to get my memories back. Everyone except her. And me. "And you think if I had these spells again, that I'd be some kind of monster." A worse one than I am now?

"I didn't say that."

"I hate wizards, Leora. The same as you. You think I *want* to be full of their spells? And I don't understand why that makes me a weapon. You're telling me I'm secretly a wizard who memorized a bunch of magic?" No wonder the Fire didn't give me an ability. I guess the Fathers and Endeil were wrong about it favoring me.

"No, Az. You don't have wizard spells. You have the spells they *wish* they had. Spells so ancient, they were lost to them. They're worse than wizard spells. They draw more energy, so much more— that's something I do remember him talking about. About how one day you . . . It was an experiment, to see how much energy the spells took, and . . ."

"Just say it, Leora. Whatever it is, I can take it."

She lifts her chin and looks me in the eyes. "You killed someone."

I stare back at her, unflinching. I don't pretend to be surprised. "So that's why you don't want to be with me."

"No! It was an accident. I mean, they made you cast that spell, and I don't think even my father knew what would happen, so how could you have known?"

I wouldn't be so sure about that—about either of us not knowing—but I don't correct her. "So I have spells more powerful than any wizard's. Ancient spells that will drain all of a person's energy and kill them." I say it matter-of-factly, still letting it all sink in. "And if no wizards have these spells, then how did they supposedly put them into me?"

"They came from somewhere else."

"Where?"

She puts her head in her hands. "I'm probably wrong. It was so long ago, I'm probably not remembering it right."

"*Leora.*"

"You should ask my father."

Just the thought makes me sick. "I'm asking *you.* You've been my best friend for over three years. You said you loved me. Maybe whatever this is changes that, but . . . I'd rather hear it from you."

"For the record, Az, I *do* love you. And you're still my best friend."

"Your best friend who you avoid. Who you wouldn't even talk to until I broke into your room. A week ago, we were *together* in this bed. And we were happy. And now you won't even sit too close to me. I know my past isn't perfect. My present isn't, either, but I didn't do anything to you. I love you, Leora. And I would never hurt you. Not if I could help it." I remember what Hadrin said, about the spell he cast on us. About both of us bleeding from each other's wounds. He thinks it could get worse if I don't stay away from her. Or maybe he just said that, in the hopes that I'd believe him and leave her alone.

"*If* you could help it," she whispers, and I don't like the skepticism in her voice.

"I deserve the truth. And I'd rather hear it from you than from the wizard who tor— I want to hear it from you."

She nods and grabs my hand, squeezing it in hers. The warmth of our skin combines, and again I remember being naked with her in this same bed and what almost happened between us. "It was the Chasm, Az." Her voice is clear and strong, but hushed, as if it's dangerous just to say the words. "All your spells came from the depths of the Chasm."

CHAPTER EIGHTEEN

I'm almost back to my room when Rathe steps out of the shadows. I'm supposed to be the one lurking in the darkness, waiting for just the right moment. But I was distracted.

Rathe's face looks pale and sallow in the torchlight. There are dark circles under his eyes, as if he hasn't slept in days. I tell myself it must be a trick of the light.

He's not alone. Bran and Letton step into the hall. Letton's got a slightly bent nose, like he's been in a few fights before. He's also taller, and his hair's a darker shade of brown than Bran's. I've seen them practically every day for the past three years, and I've never had a reason to think of them as threats. But now there's a menacing vibe in the air, and I can't help noticing they've got me surrounded.

My hand slips down to my hip, searching for the knife that isn't there. Because I left it in my room. Like an idiot. And all so Leora wouldn't think of me as a weapon. But it didn't help, and I've got something much worse inside my head, anyway.

"I *saw* you today," Rathe says. He stares at his hand, rubbing his thumb and forefinger together, like they're dirty. "When you slit open my palm."

I glance at him, then the others, at the grim expressions on their faces. Edging in so close to me. My fingers twitch, even though I know there's no knife. "I . . . had to." I did. I swear I did. "It was part of the process."

"Was *this* part of the process?" Rathe holds out his hand, showing me a wide pink scar. It runs across his palm and over the stretch of flesh between his thumb and his forefinger. Then he turns his hand over. I don't believe it at first. I was *there*, and I don't remember the knife going that far in. But there's a scar on the back of his hand. Where my obsidian stabbed right through him.

"Chasm take me," Bran whispers, staring wide-eyed at Rathe's hand. "Tell me you didn't do that, Azeril."

"I screwed up. I lost control." I want to close my eyes and pretend this isn't happening, but I don't dare look away from them. "It was an accident."

Letton glares at me. "What did you have to do to become the High Priest's apprentice? Everybody wanted the job. To go to Newhaven with him and *be* somebody. There were plenty of us more qualified. You *did* something to make him pick you."

"I saw your face when you cut me," Rathe says. "I saw how much you *wanted* to hurt me." He flinches at the memory. "Everything hurt, like my blood was on fire. The High Priest healed my flesh, but I'll never forget how it felt when you stabbed your knife through my hand. You had this awful smile on your face, and the more it hurt, the more you *liked* it."

My stomach twists into knots. I want to deny it, but I can't. I think about what Leora said. The Chasm loves chaos and violence. Darkness and pain. Maybe spells weren't the only things I got from it.

"You sick bastard," Letton mutters, clenching his fists. His face is red, the muscles in his thick neck strained. He's going to hit me. I can see the decision in his eyes.

"I thought you were my friend," Rathe says, and there's a haunted look to him, a hunger that wasn't there before. At least not before today. Not before Endeil changed him.

Before I did.

"I am," I tell him. But it's not quite the truth. I was his friend, before I stabbed the knife through his hand. Before I got carried away and he saw too much of me.

"The High Priest and I are healers. But you . . ." He closes his eyes, and when he opens them, I could swear they're black, the color in his irises completely gone. But a moment later they're back to normal. "You're a monster."

I'm backed up against the wall. I don't even know when that happened, but I try to press myself flat against it. Like I could disappear somehow if I just keep moving backward. Even if there's nowhere to go.

They want to gang up on me? Beat me up? Fine. It'll hurt, but I've had worse.

Rathe pulls out a knife from inside his robes. It's not obsidian, but its long, sharp blade glints in the torchlight.

"Whoa," Bran says. "You didn't say anything about weapons."

Rathe ignores him. He looks only at me, meeting my eyes. "Don't look so surprised, Azeril. You made torture look so pleasurable. But I guess that's only when you're the one with the knife, right?"

Letton unclenches his fists, not looking as sure about this. But he keeps his mouth shut.

"It's okay," Rathe whispers to me. "I've been bringing things back to life all day. You'll be the first human. Or at least the first monster."

My insides turn to liquid. My heart pounds, pumping cold terror through my veins. "You don't want to do that," I tell him, hoping it's true. I will myself to remember something—a spell, anything—like I did at the Silver Hound. Anything that could stop this, that could save me. But my mind stays blank.

I have to get out of here. Bran's paying the least attention, his wide eyes staring at Rathe's knife, so I dart toward him, shoving him out of my way as I make a run for it.

Bran stumbles, but Letton's quick. He slams me back against the wall, knocking the air from my lungs. He pins my arms to my sides.

I struggle against him, kicking and twisting. Gasping for breath.

"Bran!" he shouts. "Get over here!"

Bran hesitates. "You guys, I don't know if we should—"

"You can't back out now," Rathe says. "And don't worry—I can bring him *back*."

Bran moves toward me, but then he shakes his head. "I can't do it," he tells them, and takes off running.

It doesn't matter. Letton's got me up against the wall. I can't move my arms. I can hardly breathe, both because he's pressing on my chest and because of the wild terror running through me.

Rathe brings the knife to my throat. I think of Leora, covered in blood. This is how it happens. He's going to kill me.

Then he smiles and grabs my right hand instead. "You didn't think it would be that easy, did you? That quick?"

He jabs the blade into my palm. I bite my tongue hard and taste blood. "Chasm take you," I say, but my voice sounds strangled, and I hardly recognize it.

He meant to stab the knife all the way through my hand, but it's not as easy as he thinks, and he doesn't have the obsidian to guide him. He tries again, twisting the blade a little.

I scream this time. I spit blood into his face.

He wipes it away with his sleeve, grinning like a maniac. "You don't like it so much now, do you? *Do you*?!"

"If I kill you, there'll be no one to bring you back."

Letton kicks me in the shin and then grabs my throat. "You're not hurting anyone tonight, so keep your mouth shut."

"You should listen to him," Rathe says, "or I might change my mind and not bring you back at all." He starts to drive the knife in farther.

A voice interrupts him from the shadows. "Get away from my apprentice."

All three of us look over to the left where High Priest Endeil stands, glaring at Rathe and Letton. Fire flares to life in his hands. Anger blazes in his eyes.

When he steps toward us, Letton takes off down the hall. Rathe yanks the knife out of my hand and stumbles after him.

And just like that, it's over. I slump to the floor, holding my wounded hand tight against my chest. Endeil just saved my life.

—

The High Priest takes me to his office. My hand throbs, blood ooz-ing out with each heartbeat. I lean against the wall, taking slow, deep breaths. My head spins.

He paces the room. "Fire take those idiots! That ungrateful— This is how he repays me?" He stops and marches over to me. "Give me your hand."

I keep it pressed against my chest, my robes sticky with blood. "I've had enough of your magic. You're not touching me." No one is.

"Don't be stupid."

I think he's going to grab me and heal me against my will. There's not much I could do to stop him. Not without making the pain so much worse. But I would still fight him, even if it hurt, just to keep him away from me.

But he doesn't try. Instead he sighs and throws his arms up in exasperation. "I shouldn't have to worry about my apprentice getting attacked. And in the halls of the church!"

"I could say the same thing about Leora in the dorms."

Leora. I think about her palm bleeding along with mine. Of her worried about me, not knowing what's happening.

I let myself slide down to the floor, leaning my head back against the wall. The movement jars my hand, and I wince.

"And what were you thinking?" Endeil presses his fingers to his temples. "Where in the Chasm was your obsidian?"

"I'm trying something new."

"Well, don't."

"You have to fix Rathe. Whatever you gave him, you have to take it back."

"Take it back?" Endeil gapes at me like I'm insane. He sweeps his mop of blond hair away from his eyes, as if he just wasn't seeing me clearly.

"He wasn't like that before. He would never—"

"And how do you know what he would or wouldn't do? How many of your so-called friends would be shocked to find out the truth about how you really spend your nights? Even if I wanted to take his power back—even if I could—it wouldn't change what's happened. I healed that girl of yours, but I can still see the hatred burning in your eyes whenever you look at me. Even though you know I had to do it, that it was the only way—"

"You didn't *have* to do anything!"

"And you didn't *have* to cut open your friend, but you did."

I look up at the wall and see the painting of the volcano he hung up earlier. I must be remembering it wrong, because I could swear the crack in the earth representing the Chasm looks a little wider, the Fire inside it a little dimmer. Like instead of the Fire conquering the darkness, it's being swallowed up whole. Or maybe that's just how I see it, now that I know what's lurking inside me.

"Fine," I tell Endeil. "Maybe I had it coming, what Rathe did to me. But what you did to him—"

"What *we* did."

"—it changed him. It *messed him up*."

"He was the first. There were bound to be . . . complications. We'll do better next time."

The pain in my hand is distracting, so that I'm not sure I heard right. "Next time," I repeat. "You think there's going to be a next time?"

"Hundreds of them. Thousands."

I push myself to my feet. "You can't do that. I'm not going to *help* you do that."

He raises an eyebrow. "Oh really? Now the murderer grows a conscience?"

"I always had one. That's the difference between you and me."

"So noble, coming from someone who lives for the moment when you taste flesh with your knife and that sweet, dark pleasure hits you. Whether it's your worst enemy's flesh or your best friend's, or even your own—you enjoy it all the same. I know—I saw inside you. I peeked into all the wicked corners of your mind, at all the secrets you would never tell anyone, not even your beloved." He smirks. "No, *especially* not her."

Guilt slides through my chest. "What's your point?"

"The difference between you and me is that you want to hurt people and I don't. I *will*, if necessary. But I'm not going around longing for it."

But I saw the look in his eyes when he talked about getting my memories back. He wanted it to hurt. I know he did. And when he made me beg him to save Leora—that was all some twisted game to him, too. So I don't believe for a second that he's not just as sick as I am.

"I'm still not helping you," I tell him. The throbbing in my hand is getting so bad, I almost wish I had let him heal me. But then I remember how it felt when he used his magic on me. When he tore into my mind and saw the parts of me so secret even I don't know about them. And the suffocating horror I felt when that black fire spread from his hands and into Rathe.

And I have my suspicions about that black fire. After all, if my spells and everything the wizards put inside me came from the

Chasm, then where did Endeil's new power come from? He looked into my mind and saw darkness, and he came back with a magic darker and more powerful than ever.

"Oh, but you are going to help me," Endeil says. "You don't have a choice, remember?" He flexes his fingers, and dark flames appear in his palm. Silently wavering there, making it hard to breathe, making my skin crawl. I turn my head toward the wall, not wanting to see, but I can't stop glancing at the flames.

"You're going to help me, Azeril. It's not only your duty, but you and I both know I have ways of making you more"—he taps a finger against his chin, trying to think of the right word—"*agreeable*." He grins, and the flames in his hand flare up, as if in agreement. "And don't think an injured hand's going to get you off the hook. You don't get to be out of commission, because what we're doing is too important. Giving people new powers is the first step in crushing the High Guild and destroying them for good."

"And here I thought the first step was betraying the Church by writing them that letter."

"The Fire grants us one power, and meanwhile the wizards have whole books of spells at their disposal. Spells that might as well be weapons, that they sell their souls to get. Don't tell me they don't because I've *seen* what kind of damage their magic can do, sucking the life out of everyone foolish or unlucky enough to get near them. It's always been that way. How can we, with our single abilities, fight an enemy that literally sucks the life from us? They've always had the upper hand, and someday soon this is going to escalate into more than arguing over a few seats in court. You can't be everywhere at once. The wizards are out there torturing good people, and nobody has the means to fight back. I'm going to be remembered as the leader who changed all that, who was a savior. I've got the ability—no, the *duty*—to give ordinary citizens the power to turn the tide against the wizards. Let them come after us then. Let them see what it's like to find themselves on the losing side of a war. When I'm done, there won't *be* any wizards."

"And what's going to be left of the Church? If everyone turns out like Rathe?"

"They should be so lucky. Give me your hand. You're not doing either of us any favors."

"Good."

"And if a wizard finds you? Alone, in the dark, with no power to speak of? Think of all the things he might do to you if you don't have your knife. If your hand is too weak to hold it. Just a vulnerable, terrified boy who'd be at the Guild's mercy all over again. And I think you know by now that wizards have no mercy."

Cold waves of fear run through me as I remember that wizard at the Silver Hound who put his hands on me and how desperate I was to escape. I would have done anything. I would have completely snapped and given myself away. I would have been sent back to the dark room and the chair.

At least with the knife in my hand I don't have to be broken. At least if someone catches me in the dark, he'll be the one who regrets it.

I shut my eyes, fear and pain screaming at me to just let him do it and be done with it. He's right, I'm not doing anyone any favors. I'm only hurting myself. One touch from him and his dark magic and this could be over. I let him heal Leora, didn't I? No, I didn't let him—I *begged* him.

When I open my eyes, he's grinning at me like he's won. Like he knows exactly what I'm thinking and that he's got me right where he wants me. A few words from him and I'm trembling in fear, ready to do whatever he wants.

"When you're ready," he says.

But he doesn't get to win, not this time. Maybe I have to be his apprentice, maybe he can even make me help him give powers to more people. But I don't have to let him touch me. I don't have to let him use his magic on me.

Not ever again.

CHAPTER NINETEEN

I pound on Hadrin's door at the inn with my good hand, keeping my injured one pressed tightly to my side, bloody and throbbing. There's no answer, except some of the other residents opening their doors to glare at me or say, "It's the middle of the night," as if I didn't know that, and I wonder if he's gone home to the capital already. Maybe he was called away early, or maybe he abandoned me—and Leora—all over again. And after that speech about needing my help—

"For the Chasm's sake, boy!" Hadrin shouts, flinging open his door, bleary-eyed and scowling at me. "It's the—"

"Middle of the night. I know."

He gapes at me, getting a good look at my red robes, stained dark with blood. He puts a hand to his mouth.

Another door opens across the hall, an angry-looking man in his bedclothes snarling something about alerting the innkeeper. Hadrin waves him off and tells me, through gritted teeth, "Get in here, *now.*"

I follow him inside, closing the door behind me. An oil lamp burns dimly at his desk, casting shadows across a pile of open books and loose papers.

"Of course you'd break the protective spell on my daughter and then do something like this," Hadrin says. "Let me see it."

I glare at him and turn away. "That's not why I'm here." Though Leora must be freaking out by now, with her hand bleeding just as much as mine, only without knowing what's happened. She tells me my spells come from the very depths of the Chasm, and then I leave and *this* happens?

I probably should have gone to see her first, but I had to come here, before I changed my mind. "You said you needed my help."

"Yes, I did. But you don't look like you're in any shape to help anyone right now and— Do not touch that couch!" he warns.

But he's too late. The trip over here seemed so much longer this time, with my hand throbbing with each heartbeat, every footstep causing more pain. Now that I'm here, I'm exhausted. All I want to do is sit down. And never get up.

Hadrin groans as I flop down on his fancy white couch, bloody robes and all. "You think I want soiled furniture on my bill?"

"The High Guild's bill, you mean. They kind of owe me." I press my injured hand to my chest and shut my eyes.

Hadrin swears under his breath. I hear his footsteps as he crosses over to the couch. "Let me see your hand."

"You sound like the High Priest, and I wouldn't let him touch it, either."

"Damn it, boy, if you think you're going to show up here in the middle of the night and then bleed to death on my couch—" He cuts off, grabbing my wrist and wrenching my hand away. I cry out at the sudden movement and the sting of open air.

I catch a glimpse of the cut on my hand, though I didn't intend to look. It's ragged and red, and blood stains the lines in my palm. "Don't touch me," I tell him, making a halfhearted attempt to pull my arm out of his grasp. "It'll heal. I'll go to the school infirmary in the morning."

"In the morning. Hours from now. Who did this to you?"

"A friend."

He raises an eyebrow as he grabs a bag from the floor and starts rummaging through it.

"A *former* friend," I correct myself.

He pulls out a jar from the bag and untwists the lid. The slimy salve inside is dark brown, almost black. A foul, burning smell fills the room. "This will sting."

This time I do jerk my hand away from him. And it hurts—it hurts so much and I'm so tired, so much more than I realized—but he's going to make it hurt worse. Some part of me is screaming that he's going to torture me. He's going to use whatever that salve is to inflict more pain, until there's so much of it that I'm not me anymore. That I'll do anything he says to make it stop. Some part of me thinks I was stupid for coming here tonight.

"*No,*" I tell him, scrambling to sit up and get my bearings. I'm already reaching for the knife, the one that isn't there. It's still back in my room, and now I'm here, weaponless, *helpless*, just like Endeil predicted. This isn't what he meant, and I know Hadrin's trying to help. But I don't have to let Endeil touch me again, and I don't have to let a wizard do it, either.

Hadrin holds up his hands in surrender, backing off. "My daughter bleeds from your wounds. Or have you forgotten?"

"Give it to me—I'll do it," I tell him, motioning for him to set down the jar.

"Rub the salve into the cut. It will clean it out and help stop the bleeding. But it's not going to be pleasant. And don't look at me that way, boy, as if I *enjoy* seeing you hurt. I don't."

I watch his face closely, noting every muscle twitch, deciding whether or not he means it. Endeil said the same thing, and I didn't believe him. Coming here tonight, wounded and unarmed, might not have been a good idea. And yet, I believe Hadrin when he says he doesn't want to hurt me.

I must have lost more blood than I thought.

Hadrin pulls his desk chair out, as if to sit down, then turns and paces across the room instead. "So," he says. "You want to tell me why you practically knocked down my door in the middle of the night?"

The burning smell coming from the jar is starting to make my eyes water and my nose run, and I hesitate before touching the dark ooze inside. "You said you needed my help. You said I'd—" I wince, the salve stinging as I spread it on my palm. "Look, it's not like I think I should side with wizards or anything. But Endeil's crazy, and I can't be his apprentice. He wants to hurt people, and he wants me to help him do it. You said I could make a difference, when war breaks out."

"What I *said* was you'd be the deciding factor."

"So if I side with you, then Endeil loses, right?" What Endeil's doing will hurt a lot of people. It will corrupt them, the way it did Rathe. And maybe I wouldn't be too sorry if the High Priest succeeded in destroying all the wizards, but the way he's doing it is *wrong*.

Hadrin's expression is half concerned, half skeptical. "It would mean getting your memories back, Azeril."

I swallow. "Right."

He puts two fingers to his forehead, as if he has a headache, and bites his lip. "I shouldn't have asked you to do this. You don't understand what you'd be giving up."

But I do. I remember the glimpse of my past I saw when Endeil dug into my head. The dark room with the chair, the screaming. There must be more memories like that—years of torture, maybe a whole lifetime's worth—and how could the weight of them do anything but crush me? If I do this, any chance of being the boy instead of the monster will be gone. And yet . . .

My hands are shaking. I tell myself it's just exhaustion. "You said it would redeem me from my sins."

He shuts his eyes, looking pained. "I'm a foolish old man who believes in the fairy tale of making up for his past mistakes. You shouldn't listen to me."

"Can you stop Endeil without me? I know why you need my spells. Leora told me where they come from, and . . . Endeil looked inside my head. I let him—I had to—and he *saw* something. He said he touched something divine. But I don't think it was divine so much as unholy. His new powers come from the Chasm, the same as mine. It's my fault he has them, and now I'm the only one who can fix it."

"You should forget I ever came here and asked you to do this. You should just run, while you have the chance."

"Endeil wants to destroy all the wizards. He thinks he's some kind of chosen one. He's going to give people powers from the Chasm. Even if he doesn't have me there to help, I don't think that will stop him. We can't let him win. No matter what this does to me, we can't—" I pause. "Leora doesn't know, but he's the one who nearly killed her. Who stabbed her in cold blood and left her for dead."

Hadrin looks up, his eyes wide. "I'll kill him."

"No, *I* will. I said I'd make him burn, and I meant it. And if I don't do this, more people are going to get hurt."

"Including you. I know what I said, about redemption, but you don't deserve this. You don't understand what it means to remember all the horrible things that we . . . Take it from someone who *does* remember and don't do this."

"Fine, then. Tell me who you're going to get to defeat Endeil instead, and I'll pretend I never saw you."

He opens his mouth, as if to protest. But then he closes it again and shakes his head. "There's no one. You know that."

"Great. So then tell me. *How do I get my memories back?*"

CHAPTER TWENTY

I think Leora's going to hit me when I finally get back to my room. She's waiting there for me—she let herself in—pacing back and forth. Her eyes are red and lined with tears, though she's not crying. She's in her pink nightgown, wearing a white robe over it. Or what was a white robe before it was stained with blood. Big red smears run down the side and across the front.

"Where have you been?!" she demands, marching over to me as soon as I open the door. Relief flashes in her eyes as she sees that I'm still alive. Then her eyebrows furrow and her nose scrunches up in anger. Her shoulders shake, and she balls her hands into fists.

"Leora—"

"Don't." She takes a step back, away from me. "Don't come anywhere near me, Az. Not until you tell me what in the Chasm happened to you! To both of us!" Her eyes flick to her right hand. It's not injured, not like mine, but she bled from it just the same.

"I ran into trouble, but . . . I'm all right now." I uncurl my fingers, showing her my palm where I let Hadrin bandage it up.

"You weren't in the infirmary. I checked. And I don't know what's going on, but I know what happened when my father hit you. My mouth bled, too, and then something like *this* happens and you don't think to come tell me you're all right?! Didn't you think I'd want to *know*?"

"I didn't know what you'd want. Not from me. Not now that you know what I am."

"You can't really think I don't care what happens to you."

I shrug. "One minute you loved me. We were together. Then the next you find out I'm . . . That there's all this dark stuff inside me that I don't even remember, and then you don't want anything to do with me."

"That's not true."

"You were afraid of me, when you found out what I am. Admit it."

"No. I'm not afraid *of* you, Az. I never was. Just *for* you."

"For me? What does that even mean? If you know something I don't—"

But she shakes her head, dismissing the idea. She hugs herself, some of her rage leaving her, so now she just looks cold and alone. "Maybe I've been unfair to you this past week, ever since I found out. But I needed some time to think. When my hand started bleeding, all I could think about was you. The same questions kept running in my mind, over and over. What was happening to you? Were you okay? I don't care where you came from or what happened to you in your past. You're right—you don't even remember that stuff—and it's who you are *now* that matters. You're still my best friend, you're still the same person who's been there for me whenever I needed you. Nothing changed when I found out the truth. I just thought it did. But I was wrong."

A warm feeling spreads through my chest. Like maybe, just for a moment, we could pretend that none of the bad things ever happened. Things can go back to how they were. But a little tendril of guilt snakes its way through me when I think about what she said. *You don't even remember that stuff.* And I don't. At least, not yet.

"Leora, there's something I have to—"

She kisses me, her mouth soft and warm against mine. My words trail off, forgotten.

"I was afraid," she whispers, kissing my jaw, my nose, my eyebrow—as if she can't get enough of me. As if she's worried someone else will walk in and drop another horrible secret on us and ruin this. "I thought I'd lose you, that who you are meant something terrible would happen to you, but you don't even know those spells. So you can't. It won't."

"Can't *what*—" I shiver as she runs the tip of her tongue down my neck. Hot and fast, making me tingle all over. I half sigh, half groan, and pull her to me, so we're pressed up against each other. As close as we can get.

Well, *almost.*

"Your clothes," Leora murmurs. "They're covered in blood."

"Yours, too."

"So take them *off.*"

My whole body feels warm and hazy. On fire and *alive.* I take off my belt, then pull my red robes over my head and toss them on the floor. An altar boy no more. She shrugs off the white nightrobe, leaving her in just her thin pink sleeping gown.

And I'm pushing her down to the bed, not even waiting for her to take it off, I want her so badly. I hate that we've spent so many days apart. She slides her hands down my hips, practically tearing my underwear off. I pull hers down, and she wriggles out of them.

The wound in my hand is throbbing again. Sharp and hurting. But I don't care.

Being with her is like touching obsidian. My blood burns, and I can hardly think. All I know is that I want her. Here, now, in my bed. As much as the knife wants flesh.

There's no hesitation this time, no soft murmurings and tracing of scars, only a deep, all-encompassing hunger. Some primal desperation that can't be ignored. She brings her knees up around my hips, spreading herself before me, and we both gasp when I press into her, our bodies interlocking. She grabs my face with both hands and pulls me down to her, kissing me hard. Her breathing's heavy as her whole body arches against mine. We move together, over and over—frantic, impatient. And like with the knife, there's a euphoria. A sweet, sharp pleasure that rips through me, only so much better. Leora's fingers dig into my back, her nails biting into my skin.

And then it's over, both of us tired and panting. It's only now that I realize my hand started bleeding again. That hers did, too.

"We could have been doing that for *years*," Leora murmurs. She grins. "You should have fallen in love with me sooner."

I smile back. "I did."

She notices the fresh blood on her hand. She swears and sits up, but it's me she looks at with concern. "That looks bad."

"It's fine. I'll have it looked at in the morning."

"It's morning now."

"You know what I mean." Hadrin said it would need stitches. It feels hot, inflamed. I curl my fingers up and try not to think about how long it might be before I can hold the knife again. How long I'll be helpless, just like Endeil said.

"Okay. But you're *going* to tell me what happened."

"It's a long story. One that involves me doing something I shouldn't have." Like listening to Endeil and hurting a friend. I lick my lips, my mind already racing, wondering how much to tell her.

"Yeah, well, in case you haven't noticed," she says, "I'm not going anywhere. So spill it."

"I will. I promise. But, before that . . ." I take a deep breath, remembering what Hadrin told me. About how I can get my memories back. About how it involves Leora. "I need to ask you for a favor. And . . . you're not going to like it."

———

Leora gapes at me after I finish telling her Hadrin's plan. About the upcoming war and my part in it. And hers. She presses her palms to her forehead.

"Say something," I whisper, hating the tense silence that's filled the room.

"I just got you back," she says. "And now you want me to . . . I must have heard you wrong, Az, because you couldn't have asked that."

"I don't want you to unlock my memories. I *need* you to. I—"

"I've only ever unlocked doors before, Az. Physical, mechanical locks. Not a mind. Not . . . not this."

"Hadrin said you could do it, that it's the only way."

"My *father* said it was the only way, and you believe him?"

"Does it matter if there's another way? If this will work, then—"

"Of course it matters!" She shakes her head and draws the blankets up around her, as if they can protect her from this. "You think I want to be responsible for ruining you?"

"You won't lose me, Leora. I love you—I'll always love you—no matter what happens."

"If you get your memories back, then who will you be?" A tear slides down her cheek, and she quickly wipes it away. "It will change you, Az. You know it will. So don't sit there making promises to me you won't be able to keep."

I slip my fingers between hers, locking our hands together. "I don't know who I'll be, but I do know there's going to be a war. And that people are going to die."

"So you're going to get your memories back, and all those spells, and become a super weapon for the wizards? You're an *altar boy.*"

"Endeil looked into my head. Into the darkness. He took something from it, and now he's got this new power, straight from the Chasm. He's going to spread it to everyone he can. He's not going to rest until he's wiped out all the wizards and given unholy magic to everyone else. The spells inside my head are my only chance to stop him and make things right."

"Your spells kill people," Leora says, her voice quiet. "They take so much energy that they actually *kill* people."

"I'll be careful."

"They'll kill *you.*" She bites her lip. Another tear falls, but she makes no move to wipe it away this time. "You don't know how to control the spells. You didn't then and you won't now."

She doesn't know that. "I wouldn't ask you to do this if it wasn't so important. I wouldn't risk losing you, or . . . myself . . . if I had any other choice."

"You could walk away. It doesn't have to be you—"

"But it does. You know it does."

"I know." She squeezes my hand. "And that's why I'm going to do it. Just . . . don't think I like being part of this. And don't think that if you're not you anymore, or if you die . . . don't think that's not going to break my heart. But that's love, isn't it?" She smiles through her tears, the corners of her mouth wobbling. "I would break my own heart for you, Az. That's how much I love you. And I know you would do the same for me."

"A thousand times."

She nods, her shoulders shaking.

"I wish I didn't have to ask this," I tell her. "If there was any other way . . ."

"But you do and there isn't. So I'll do it, because you asked me to. Because it's that important to you. But not yet. Right now you're going to put your arms around me, and we're going to lie here like two normal people whose lives aren't about to be shattered. Like just another couple who have everything still ahead of them. I'm going to lean against you and feel your heart beating and know you love me. And I'm going to remember this moment for the rest of my life. You and me. No matter what happens."

CHAPTER TWENTY-ONE

I leave my red robes behind when we go to the inn, not intending to return. I dress in black, the same as when I went to meet Hadrin at the Silver Hound. Or maybe because I feel like I'm going to my own funeral.

Hadrin paces the room, wringing his hands and looking pale.

"Maybe you shouldn't be here," I tell him, sounding a lot calmer than I feel. I sit down on the edge of the bed—which is even softer than it looks—next to Leora. She has her hands on her knees and takes deep breaths.

Hadrin's gaze flicks over to the obsidian at my waist. "You had to bring that?"

"Yeah, I did." I'm never going back, and I couldn't leave it behind. I feel vulnerable enough as it is. I hold up my right hand, fresh bandages covering the stitches they gave me at the infirmary. I told them it was an accident, self-inflicted, though I don't think they believed me. "Why? You afraid I'm going to use it?"

He glances at Leora. "Yes," he says. "Get rid of it."

"I'm not going to—"

"*Get rid of it*, or this doesn't happen."

"He's not going to hurt me," Leora says.

But I get up and drop the knife into the desk drawer. Maybe I wasn't going to hurt anyone with it, but just knowing it was there, that I could graze my fingers along the hilt and feel that familiar rush at any time . . . It made this situation and what's about to happen seem almost doable. Without it, I feel alone, but I take a step back, letting Hadrin lock it up.

Leora's watching me, and I know that I'm *not* alone. I sit down again and slip my hand into hers.

"Will it hurt?" she asks. "When I . . . If it hurts, tell me and I'll stop."

I nod, even though I have no intention of stopping her. We've come too far for that.

Hadrin's still pacing, looking more nervous than ever. "As soon as it's done," he says, nodding at Leora, "you get out of here."

She glares at him. "I'm staying. You know that."

"Besides," I say to Hadrin, "you're the one I made the promise to." I don't mention it was the promise to kill him. I don't need to. "So maybe you're the one who should go."

"And leave her alone with you?"

"Dad! For the Fire's sake, he's not psychotic. And he's unarmed. What more do you want?"

"He's never unarmed," Hadrin mutters, but then he shakes his head. "It doesn't matter. I'm not going anywhere." He looks me right in the eye as he says it, making it not just a statement, but a threat.

"Great," I tell him. "You do that."

Leora squeezes my hand. She leans in close and whispers, "You're sure about this?"

"I'm sure that this is the only way to stop Endeil." Which isn't exactly what she asked, but at least it's not a lie. "Let's do this."

She nods, not looking all that ready, but she steels herself and puts her hands on either side of my head.

And then I feel it. It's not like when Endeil's magic ripped through me, shining a bright, intrusive light on all my shadows. It's more of a probing feeling. Like someone's tinkering with my thoughts and making them not fit together the same way as before. A wave of dizziness passes over me. I shut my eyes.

The feeling stops. Leora pulls her hands away. "Az, are you—"

"I'm fine. It just feels weird, that's all."

She looks skeptical, but she puts her hands back where they were and keeps going. As soon as she does, the feeling returns. My thoughts shift again, and then it's like my mind is being torn in all directions. I grit my teeth, trying not to show how much it hurts.

But Leora's eyes are closed, not watching me. Her mouth slips open, her forehead wrinkling in deep thought. She always says the process is like solving a maze. I imagine the hedge maze in my brain being so overgrown that not all of the pathways are still open. Brambles grow along the ground and through the bushes.

A sharp pain in my head. Leora, tripping on one of the brambles and snagging her sleeve.

A dull ache. Leora hitting a dead end.

A white-hot poker stabs through my thoughts. It's Leora, tearing through an overgrown path.

Except the burning feeling doesn't go away like the others. It flares hotter instead.

And then I forget all about the maze because I'm in the chair. I don't know how, but I am. My feet are numb, and I feel the leather straps chafe against my wrists. Hadrin's here, the worst of my tormentors. The one who's responsible for all of this. He's the one the others listen to—the one who could make this all stop. But he doesn't. He never does. He *wants* me to hurt. It's the only way they can get the spells in.

He's staring at me now, as if he doesn't know who I am. Like he wandered into the wrong torture chamber. Maybe he could forget me, but I could never forget him. Just the sound of his footsteps fills me with dread.

And then another wizard puts his hands on me. I jerk away and find that my hands are free. I don't know how or when that happened, but I'm not wasting what might be my one chance to get away. Or to at least do some damage before they can lock me up again. The words to a spell are ready on my tongue. A spell that will turn his skin inside out, and I'm praying this wizard isn't part of Hadrin's team, the ones with the tattoos that keep them safe—

"Az!"

The wizard shouts in my face. No, not a wizard. "Leora?"

She smiles in relief. "For a second there, I thought maybe I messed up. Something changed, in your eyes, and then it was like you couldn't even see me. Like I wasn't here at all."

Or like I was somewhere else. I realize I'm still sitting on the bed, safe and sound and not anywhere near that chair and its straps. "You solved the maze?"

"Part of it. I couldn't find the way. There were so many paths. I made a lot of wrong turns, but then I finally found a . . ." She holds up her hands, squeezing the air, as if she could shape the word she's looking for. "Okay, it was like there were all these different paths, only none of them went anywhere. As if they'd all been blocked off. But then one of them was like a door. It was locked, too. A maze within a maze. But then the— I got it open. Just one path, and I don't know where it led, but that's when something changed in you. Like you weren't here anymore, and you were mumbling something. I thought at first I'd opened the wrong door and screwed something up in your brain. I had to stop, Az."

"But you opened up *something*."

Images flash through my mind. Hadrin bringing me to live at the High Guild when I was really young. An orphan, only a few years old. They didn't put me in the chair then. The experiment was still hypothetical.

"So, it worked?" Leora asks.

Hadrin's standing behind her, frowning. The image of the chair might not have been real, but he is. "It worked," he says, not waiting for me to answer. He exchanges a look with me, then glances away guiltily. Things have changed. I'm his tormentor now.

"I think so," I tell Leora, ignoring Hadrin. She meant to open a floodgate, but instead it's like she poked a hole in a dam, letting out a trickle. Spells lurk beneath the surface of my thoughts. I can feel them, heavy and strange, but at the same time so familiar.

More memories fill my head. The cramped room where I slept. No, not a room so much as a cell, where they locked me up at night. The way they had to bind a cloth around my mouth once I started learning the spells, to keep me from using them. I smile a little, remembering the wizard I took by surprise one day. He was one of my torturers, until I turned his lungs to ash. That's when they gave me the tattoo on my wrist, and when Hadrin and the others got ones to match.

"And you're . . . you?" Leora asks.

"I'm still me."

"Uh-huh."

"Seriously. I'm *fine*."

I remember what happened at the High Guild. The way they used me as a vessel for the Chasm's spells. The Chasm feeds on violence and pain, so they made sure I got plenty of both. But the joke was on them because the spells they summoned and put inside me were so old, they couldn't even understand the language. The spells were useless to them. But not to me.

"Wonderful," Hadrin says. "You've just had your mind turned upside down and rearranged, had who knows what dredged up, including spells you don't know the first thing about, but you're *fine*. You expect us to believe that?"

I shrug. "You'd rather I totally lost it? If I was huddled on the floor, crying and inconsolable, would that make you happy?"

"No. But . . . I'd have an easier time believing it."

Leora rolls her eyes at him. "It was your idea for me to unlock his memories, and now that I have, you're upset that nothing went horribly wrong?"

He ignores her and looks me in the eyes. He and I both know all the awful things that happened at the High Guild.

"I know what you were worried about," I tell him. "What we were *all* worried about. That I wouldn't be me anymore. But it's not like that." I'm both the boy and the monster. We were never different people—always one and the same. "I'm starting to remember everything. Isn't that what you wanted?"

Hadrin nods, but I know that, deep down, part of him hoped this wouldn't work. "You're going to need training, to master your spells and reach your full potential."

Leora makes a disgusted sound, clearly not liking that idea any more than I do.

"I don't think so." I hold out my injured hand. "I'll be taking my knife back now."

Hadrin glances at me, then at the drawer. "You don't need it."

"I always need it."

He snorts. "Forgive me if I don't go rushing to give it back to you. Perhaps when I don't feel you're in such a hurry to use it."

"I'm not. Like you said, I'm never unarmed." I grin at him, getting up from the bed and flexing my fingers. "And I don't *need* the knife for this." It would just make it that much more fun.

Hadrin's eyes go wide. He inches forward, as if he's going to plant himself between me and Leora. Like he thinks she needs protecting from me.

Clearly she doesn't agree, because she gets up from the bed to thwart him.

"And what, exactly, don't you need it for?" Hadrin asks, never taking his eyes off me, like I'm a snake about to strike.

And I am, but he's not my target. "Why, wizard, can't you guess?"

He shakes his head, and now he really does move between us. As if he believes I've completely lost it.

"The reason we did this in the first place," I tell him. "I'm going to stop Endeil."

CHAPTER TWENTY-TWO

"You will do no such thing," Hadrin tells me.

"And why not?" I ask him.

"You're not ready. I could count on one hand the number of spells you've cast in your entire life."

The few times he couldn't stop me, he means. "I healed my arm, didn't I?"

"And what is your plan? Waltz into that church and take him prisoner? Or are you going to kill him in front of everyone? You think you'll waltz back out so easily?"

"I'll get him alone. In his office. It won't be hard—I'm his apprentice, remember?"

"Az," Leora says. "Maybe you should think about this."

"I said I'd make him pay," I remind Hadrin. "And if I take him out now, then there doesn't have to be a war."

"Right. And when some acolyte finds his body and it's obvious he was attacked with wizard magic, do you think the Church will really let that go?"

"But without the High Priest, no one else will have powers from the Chasm." *No one but me.*

"So the Church will be on the losing side, but there will still be a war."

"Fine, maybe I can't stop the fighting, maybe it's inevitable, but I can at least stop *him*."

"Can you?" Hadrin asks. "Your technique is sloppy. Powerful but unfocused. And when you healed your arm, you took energy from yourself to do it. Are you going to do that now? Will that even be enough? Or will you merely end up killing yourself?"

"Give me the knife back and I won't need to cast anything."

Leora's fingertips brush against my elbow. "Az. You *just* got your memories back. We don't even know if you're . . . I think you should listen to him."

"The knife," Hadrin mutters. "You can barely hold it with those stitches in your hand. Let me put it this way. If you start a fight and lose, what happens to my daughter? Like it or not—and I *don't*—your lives are intertwined. If you bleed, so does she. And if you die . . . I haven't come this far just to have you run off prematurely and get both of you killed."

I hadn't thought about what might happen if I failed. Losing hadn't crossed my mind. I can take on Endeil—with all these spells that are coming back to me, I *know* I can. But what if Hadrin's right? What if I'm not ready?

"You're untested," he goes on. "And you've had no training. You might have cast spells before, but you don't know the first thing about it. And if you think you're going to battle someone like Endeil, and possibly everyone in that church, *alone*, then—"

"You're right, okay? It's too dangerous. And as much as I want this to be over, it's not worth the risk. Not to me or to Leora." I slip my hand into hers. And even that's enough to make my wound flare up, tender and sore. If I can't even hold Leora's hand, how am I going to wield the knife?

"Well . . . good," Hadrin says. "I'm glad you've come to your senses."

Leora reaches up and flicks me in the forehead.

"Ow!"

"Don't get yourself killed, Az. And don't do anything stupid. If you do, there's more where that came from."

———

I wait until the middle of the night, after they've both fallen asleep—Hadrin in his bed and Leora on the couch—before getting up from my pile of blankets on the floor and sneaking out of the room. I make my way across town, back to the Church of the Sacred Flame. I meant to stay put, to not do anything stupid, like I promised. But I can't stop thinking about the way Endeil nearly killed Leora, just to prove a point to me. And the way he tore through my mind, greedily seeking out the dark places.

I might have been the one who hurt Rathe, but Endeil's the one who ruined him. And he did that, like he did everything else, without a second thought. So why should I hesitate to take my revenge? When I have all these powerful spells coming back to me, begging to be used, and I know exactly where he sleeps?

The church is quiet when I arrive, the halls empty. There's a twinge in my hand as I remember being caught here, alone and vulnerable. That's not going to happen again—I won't let it—but I still feel a flicker of dread as I move through the darkened hallways.

My hand might be injured, but there's no reason for it to stay that way now. I pause in the shadows, only needing to think of the healing spell before the words are falling from my mouth. I have no idea what they mean or where they come from, only what their effects will be. An electric feeling builds up in my arms and legs as I recite the spell, a surge of energy flowing into my hand to heal it. It hits me hard, stealing my breath and sending a dizzying wave of nausea through me. But the feeling doesn't last and at least my hand is healed and is no longer a distraction. I flex my fingers, half expecting searing pain to flare up in my palm under the bandages. It doesn't, and I think maybe I could have taken the knife, after all. Not that it matters—I'm going to kill him either way.

There's no one around to stop me when I silently open the door to Endeil's bedroom—not that anyone would. I'm his apprentice still. No one here knows that I've defected and joined forces with a wizard. But maybe once Endeil is gone, I can come back to the Church. No one has to know I killed him. And who would ever suspect *me* of using wizard magic? Of casting dark spells even more powerful than the wizards'?

Hadrin thinks I don't know how to cast properly, but that's just something he tells himself so he can still feel in control, like he has something I don't. But he doesn't—none of those Fire-forsaken wizards do—and how can he possibly teach me *anything* about magic when the spells I have floating around in my head are so far beyond his comprehension?

Several spells come to mind as I creep into Endeil's room. It's too dark to see, and I pause to listen for his breathing. But there's nothing, only silence. I mutter a spell, again not comprehending the words, yet still knowing exactly what they will do. I feel a spark of energy run through my arm as a little ball of light appears, casting a pale, sickly glow over the bed.

I hold my breath, but the bed's empty. I wonder for one awful moment if he anticipated me and what I've come for. He could be standing right behind me.

I whip around, my heart racing. But I'm alone. I douse the light—though not before moving to the door and putting my hand on the knob, ready to bolt—and make my way to his office instead.

Torchlight peeks out from under the door, and I know this time I've found him.

He glances up from his desk when I come in, his head in his hands. His eyes look almost sunken. "Azeril," he says, blinking and taking in the fact that I'm not wearing my red acolyte robes. Then his gaze flicks away, as if he has more pressing matters to think about than why I'm here.

I shut the door behind me. He's off his guard. All I have to do is make my move and cast something before he knows what hit him. So why don't I? But I just stand there, silent and afraid, both of him and of myself and what I'm about to do. He deserves it, I know he does, but I can picture Leora's face, disappointed, hating me for being a cold-blooded killer. I could still turn around and go back to them. I could go back to the inn and fall asleep and no one would ever even know I'd been out.

But I don't do that, either. I stand frozen in the doorway, too unsure of myself to move forward or go back.

"I've been wondering when you'd turn up," he says. When I don't respond, he adds, "And my apprentice *doesn't* lurk in doorways."

I take a breath and step inside his office.

He steeples his hands. "The Fathers wanted to know where you were today. You didn't show up for your duties or for class. Father Gratch, in particular, was ready to have you expelled, but I stepped in. I told them you were absent because of your injury." He pauses, waiting for something. "Well?"

"Well what?"

He sighs. "Well, come here and let me fix it. Obviously it's more serious than you wanted to believe if you had to miss an entire day."

I curl my fingers, pressing them against the bandage on my palm, where my injury used to be. There's no way I can let him see it now. "It's fine," I tell him. "That's not why I was absent."

"Oh." He presses his fingers to his temples. "So this is about Rathe."

"Don't sound so surprised. He *did* try to kill me. And I've been thinking. When you looked into my head, when you saw everything and got that new power . . ."

Endeil stares down at his desk, as if he knows what I'm going to say and doesn't want me to go on. But then he looks up, his green eyes meeting mine. "Yes?"

"You said once that you knew where my ability with obsidian came from. That you saw it. And if that's true—"

"I assure you, it *is*."

Then he knows. He *must* know that the Fire didn't have anything to do with his new power. That it was just the opposite. "I want to hear you say it."

"What?"

"Tell me where the power came from."

"Mine or yours?"

"Both. Just tell me. I'm ready to hear it."

He gets up from the desk, combing his hands through his hair, smoothing it off of his forehead. "Why aren't you in your robes, Azeril? The High Priest's apprentice can't be seen skulking around in black. It gives the wrong impression."

"But I think it suits me. And, anyway, my robes were covered in blood." I almost hold up my hand to remind him, but I don't want him getting any more ideas about trying to heal it. If he looks under the bandages and sees what a miraculous recovery I've made . . . "You said you saw darkness, when you looked inside my head. That it was *divine*. But what happened to Rathe . . . That's not how the Fire bestows its gifts on people. With pain and violence? And it doesn't corrupt a person like that. So I think you'd better tell me where the power really came from, because—"

"Stop. Consider what you're saying, apprentice."

"I think you've known all along—you must have—and yet, you want to go on like you're some sort of chosen one."

"I *am*. Doubly chosen."

"But you can't even speak its name."

His nostrils flare, his mouth going taut. "The Chasm," he whispers. "I was chosen by the Fire, and then by the Chasm. Blessed by both."

"There's no such thing."

"Isn't there? And what about you? I know what you're getting at, that if I saw darkness inside your head, then your power must come from the Chasm. But obsidian is a blending of both. It's fire and darkness, order and chaos, together as one."

"And which power did you use on Rathe?"

"It's us against the wizards. I did what I had to."

"You used Chasm magic, you mean. Do you even still have your power from the Fire? Or did it revoke that ability the second you accepted the darkness?"

"How dare you say that to me! This isn't how an apprentice should talk to his master."

"Then maybe I'm not your apprentice." And he's definitely not my master. I instinctively reach for the knife that isn't there. And now I wish I'd brought it, because even if I do remember all these spells the wizards put in my head, I have a lot more practice with the knife.

"You pledged yourself to me. You promised to do anything. And here you are, going back on your word. We made an exchange. You became my apprentice and I healed her. Wouldn't it be a shame if I undid that?"

My blood burns with rage, even without the knife. Spells swirl inside my head, faster and faster. "If you ever hurt her again—"

"Ah." He taps his chin, as if he just thought of something. "But I wonder which would hurt her more. Undoing that healing magic, or telling her the truth?"

My insides go cold at the words. I try to hide it, but he must see the fear on my face.

"That's right," Endeil says. "How would you like for everyone to find out the truth about you? Rathe found out and then he tried to kill you. You say it was the Chasm that changed him, but I wonder. Was it really, or was it your betrayal?"

The spells that were at the surface of my thoughts, ready to be used, now collide and jumble together. It was *his* magic that corrupted Rathe. But I can't say that Rathe finding out the truth about me had nothing to do with it. The way he looked at me, when he saw me hurting him, *liking* it . . .

"Perhaps he saw the real you. And he couldn't take it. Perhaps it was your darkness that hurt him, not mine. Just like it's yours that's going to hurt *her* when I—"

The words to a spell come to life on my tongue. It's his skin I'll turn inside out. And then I'll turn it right-side in again and get my knife and do it all over by hand. And when I'm done, I'll turn his lungs to ashes, like I did to that wizard years ago.

Endeil makes a choked, gasping noise.

It's a complicated spell—not as quick as casting a light or healing my hand—but I'm so much stronger than he is. I can *feel* it. I can sense his energy in the room, but it's something to draw from, not anything that poses a threat.

Endeil holds up a trembling hand. A strip of flesh turns pink and raw, running down his wrist and then his arm. He screams in agony. His face is mottled, pale in some spots and an angry red in others. I concentrate on his throat, on stopping the screaming.

I hate what Leora might think if she could see me now. I want to look away from the agony on his face, but I make myself stay focused. This might not stop the war, but it will stop Endeil from corrupting anyone else.

Black fire blazes in Endeil's palms. Too late. Way too late.

And then the flames suddenly flare up. The room goes pitch black. The scent of decay fills my nostrils. Damp earth and rotting blood. Just like in that room in the basement. I feel the chair's straps tightening around my wrists. Then my ankles. I can't breathe. Then Endeil's office comes into focus again. I've stopped casting the spell. The black flames in Endeil's hands climb higher and higher, building a barrier to block me out, so that the only energy I can draw from is my own.

He smiles. The strip of exposed flesh on his arm heals. He's able to speak again, his voice only slightly hoarse. "So you discovered your wizard magic, did you?"

The flames creep from his hands to the floor, growing into dark walls that spread through the room. I'm surrounded by darkness, by magic that makes my skin crawl. I struggle to start up the spell again. It's not fair. One moment, I was easily overpowering him. And the next he throws some vision at me.

The wall of fire closes in. I feel like my bones are being ripped apart. Every part of me is on fire. Not the addictive fire of obsidian, but an excruciating pain that leaves me screaming too hard to cast, even if I could focus enough to call up the words. I haven't felt anything this agonizing since my days at the High Guild. And here it was Hadrin, my old tormentor, who warned me not to confront Endeil. That I wasn't ready.

Sweat pours down my forehead. My shirt sticks to me like it's the hottest day of summer. I'm on my knees on the floor. It's so dark and there's so much pain, for a moment I think maybe I never left the wizards' guild at all. Maybe everything since then has been a dream. They've driven me so mad, the only way to exist is through some wild delusion.

And then Endeil approaches, stopping just outside the wall of fire, and says, "Would you like me to stop?"

The pain eases, just enough for me to answer. "If you stop, I'll kill you." It's the truth. I've always been a terrible liar, anyway.

He laughs, and the flames turn an even darker shade of black. "I'd like to see you try."

I feel like my skull's going to crack apart. I press my hands against my ears, as if I can stop it, as if I can hold it together—my bare hands against his magic. This is it. He's really going to kill me. I'll never see Leora again. And what will happen to her, if our lives really are so intertwined? I never should have come here. Not without my knife.

"*What* is going on?!" an angry voice shouts from the hall.

The dark flames disappear, as if they'd never been there at all. I'm left crouching on the floor, dazed and sweating and clutching at my skull.

And then Father Gratch, of all people, storms in. He takes one glance at me—me, his least favorite acolyte, to put it lightly—and scowls in disgust. As if to say, *Oh, it's you.*

Why did it have to be him? Why couldn't it have been Father Moors? He's always protected me, looked out for me. He's never tried to get me expelled from school or kicked out of the church.

But then Father Gratch glares at Endeil. "High Priest Endeil, what were you doing to this boy? Everyone could hear him screaming bloody murder all the way at the other end of the hall!"

"I'm sorry," Endeil says, rubbing his eyes and yawning. "I was wrong about him. He spent the whole day shirking his duties and lazing about on a whim. And it appears," he goes on, giving me a sharp look, "that his hand is completely fine and he was faking his injury. I've only just now caught up with him, you see—hence the late hour."

He must suspect the truth about my wound, because I had my hands pressed to my head so tight. Or he doesn't really know and is just making up an excuse for why he'd be punishing me. But then I glance down at my hand and see that the bandage has come loose, exposing the healed skin underneath.

Father Gratch doesn't look like he quite buys Endeil's explanation, but he nods anyway. "Doesn't surprise me. I knew you'd picked the wrong acolyte for your apprentice. I've had this one on my list ever since he got here."

If only he knew. Another few moments and he wouldn't have had to worry about me ever again. I glance at the door, wondering if I could make my escape. Would Endeil risk using his dark magic in front of Father Gratch? But he wouldn't have to risk it. Father Gratch is standing between me and the doorway, effectively blocking my exit. He'd grab me before I could get past him.

"Then you understand," Endeil says. "If you'll shut the door on your way out, I think you'll find the noise to be an acceptable level."

"You want me to leave, so you can continue torturing him?" The words come out a growl. Father Gratch takes a few steps forward to stand in front of me. "I don't know what kind of practices you keep in Newhaven, but that's not how we do things here in Ashbury." He reaches out a hand to help me up.

My mouth falls open a little. Father Gratch doesn't look at me, keeping his eyes on Endeil, but he doesn't take his hand away, either. I consider not taking it, but then I think maybe I need all the help I can get, and slowly, my legs wobbling, I manage to get to my feet.

"Torture," Endeil repeats, his expression souring on the word. "I think you misunderstand, Father. I was merely reprimanding the boy."

"Were you, now?" Father Gratch scoffs. "If that's what you call it."

"He overreacted. He's nothing more than a liar and a cheat who would love for you to think something terrible was happening to him. In fact," Endeil says, "*he* attacked *me*. He even threatened to kill me. Didn't you, Azeril?"

My eyes dart from Endeil to Father Gratch, not knowing what to say. He's painted me into a corner, so that either the truth or the lie would condemn me. My voice comes out a desperate whisper. "I wish you had expelled me," I tell Father Gratch. "I wish you'd done it before he ever came here."

Father Gratch raises an eyebrow at Endeil. "Seems you've kept the upper hand."

"I should hope so. I should hope the High Priest wouldn't be thwarted by one *powerless* boy. Now, if you'll excuse us, we can finish up here and everyone can get to bed."

"And leave him here alone with you? I think not."

Endeil eyes us both. "Do I need to remind you, Father, that I outrank you?"

"That depends. Do I need to remind you that we don't torture children here?"

This from Father Gratch, who's made me scrub the floors until my hands bled. I never thought I'd feel so grateful to him.

"I can make you regret this," Endeil says.

Father Gratch sighs. "I already do. Come on, Azeril. We're done here." He shoots one last hateful look at Endeil before steering me into the hall, making a point of closing the door behind him.

"Thank you," I whisper. I'm still trembling all over. I half expect Endeil to burst through that door and kill us both.

"This doesn't change anything," Father Gratch mutters. "You'll likely be expelled. And I don't know what went on in there, but if one word of what he said was true . . . You'd better run, boy. Run like the Chasm itself is at your heels."

He doesn't know just how right he is. And I don't need him to say it twice. We share a look of understanding, just a glance, really, and then I'm out of there.

For good this time.

———

Hadrin's tearing the room apart when I get back to the inn. Or at least that's what it looks like. He's in the middle of yanking some clothes out of a drawer and stuffing them in a bag when I walk in.

"Hmph," he says, shooting me the barest of glances—but obviously disapproving of what he sees—before adding, "Those do not sound like the triumphant footsteps of a victor."

Leora's sitting on the bed, wringing her hands. She looks up at me and bites her lip. "Az. You didn't . . . You didn't kill him." It's not a question. It's what she wants to believe.

"Oh, no, he didn't kill him," Hadrin says, pausing from his rummaging—no, packing—for a moment. "But don't think he didn't *try*."

Leora glares at him. "And you should know. You're the one who put all those spells in him. You're the one who wanted him to be some kind of weapon. So don't act so high and mighty, like you're better than him."

I stare at her in shock. "Leora—"

"Save it, Az. I *know* you're not like that. I know you're not a weapon. I get that. I was just making a point, because you going after the High Priest doesn't give him the right to stand there and act like he's above it all."

"Here," Hadrin says, pulling a set of blue robes out of a drawer and tossing them to me. "Put those on."

I hold the robes as far away from me as possible. "You want me to dress like a wizard? Like *you*?"

"Oh, so you didn't confront Endeil tonight? You actually had the sense to turn around before you went anywhere near him? *Well?*" he asks, when I don't respond. *"Did you?"*

Leora massages her forehead with her palms. *"Dad."*

"No," I tell Hadrin. "I fought him and I lost. Is that what you wanted to hear?"

"That I was right and you weren't in the least bit ready?" He hesitates, then takes a deep breath, calming himself. "No," he admits. "I wish you would have stayed here, like I told you. But I'm not glad to have been right—not this time. And you'd better put on those robes. Unless you want to be recognized, or worse, killed."

"I don't need you telling me what to do. I can take care of myself. I have my spells now, don't I? And my knife." I gesture to the drawer. And I *could have* killed Endeil tonight. I was strong enough. He just . . . got the better of me. I think.

Hadrin rolls his eyes and makes a point of not offering up the key, but Leora stomps over to the desk and unlocks the drawer with a touch just to spite him.

"You can take care of yourself," he repeats with a derisive snort, as if it's the most ridiculous thing he's ever heard. "If you'd listened to me earlier, we wouldn't be in this predicament. And you'd better listen to me now. Endeil's going to be looking for you, and a wizard is the last thing he or anyone else would ever expect you to look like. So get dressed. Now. We're leaving."

"Leaving?"

"We're going home."

I thought I was home. "And where is that?"

"To the capital," he says, as if it should be obvious. "To the wizards' guild."

CHAPTER TWENTY-THREE

Two days and a long, bumpy carriage ride later, I'm standing in Newhaven, the capital city, staring at a two-story wooden house. Leora's house, where she and her mother lived. And Hadrin. And . . . it's also where her mother died.

The house is in a quiet neighborhood, on a street lined with beautiful houses, all with cobblestone walkways and hedge fences. Unlike its neighbors, though, this one has seen better days. It could use a new coat of paint, and a few of the shutters need replacing, and it's obvious no one's lived here for a few years at least. When Leora opens the front door, the movement stirs up a cloud of dust that makes us both cough and cover our noses.

I pause, standing just inside the doorway and gaping at the staircase with the intricately carved banister. At the shelves in the living room lined with expensive, leather-bound books that I wouldn't even be allowed to touch back at the church. The couches—there's more than one of them—look too nice to sit on, even with several layers of dust settled on them.

"Az," Leora says, squeezing my hand, "I'm *home*." She closes her eyes and just soaks it in for a minute.

"This is where you *lived*?" I can't help sounding incredulous. Though I don't know what else I expected. Even back then, Hadrin was a high-ranking wizard, running a top secret experiment. The Guild must have paid him well to torture me.

I picture the cramped cell I used to sleep in. The small bed with the thin, hard mattress that took up most of the space, so that there was hardly any room left to stand. I didn't know any better. I thought that's how everyone lived, until . . .

I press a hand to my forehead, remembering the day I discovered I was a prisoner and that the wizards all went home at night. Some of them lived at the guild, but most of them lived in houses, with families. I was six, maybe seven. I'd been in the wizards' custody for a few years. I don't know where I lived before that—if it was better or worse. A couple of wizards were locking me up for the night, and, innocently, I asked them who locked *them* up when they went to bed. After all, if they were tucked away in their cells, who would turn the key? But they just laughed at me. A cruel kind of laughter that filled me with doubts about my situation.

Not that I thought everyone spent their days like I did, being tested and prodded and made to recite things I didn't understand. That was before the chair, of course. They saved that for me until I was a little older.

"It must be weird for you," I say, pushing those dark thoughts away. I'm glad Leora had a nice place to live. I'm just not glad that Hadrin did. "I mean, you haven't been here since your mother died. Have you?"

She shakes her head. I follow her into the dining room, where there's a long wooden table surrounded by fancy wooden chairs.

"Wow. Did you have the king and queen over for dinner *often*?"

She rolls her eyes at me. "It's exactly how I remember it. I doubt my father's stepped foot in the place in years. Probably not since he left us. He's certainly not here *now*."

It's true. Hadrin went straight back to his rooms at the High Guild as soon as we got to the city. He asked Leora if she remembered how to get here, double-checked that she remembered his room number if she needed to contact him—45B—and then abandoned us. Though not without a stern reminder that there was a guest room I should stay in, *alone*, and that if I even thought about touching his daughter, he'd drag me back to that chair himself. He said all this while Leora was in her favorite bakery, buying some twisty-looking pastry they apparently don't have anywhere else. I refused to make him any promises, and he glared at me and clenched his teeth until I thought I heard one of them crack.

Now we're here alone, and Leora's grinning from ear to ear at everything in the house. She might have some pretty terrible memories associated with this place, but it's obvious her life here wasn't all bad. There must have been a lot of good times, too.

"And this was mine," she says proudly, dragging me to a room at the end of a long hallway.

There's a bed. A girl's bed, the blanket embroidered with roses and ladybugs. Ratty, well-loved stuffed creatures are piled at the foot of it and on top of a dresser. They're all links to her past, to all the moments I wasn't a part of. But I barely glance at any of them, my eyes drawn instead to a dark stain on the wooden floorboards in the middle of the room.

The smile on Leora's face melts away when she sees what I'm staring at.

"What's that?" I ask, though I already know the answer.

"It's nothing. Just a spill. An accident."

"It looks like blood." Dread seeps into my stomach. I can't stop staring at the spot.

I didn't know it mattered, that you'd be . . . linked. Not until I came home that night to find my ten-year-old daughter, my little girl, covered in blood.

"You weren't hurt," I tell her. It's a statement, not a question, because we both already know it's true.

"It was a long time ago. It doesn't matter anymore. Don't *think* about it."

"It matters to me." It's her blood staining the floor, but it might as well be mine.

Hadrin said he needed the hair of a maiden to work the spell. And now I remember just what that spell was. It was a sacrifice to the Chasm. That was the day they opened up a channel between it and me. That was the first day they put me in the chair, when they made me *bleed.*

It wasn't just hair they needed. It was a blood sacrifice. No wonder we're linked now.

I shudder. And then I'm there again, in that dark room, naked and strapped into the chair. The leather's too tight on my wrists. Two wizards stand in front of me, holding sharp knives. Bringing them closer.

I'm sick and shaking. Terrified and powerless. I scream. I beg them not to do this, but they act like they can't hear me, like I'm not even there. I pull against the straps, but it's no use. I keep expecting them to put the knives down and admit it's just another test, just to see how I'd react if something like this was really happening. But the intensity radiating from them, and the way they won't look at me, lets me know it's not a test. There's no getting out of this, and just the thought turns me into someone else. Something else. Wild and crazed, like a trapped animal. My only thoughts are of how to get away. Of how I'd do anything, anything, to get out of here, to not let them touch me.

Or maybe that was the real me all along. Maybe everything else—all the outer layers, the parts people see—was all just for show. A few moments of fear and it's shucked all away, leaving a raw core of violence and desperation. A gnawing madness that won't be calmed.

Hadrin stands off to the side, supervising the whole thing. Listening to my terrified pleas and watching me suffer. I look to him, to see his face, because I know he outranks the others. I know he could stop this. Maybe it's not going to happen. Maybe he'll change his mind, because he can't really stand there and watch these wizards do whatever it is they're going to do to me. He has to call it off.

I silently pray for him to call it off and let me go.

But he doesn't. And when one of the wizards looks up, waiting for his approval to start the next step, he nods. He nods. And then—

I'm back in Leora's room. Trembling all over. There are tears in my eyes, but I quickly rub them away with the palms of my hands. I reach for my knife, my nerves jolting when it's not there. It wasn't enough just to wear the blue robes. Hadrin insisted that the knife would be too recognizable. If Endeil was looking for me, if we got stopped by a guard on the way out of town . . . One glance at my obsidian and it would all be over.

Leora's staring at me, her eyes as wide as I've ever seen them. She opens her mouth, but no words come out. Then, her voice shaking, she asks, "What were they going to do?"

I turn away from the bloodstained floor, rubbing my arms, suddenly freezing. That's what I remember most about afterward, when they were done with me. Being so, so cold. "What was who going to do?"

"It was like you were having a nightmare, only you were awake. You said, 'Don't let them do it.'"

"It doesn't matter. I don't remember, anyway."

"Az," she whispers, "don't lie to me."

"Do you still have my knife?" I wrapped it up carefully, so there'd be no chance of her touching it, before she packed it away in her bag for me.

"Yeah," she says. "Of course. It's with the rest of my stuff. Let me go get it."

She steps into the hall. I put a hand on her wrist. "No. That's not . . . I don't think you should give it back to me."

"*What?*"

"Just . . . put it somewhere safe and don't tell me where it is."

"Is this because of what my father said? Because we're not in Ashbury now, and even if the High Priest is looking for you, which we don't even know if he is, that doesn't necessarily mean—"

"No. That's not it. I just . . ." *I just don't trust myself with it right now.*

Leora's raising her eyebrows at me, waiting for an explanation. "You and that knife have been inseparable ever since I met you. You almost didn't take it off when we . . ." She trails off, her cheeks going red. "And now you're telling me what? That you don't even want it back? *That'll* be the day."

"I didn't say I don't want it."

"That's what I thought. So I'll put it on the dining room table, okay? If you want it, you can take it. If not . . ." She shrugs, already on her way down the hall.

I watch her go, not stopping her, not arguing. Already my resolve to stay away from my obsidian is crumbling, because *of course* I want it. It's better this way, her leaving it out for me. Not putting it directly in my hands, but not keeping it from me, either. Pretending I have a choice. I'll go mad without it, and what was I thinking, telling her not to give it back?

An image flashes through my head. The one of Leora, sobbing, drenched in blood.

And I wonder if we both haven't just made a horrible mistake.

CHAPTER TWENTY-FOUR

I'm walking up Market Street with Hadrin a few days later. He's been coming to the house every morning—to the house, but never inside—and we've been going to the wooded park nearby, talking in hushed voices about magic. It's a nice park, part of their fancy neighborhood, with hardly any people in it, at least in the mornings. A couple of neighbors have recognized him, from years ago, and given their condolences for his late wife. When anyone asks about me, he says I'm his apprentice. He doesn't tell them my name, or that his daughter and I are together.

That's what we've *been* doing, but today I had something else in mind. Today, I want to see the guild.

We're on our way there, headed up the hill, when I start catching snippets of conversations. Not much, just a few words, but they're enough to make me pause. Phrases like "new power" and "the High Priest."

I shouldn't be surprised. After all, Rathe can bring back the *dead.* It was only a matter of time before everyone heard about it.

I'm stopped in the street, straining to hear more, but then Hadrin glares at me and grabs my arm, practically dragging me along. He must not have heard what I did, or he'd be stopping to listen, too. "We're never going to get there if you keep gawking at everything," he growls. "Do I need to remind you that coming here today was your idea?"

"No," I say, jerking my arm out of his grasp, "but it hasn't stopped you so far."

"Let's just get this over with."

I follow him. Maybe this is the stupidest thing I've ever done—something he's already told me several times this morning—but I can't stop thinking about it. About the wizards' guild. Ever since I started getting my memories back, it's been on the edge of my mind, never quite leaving me alone. I thought that I'd have all the answers now, that I'd know all the missing pieces, but I don't. And now that we're here, in the capital, the thought of the guild being so close haunts me. It walks up my spine like spiders every night as I try to fall asleep. It brushes over my skin, making me shiver.

"It won't fix anything, you know," Hadrin says.

"I have to see it," I tell him. "I *have* to, just to prove I can look at it and walk away again and still be all right. Just to . . ." Just to prove to myself that it doesn't have any power over me. That it's bigger in my head than it is in real life.

"You're making a mistake." He sounds worried. Not snide or judging. Like he actually cares what happens to me.

I glance over at him. I could have gone alone. It's not like the High Guild is hard to find. Or I could have brought Leora instead. She would have held my hand when we got there and yelled obscenities at the building, or at wizards passing by on their way to work. She would have told me it doesn't matter what happened there—not a moment of it—because she loves me anyway.

It's not that I wouldn't have wanted to hear that. It's not like I wouldn't have smiled at her and felt lucky and grateful and like maybe, just maybe, there was a chance that what she said was true. That it really doesn't matter. Even if I know that it does. It matters too much, and I don't want her to see me like that. To look over at me and *know* how much of me died inside that building.

I have to face it, to show myself that I can, and yet . . . I can't face it alone.

"You shouldn't be doing this," Hadrin says. "I shouldn't have let you come this far."

"Let me? As if anything I do is your—"

A nearby conversation makes me stop in midsentence. We both hear it this time. A woman says, "She has a second power now, thanks to the High Priest," and Hadrin and I both turn to stare at her.

She's standing with a friend in front of a bakery. "It's a miracle," she goes on. "My niece can make all the weeds in the garden just wilt away." She snaps her fingers. The other woman's eyes widen, and she gasps, but it's not a horrified gasp—it's more like she's in awe.

I want to run over there and tell them that it's not a gift, that it's from the Chasm, of all places, and that if her niece turns out anything like Rathe— But what good would it do? Going up to a complete stranger and saying I overheard her conversation and her niece is probably evil now, so she'd better watch out? Instead I keep walking, my pace quicker this time.

Word about Rathe's new power getting out—that was inevitable. But this is much worse. "Endeil's found a way to keep doing it,"

I tell Hadrin. Not that I'd believed he wouldn't, or that, without me, he'd just give up the whole thing. Maybe he got someone else to do the obsidian part. Someone less skilled, but more willing. Then again, I underestimated how powerful his magic was the other night, and he almost killed me. He would have, if Father Gratch hadn't walked in. Maybe his magic is strong enough now that he doesn't even need the obsidian.

If he ever did. I wouldn't put it past him to have told me the obsidian was a necessary step, that he needed my help. All so he could play some sick mind game and get me to willingly cut into my friend. But I push that thought away. He needed me—he *did*. He's just found some other way now, that's all. What I did to Rathe . . . that wasn't for nothing.

"All the more reason," Hadrin says, "why he needs to be stopped and why you should be preparing to defeat him. Not out on some crazy mission to drive yourself mad." He pauses, putting a hand on my arm. "Listen, Azeril. When I said this wasn't a good idea, I meant it. I know you think I'm the last person you should trust, but I don't want anything bad to happen to you."

"Because I'm a weapon. Because you need me in working condition."

"Because you're only a boy and you need someone looking out for you. Someone older and wiser who doesn't want to see you get hurt. Not any more than you have been already. And going there *is going to hurt*. You've been through enough. So let's turn around and go back and forget this."

"You're telling me you care what happens to me. *Now*, after everything you did. You could have stopped the experiment at any time. You never had to let it go that far, but you chose to anyway."

"All the more reason to stop this. I know what we did to you. I know everything you endured in that Fire-forsaken basement, and I *won't* let you relive it. It's bad enough you have your memories. Dredging up the past any further will only cause you more pain. We've both changed since then. I'm not the same man who stood by and watched you get hurt. I will *not* watch it happen now, and that means we're turning around and going back home."

My home is in Ashbury. Even if I've left for good, it still feels like home. And his is up this hill, at the guild itself. But I know what he means.

I open my mouth to say, "Okay," but the word dies on my lips as I look up and see the tallest spire of the guild looming over the nearby buildings. It's just a glimpse, but it sucks the air out of my lungs. A wave of fear passes over me, so strong that my vision blurs.

And suddenly I remember the last time I was here, in these streets. I was running. Knowing that at any moment someone would realize I was gone and send the whole guild after me. And if they found me . . . But I had the knife. I would have killed myself before I let them take me back. And I'd have taken down as many of them with me as I could.

Getting anywhere near this place was a mistake. I feel like I'm back there, the day I escaped, and that it's only a matter of time before the wizards find me. And when they do I'll be too scared to move, to reach for the knife, and then I'll be back in the chair—

"Azeril?" Hadrin peers at me, his face lined with worry. He's right there, only inches in front of me, but he sounds so far away. "Are you all right?"

I can't even speak. All I can do is shake my head before I turn and run in the other direction.

———

Hadrin finds me hiding in an alley at the bottom of the hill, my arms wrapped tightly around my knees, taking deep breaths.

He's out of breath himself, and his face is red, his chest heaving.

The alley is narrow, wedged between two gray stone buildings. It smells like garbage and urine. I can hear a rat scrabbling around in a discarded basket somewhere behind me, while a blackbird squawks from the rooftops.

I know the wizards aren't coming for me. I *know* this isn't that day three years ago, and yet I can't shake the terror. My thoughts won't sit still, and my body won't move.

"Don't tell me 'I told you so,'" I mutter. "If you even so much as *think* it . . ." But my threat sounds empty, even to me.

Hadrin squats down in front of me, so our eyes are almost level. "I know I've made mistakes in the past, and I know this doesn't even begin to make up for them, but I would never let them take you. *Never.* Do you understand?" He presses a hand over his heart. "No matter what happens, you will never have to go to the guild or down to that basement again."

"To the place where *you* tortured me, you mean?"

"Yes, that's exactly what I mean. I would die first, before I ever let anyone take you there."

"And I know what a wizard's promise is worth." I rest my forehead on my knees, not looking at him. I think about my obsidian and its comforting fire, but I don't move to touch it. Partly because I'm still too frozen with fear, and partly because I need my thoughts to stay focused as I try to remember exactly what happened the last time I was here. I glance up at Hadrin. "I remember running,"

I tell him. "Running through this strange, unfamiliar city, with all these sights and smells and noises, and . . . and *light*, and knowing I would die if I stopped. If I didn't run fast enough or far enough before they figured out I was gone and caught up to me."

They did, in Ashbury. Those wizards that Father Moors saw me kill. That was my first memory. I'd blocked out everything else, or something had blocked it out for me. That part's still fuzzy. One minute I knew who I was, and then there was a burning feeling in my head, and it all went away.

"But what I don't remember is how I escaped."

"Someone left your cell unlocked that night. Terrible mistake. The wizard on duty was fired years ago."

"No. He locked it. Like he did every night. I *saw him* do it. Do you think I wasn't watching? Waiting for the time someone would make even the slightest mistake and I'd have a chance of getting away? Every night I tried to open the door, even though I knew it wouldn't open. Even though I'd watched my keeper lock me in. It hadn't opened that night. I fell asleep, but I woke up in the early morning. There was a noise or something, and my door was ajar."

"Perhaps you were wrong," Hadrin says. "Perhaps it wasn't locked after all, only jammed, and came free in the night."

"It wasn't the only door that was unlocked. There were several more I had to get through to escape. If even one of them had been locked properly . . . but they were *open*. You can't tell me that's just one act of carelessness."

He glances away, wincing as he gets to his feet. "I'm too old to be kneeling down in the gutter. Come on. I assume you've had enough of this foolishness and we can go back?"

I don't move. My voice is quiet, strained, afraid to say the words—but I say them anyway. "Was it you?"

"*What?*"

"Was it . . . Were you the one who—"

"I understood the question! You think *I*, a high-ranking official of the High Guild"—he tugs at the collar of his robes, indicating the little gold symbols sewn there—"would ruin years of hard work and risk my career for some pathetic boy?"

"Someone let me go."

He snorts. "And you think it was *me*? How *touching.*"

Slowly, I get to my feet. My legs are still a little wobbly, but I can move again. "You said you'd never let me go back. Maybe you're the one who let me escape in the first place."

His voice is dangerously low, burning with rage. "You think I would sabotage my own top secret experiment and let a weapon I created—a killer with ties to my *daughter*—loose on the streets?"

"And yet," I say, keeping perfectly calm, despite his outburst, "those are exactly the reasons why you would have done it. I was *your* project, and you knew what you were doing to me was wrong. The guilt was eating you alive, wasn't it? You'd cast a spell to keep Leora safe from me. You didn't know I would find her." Or be drawn to her. And now I wonder if it was a coincidence I ended up in Ashbury, in the same town as her, or if it was something else. Except I refuse to believe that. I'm meant to be with Leora, and not because of some spell. "The first day you put me in that chair, when you made the blood sacrifice to the Chasm, you didn't know it would be her blood you were sacrificing, too. When you went home and found her bleeding all over, in all the places you'd cut me—"

"I didn't." Hadrin's voice shakes. "I never held the knife. I never touched you!"

No, not then, and not with the knife, but he told them what to do and he was the only one with the authority to stop it. "You were scared. You were worried about her. But you were worried about me, too. You saw how terrified she was, and she wasn't even in any pain. You must have thought about me then, about how I had no one—"

"*Enough.* This is all speculation. And that was years before you escaped. You know that."

"So you let me suffer for years, the guilt building up in you day by day, until you couldn't take it anymore."

"It wasn't my job to coddle you. In order for the spells to take, we had to make you suffer." He glances up at me, then looks away.

I take a step closer to him. He flinches, as if I've made a move to attack, which I haven't. I think if I'd drawn the knife he would have held still. "You ranked high enough." My voice is a whisper, as if we're talking about something shameful. "You could have gotten the keys to all those doors. You would have known who'd be on duty and made sure they were on break or something. It's funny that no one got hurt, don't you think? That all the timing worked out so I never had to confront anyone. Not until later, when they'd come after me."

"You're saying that out of the entire guild, you think I'm the only one who could have done it?"

"No. But you're the only one who had a reason to."

"It could have been anyone. A janitor. A guard. Someone who felt sorry for you. Some misguided sap who thought he was doing a good deed by releasing you."

"I don't understand why you can't admit it. It's not like I'd tell anyone, not if you don't want me to, not even Leora."

"No matter what you want to believe, it wasn't me."

"Chasm take you! You saved an innocent kid. I didn't deserve to be there, and you let me go. Why can't you admit it? What's so horrible about it, about *me*, that you'd fight so hard to deny it?!"

He's quiet for a minute, just watching me. Then, his voice heavy, like speaking at all takes a great effort, he says, "Because I was the one who brought you there. I was the one who ordered all of the horrible things to happen. And I was the one who thought about calling it all off a thousand times, yet never did. And then it was too late. The Guild decided the experiment was a failure. You were too dangerous, and we didn't get the spells we were after. One day there was an order from higher up that my team was to permanently end the experiment. I was supposed to kill you, Azeril."

"But you didn't." He could have. He'd already cast the spell to keep Leora safe.

"You'd been through enough. All because of me. But I won't say I let you go, because if you ever thought I had done something to bring about your escape, then you might start to think you had a reason not to hate me. That I was somehow even the least bit worthy of your forgiveness, which I am not."

"Lucky for you, I would never think that."

"I should hope not," he says. "But, thankfully, there's no chance of it, since, like I said, it wasn't me."

"*Right.* It wasn't you."

"I'm glad we understand each other." He brushes off his robes. "Now, we'd better be off. If you're done with your little diversion, we have a High Priest to thwart."

CHAPTER TWENTY-FIVE

I wake up in the night, sweating and terrified. I kick the blankets off, struggling to get free, gasping for breath.

Leora stirs next to me. Here in her bed in her room. She pulled a rug over the dark stain on the floor, so neither of us has to see it. I would have slept in the guest room—not because Hadrin wanted me to, but because of that stain—and had her come with me, but the guest room felt so impersonal. There's something comforting about being so close to her here, near all her old toys, the remnants of a childhood I never had.

I take a few breaths, trying to calm back down. I dreamed I was there again, at the guild. Not surprising, given what happened today. Just catching a glimpse of it sent me running.

I rub my face with the heels of my palms. Maybe some fears are meant to stay. Maybe they get so ingrained that they become a vital part of you, like a second heart, so that if you actually got rid of them, you wouldn't be able to function anymore. I slide out of bed. My heart—my own, real heart—is still racing from the dream, and I don't think I'm going to fall back to sleep anytime soon.

The floor is cold against my bare feet. Leora stirs again, and I pause, waiting to see if she's awake, sort of hoping that she is. If I could hear her voice, maybe it would banish the lingering feeling that it wasn't just a nightmare—that the wizards' guild is the reality and this place, this dark room with blood staining the floor, is the dream.

But she doesn't wake up, and I slip out into the hall. It's so dark out here. It could be any hallway. It could lead anywhere. I swallow down a growing sense of unease and consider going back into the room. But I hate myself for being so afraid. I couldn't even look at the guild, and now a *dream* is going to make me a prisoner?

Okay, so I *do* slip back into the room, the door making a slow creak as I push it open, but only to grab my belt and my knife. She left it out for me the other day, on the table, like she said, and I didn't last five minutes before taking it. Its familiar heat flares to life in my hand as I grip the hilt. Its fire creeps through my veins, burning my skin and lighting up my brain. Any traces of fear vanish. I exhale, finally myself again.

The boy creeps back into the hall, a wicked smile tugging on one side of his mouth. Let the wizards come for him now that he has the knife. Just let one of them run into him here, in the dark. The spells are fun, but they take too long to kill them. The spells make them scream, but the boy must stay unnoticed. Some of the wizards have those spiral tattoos, like the one on the boy's wrist, that protect them from his magic. But the knife . . . The knife is silent. Always. Most of them don't get a chance to scream, not if he doesn't want them to. And the knife's so good at slicing through their fragile skin, right through those tattoos they love so much, rendering them useless. Just let them try and protect themselves from him with the knife in his hand.

I blink, though the hall is still pitch black, trying to get my bearings. Something's not right. I'm mixing things up. And . . . there are no wizards here, are there?

But . . . I was there, just now. In *that room.* They had me in the chair. I *remember.* I don't want to, but I can't forget. That was too real to have been a dream. So I give in a little more to the knife's heat, letting it sear away all the thoughts I don't want to have.

The boy presses forward, through the silent hall, his heartbeat loud in his ears.

There's a creaking sound behind him.

Fire races along his nerves. The hairs on the back of his neck stand on end. He holds perfectly still—a boy, a weapon, a murderer—there, in the dark.

The creak came from the room. The one with the blood. With his blood spilled across the floor, from when they cut into him. He closes his eyes and still feels their knives. How they were so sharp it didn't hurt at first, and he thought maybe nothing had happened. But he was wrong—so, so wrong—and now they're back for more. So the boy presses himself against the wall, silent and waiting.

He holds his breath for a long time, his whole body tense, but nothing ever comes. It was just a sound. Just the walls settling. The boy thinks about casting something, feeling for energies to draw from, just in case. There's only one source besides himself, one life to drain. But that doesn't mean anything, not here, not when they have those tattoos. There could be a whole slew of wizards, just waiting for the boy to let his guard down, their energies hidden from him by the spiral marks.

The boy listens, straining to hear even the slightest hint of breathing. Anything that might mean they're here, coming for him. But there's nothing, not a sound, and the air only smells of dust, not of bitter herbs.

He starts to wonder if maybe there aren't any wizards here, after all. No . . . not here. But close. They're not all that far from here, over in their guild, asleep in their beds. And here the boy lurks with his knife and his spells, and they have no idea. He wonders how many of them he could kill before they managed to stop him.

It wouldn't be enough—it wouldn't be all of them—and yet there's really only one that matters. The boy doesn't even have to think about it, to know which wizard he would kill if he could hurt only one.

And he knows exactly where to find him.

——

The boy walks up the hill to the wizards' guild, right up to their front doors. Four wizards stand outside the main entrance—four bright spots of energy to be drained. They're here, even though it's the middle of the night, talking and laughing.

Not for long.

The wizards see him coming, but they don't know to stop him. They don't recognize the monster they created, finally coming home. He gets close—way too close—before one of them holds up a hand and says, "Kid, you can't—"

But that's as far as he gets before the words to a spell are on the boy's lips. The first spell he used to kill. The one that turns the lungs to ash. He pulls from the wizard's own energy to destroy him and watches as he falters, choking, taken by surprise.

The other three wizards rush toward the boy. One of them tries to cast a spell to silence him, but the boy draws the knife and slits his throat. It feels so good for the knife to taste flesh. Blood sprays from the wizard as he falls to the ground, joining the first, who's no longer moving. The blood sizzles when it touches the blade and burns away.

Two wizards left. They try to run. The boy recites a different spell, one that makes the blood vessels in their feet shrivel until every step causes insufferable pain, like walking with broken glass in their skin. The wizards stumble, screaming for help. For the hundreds of others inside the guild walls who might save them.

Might, but won't. Not tonight.

The boy catches them and slashes their throats, one and then the other. He sees the fear in their eyes, the moment when they know their fate is decided. And then they lie on the ground, silent and unmoving.

He doesn't even try opening the doors. They might be locked. But the boy doesn't need to find out. He casts a spell that makes the doors wither and decay so fast they explode into dust. A surge of power made possible by having so many wizards nearby to draw from. Wizards who can't see him, who don't yet know he's here. So many sources of energy, so that his spells seem limitless.

It feels almost as good as the knife's fire, letting his spells take over.

A door in the hallway opens. A wizard rushes out, terror on his face. The boy knows that he heard the screaming outside. He casts the spell to desiccate him. To shrivel his organs until he's only a husk. It happens so fast. The wizard never gets anywhere near the boy, doesn't even know what's happening to him, and then he's crumpled on the floor.

The boy smiles. Another wizard appears, coming at him from behind, from another hallway. The boy feels the wizard's energy before he sees him. He twists and buries the knife in the wizard's chest. His hands shake from the euphoria. From the sweet pleasure of cutting into this wizard, especially so soon after the others.

But there will be more flesh to cut, more pleasure to be had, when he finds the one he came for.

The boy sees a map on the wall. He locates the living quarters, where the wizard will be. It would be easier to get there without the wall in the way, so he casts the decaying spell again and blasts a hole through it. The spell is silent, the wall in front of him disintegrating into dust. Now he's in another hallway. One with numbers on the doors.

45B flickers in his mind. It's where the wizard sleeps. The wizard. The one that deserves to die more than all the others. The boy doesn't remember how he knows this number, but it doesn't matter. The wizard will be there, in that room.

The boy turns a corner. A wizard standing in the hall stares at him, his mouth open, not sure what he's seeing. There are so many energy sources here, in this part of the guild, that the boy can't tell which ones are in their rooms and which are lurking in the hall, like this one.

The wizard hesitates, fumbling at his belt for ingredients to a spell. But then fear takes over as the boy gets closer, as the wizard sees the knife in his hand and the blood on his clothes, and then the wizard is going to scream. The boy considers letting him. Let them all come for him. Let them all die.

But if that happened, he might not get to spend time alone with the one he came for. That one might get away. Or he might die a quick death, and then it would be over, and that would not make the boy happy.

So he casts the decaying spell on this wizard before he can make a sound. One moment the wizard is drawing a breath to scream, and the next he's a pile of dust. When the wizards wake in the morning, they won't even find his body. They will never know what happened to him.

The boy moves on. He finds room 45B and uses the door to get in, so he can close it again. So no one will interrupt.

The wizard is asleep in his bed, as the boy knew he would be. The boy crouches next to the bed, the obsidian burning in his hand, begging to be used. The wizard said he never held the knives that cut the boy. He only pulled the strings. But none of it would have happened without him. The boy would have stayed whole, unbroken, if it weren't for this wizard. And the boy has his own knife now, and the wizard's throat is right there, only a hand's breadth away. One quick movement and he could slice it open. The wizard would wake up just in time to bleed out all over his bed while the boy watched. He'd see the recognition in the wizard's eyes. And the wizard would wonder at first if this was really happening, because it couldn't—it couldn't—be real, but it would be.

Except that would be too quick. And the wizard deserves so much worse than that.

The boy whispers the words that make a little ball of light appear in the air. There's a zap of energy that runs down his arm, since he can't use this wizard's life against him—not with the tattoo—but the knife's fire burns so hot he barely feels anything else.

The sudden light wakes up the wizard. He raises a hand to shield his eyes and scrambles to sit up. Then he notices the boy. "Azeril?" He glances around the room, as if he's not sure where he is. "Chasm take me, did something happen to Leora?"

"Oh, the Chasm's going to take you, all right."

He squints at the boy. "I can think of only one reason why you'd be here. Is she—"

"I don't know who you're talking about. It couldn't be anyone important—the wizard doesn't have a heart. Or does he?" The boy gestures toward the wizard's chest with the tip of the knife. "We could find out."

"Azeril?" There's a tremor of fear in his voice. A sound the boy has never heard before. It's like the wizard doesn't recognize him when he's not in the chair.

The boy smiles. The obsidian blade gleams in the light he cast. "You're right. There is only one reason I would ever come here again. I think I'll start with your stomach. Long, shallow cuts at first. Though it will be difficult. The knife will want to go further than that. I might lose control of it. But don't worry—if I do, I'll heal you up and start again. Oh, but wait. I can't. Not with that tattoo on your arm." The boy flashes the matching one on his wrist. "So maybe I'll start with that instead. Should I slice through it, or should I cut it out of your skin completely, just to be on the safe side?"

The wizard stares at him. At the blood that stains his hands, that's spattered on his clothes. His mouth moves a little, but no words come out. Then he says, "This isn't you."

"Because I'm not screaming? Or bleeding?" The boy laughs. "You've seen so much of me. So much of my blood escaping to the floor. But it's only one part of me. And I've only seen one part of

you—just the outside. Tonight we're going to trade. You're going to watch me *slowly slice you into pieces, and I'm going to see what's inside you."*

"Azeril, listen to me," the wizard says, his voice steady and almost maddeningly calm, though his face is pale. *"You don't want to do this."*

But he does. There's nothing else he wants more. *"Don't I? You never showed me any mercy. I was innocent then, I didn't deserve any of it, and* you didn't care. *So why should I spare you now?"*

"Because you'll regret it tomorrow. When you're yourself again."

"This *is who I am. Get up. Off the bed. Now."* The boy motions for him to move.

The wizard hesitates. His eyes dart to the boy's, searching for something. The boy doesn't know what it is, but he's certain it isn't there.

Then the boy reaches out with the knife and slashes the wizard's arm, cutting right through the spiral tattoo that protects him. The wizard cries out.

There's a surge of ecstasy from the blade as it hits flesh, and then a wave of emptiness as it already longs for more, despite having fed several times tonight. But it will have plenty more later, so the boy pushes its desires away, chanting a spell instead. Using the wizard's own life force against him.

He has waited so long to do this.

The wizard gasps for breath, clutching his hands to his chest. His mouth moves silently, so that the boy can't tell if he's trying to form words, or if he's just struggling with the pain of his lungs starting to burn, flaking into ash. He coughs. His eyes find the boy's again, and *the boy expects them to be pleading. Quietly begging him to stop. But instead all he sees is sadness. And disappointment.*

The boy snaps his mouth shut, suddenly stopping the spell. The wizard sucks in a heaving breath.

"Get up," the boy repeats, and this time the wizard does what he's told. The boy gestures at a desk chair and motions for him to sit. It's a plain wooden chair, no straps built in, but it will do. He considers making the wizard take off his night clothes, to force him to be naked and bare like he was once, but there's no need. The knife will cut him just as easily.

There's a belt sitting by the bed, next to his perfectly folded robes. The boy takes it and secures the wizard's hands behind the chair. That part will be the same. "Now," he says, circling him, "where should I start?"

"You should start by figuring out what you're going to tell her in the morning."

"Maybe I should break your fingers, one by one. Do you remember when you did that to me? Not until after I could heal myself, of course. You couldn't risk breaking all the valuable pieces until then. I refused for a while. Imagine the only control you have in your life, the only freedom, is the choice to hurt. But my defiance didn't last long, did it? The pain was too great. And it was the knife hand. The one I planned to kill you with. So, you see, I was kind of invested in it."

"Break every bone in my body, if that's what you have to do," the wizard says, his voice quiet and choked, but sincere. "The Fire and the Chasm both know I deserve it. But what will you tell her?"

"You keep saying 'her.'"

"My daughter. Leora. What will she say when you tell her you killed her father?"

"What do I care what a wizard's daughter thinks?"

"Because you love her. Damn it, boy, you might not remember it right now, but you do."

He's not making any sense. How can the boy love someone he's never met? And the wizard's daughter, no less. *"If you've treated her anywhere near the way you've treated me, she won't be sorry to see you gone."*

The boy moves closer to him, his hand shaking with the effort of holding back the knife, already so desperate to be cutting again.

"I don't know that she'll be sorry for me," the wizard goes on, *"but she will be for you. She loves you, and you'll break her heart if you do this."*

"If I do this, you mean?" The boy leans in close, trailing the tip of the knife down the wizard's cheek. The wizard gasps a little at the burn. Blood trickles down his skin in its wake. *"And I don't love her,"* the boy says. *"I don't love anyone. I'm a weapon. Nothing else. A weapon can't love."*

"You're not a weapon. It may be my deepest regret that you think you are."

"Oh, so the wizard regrets, does he? And I am. I'm exactly as you made me to be. You never thought I'd be back for you, that I'd ever have the chance to show you firsthand all the gifts you gave me. But here I am. Which one do you want to see next?"

"You are so much more than anything I ever made you to be. The boy we kept here . . . perhaps he wasn't capable of love. Of trusting anyone enough. But that's not who you are. Not now."

"What you should be asking yourself is if I'm capable of mercy."

He shakes his head. "I don't have to ask that. I know that you are. Even if I don't deserve it. If there's one person in the world who doesn't deserve your forgiveness, it's me. But I worry how you'll feel if you lose her. I worry for you."

"Enough." The boy opens the dresser and pulls out a sock. He would have preferred a dirty one, but those are still on the wizard's feet. So he stuffs the clean sock in the wizard's mouth. "To muffle the screaming," he explains, as if the wizard doesn't already know. As if he hasn't done this to the boy a thousand times. "Because there will be screaming, and I don't want any interruptions. I don't want you alerting the entire guild." Anyone who saw the boy in the halls is dead now. And even though it's only a matter of time before someone finds the bodies and the hole in the wall and the missing doors, for now the guild sleeps. Leaving the boy free to do his work.

The wizard tries to speak, but the sound is too garbled with the sock in his mouth and the fear straining his throat.

"Shh," the boy tells him. "There's nothing you can do to stop this. You made this choice long ago." He holds up the knife. It's burning him alive, and all he wants to do is give in to it. To let it sink into this wizard's flesh. He'll try not to kill him, not all at once, but there's no telling what will happen once he starts cutting.

A mixture of horror and dread spreads across the wizard's face. He looks like he might pass out. But he'll wake up again, when the knife slices into him. The boy knows. He's been there.

Tears fill the wizard's eyes. A wizard. Shedding real tears. And here the boy thought they didn't exist. He thought they would be made of dust. Then the wizard moves his mouth again, trying to speak.

The boy pulls out the sock this time, to hear his last words. Because after this it will only be screaming.

"Tell Leora I love her. I . . . I love you both. She's my daughter, and you . . . you've become like a son to me. Yes, you," he says when the boy flinches at the words. "Azeril. The boy I broke. I would do anything to take back what I did to you. If killing me will make you whole again, then for the Fire's sake, do it. It's my fault, after all. Make sure you tell her that. She might understand, if you put it that way."

But she won't. I know she won't.

And with that thought, with that one clear thought of her, the world shatters. I'm suddenly aware of my surroundings. Of what I'm about to do. I drop the knife to the floor, my hands stained with blood. "Hadrin," I say, feeling out the word, the one I wouldn't dare speak just a moment ago. "I don't know what I was doing—I don't even know how I got here!"

Except that I do. I wasn't myself, not really, but I remember coming here. Slaughtering wizards to get to him. It's like it happened to somebody else. But it was me.

Just knowing I'm inside the guild makes the walls feel closer, more cramped. A desperate feeling crawls up from my stomach and through my chest, making me want to run. To get out of this place as fast as possible. But I force myself to stay and unbind his hands. It's difficult, because my own hands are trembling so much.

"I wouldn't have done it." The words come out too quickly, all jumbled together, and not sounding at all believable, especially not with so much blood on my hands. "I wouldn't."

Hadrin touches the cut on his cheek. His fingers come away bloody. "Yes, you would have," he says. "And with no remorse. But I—"

I shake my head, grabbing the knife and running for the door. I can't stand to be here even one more second. With him, telling me what a monster I am, as if I don't already know.

"Azeril, come back!" he calls after me.

But I'm gone. Fleeing the wizards' guild for the second time in my life.

CHAPTER TWENTY-SIX

I run through the hole in the wall. I run past the bodies. I don't stop running until I'm at the bottom of the hill, back on Market Street. It's only now that I realize my feet are bare. The street feels wet and gritty—it must have rained earlier—but I didn't notice until now.

I don't know who I was tonight. It was like the past three years never happened, like I never knew Leora or Rathe or Father Moors. Like I was only a weapon, only the monster. I could have killed him. And the world might be a better place without him in it, but . . .

Did he really say I was like a son to him?

It's too much. I should go back to Leora and pretend to be normal. Pretend like I didn't just slaughter half a dozen people. But I don't.

There's a church not too far from the house, only a few blocks away, on the corner of Yarrow and Front Streets. I noticed it the day we first came to Newhaven. Hadrin told me before that the church wasn't the sanctuary I thought it was, but he meant the one in Ashbury. He didn't mean all of them. He didn't mean *tonight*.

My feet are cold and damp when I get there. I dip my hands in a rain barrel outside, rubbing them together, the water turning pink. There's nothing I can do about the blood on my shirt. I just hope there's no one around to see how crazy I must look. Or how crazy I actually *am*.

The door's unlocked. Prayer candles flicker along the walls when I walk inside. This church is smaller than the Sacred Flame, with no school associated with it. But mostly it feels the same. Safe and familiar. The logs in the hearth are stacked the same way. The candles give off the same faint smell of beeswax. The altar looms at the end of the aisle, smooth and worn.

I pick up an unlit prayer candle from one of the dusty boxes in the corner. I remember the one I tried to light for Leora's mother—how it didn't take. How the Fire refused to acknowledge me. Not that I could blame it. Not then and not now. I'm not even an altar boy anymore.

But I still cup the little off-white candle in my hands and kneel, bowing my head. I wasn't myself tonight. I could have hurt Hadrin, like he hurt me. I killed seven wizards. I gave them quick but painful deaths, and I was going to drag Hadrin's out as long as I could. I was going to make him suffer. And I would have done it. I have no doubts about that, no matter what I said to Hadrin.

I didn't even know who Leora was. What if she'd seen me like that? Would I have known her then? Would I have remembered how much I love her? Or would I have . . . ?

"Please," I whisper, closing my eyes and picturing Leora. "Please keep her safe from *me*." I will the Fire to listen. It might condemn me and Hadrin—it has good reason to—but not her. It's not her fault either of us loves her.

"Can I help you?" a man says behind me.

Reluctantly, I open my eyes, not wanting to see that the candle hasn't lit, that the Fire hasn't listened to me. But I don't feel any warmth from it. I don't smell the flame. And when I open my eyes, I'm right—it hasn't changed. But a little jolt of disappointment runs through me all the same.

The man wears the red robes and the flints around his neck that mark him as a Father. His hair is gray, his face wrinkled with lines from a lifetime of laughter. There's a tiredness about him. His eyes are bloodshot and have dark patches beneath them, like he hasn't slept in days. He startles a little at the blood on my shirt.

"Are you hurt?" His voice is soft, concerned but friendly, even though it's the middle of the night and he didn't ask for some crazed kid to show up. Though obviously he wasn't sleeping, either.

I shake my head and get to my feet, still clutching the candle. "I was just . . ."

"In need of guidance?" he offers.

"Something like that." It's close enough. And suddenly I picture Father Moors's office. The green rug by the fireplace with the burnt specks in it. The way it always smells funny in there, like he was making soup but forgot about it. A pang of homesickness hits me. Not just for the place, but for the way I was, before I met Endeil. Before Hadrin came back into my life. It was inevitable that my past would catch up to me—I see that now. I just wish it could have waited a little longer. "Do you think it's possible for people to change?" I ask this stranger. "I mean, do you think it's ever possible to really put the past behind you? For it not to matter?"

"Ah." He takes that in slowly. "I do believe people can change. That is what it means to be human, after all. The Fire flickers, its

239

light ever-changing, and so do we. It is only the darkness that remains the same."

I don't know if I like that answer. It means there's hope, but is there hope for *me*?

"The best way to change is to let more light into your life," he goes on. "I don't know if you've heard the good news, but the High Priest was here earlier today, doing just that."

"He was *what*?" I glance around, like Endeil might be lurking in the corner.

"Oh, yes, he graced our little sacred space with his presence this morning. He brought new light to us all, myself included. He put his hands on me." He shuts his eyes, smiling at the memory. "Now see how blessed I am." He holds his hands up in front of him, his palms facing each other. An arc of lightning crackles between them. "He can give you new light, a new hope. He'll be here again tomorrow. Let him help you become who you're meant to be."

I'm clutching the prayer candle to my chest, the wax warming in my fist, as if I could use it to ward away the crazy.

"You can stay here tonight," he says, taking a step forward. "Whatever's wrong, he'll fix it. You'll see—" He stops, suddenly squinting at me in the candlelight. "Wait. Wait, wait, *wait*." His eyes narrow, his mouth twisting. "You're that *boy*."

Chasm take me. My free hand hovers over the hilt of my obsidian. I glance at the door, planning my path of escape. Several spells are already surfacing in my mind, all of them deadly. I'm ready to use them at the first sign of trouble, I'm ready to use the knife, but I don't actually want to *kill* this man. I've killed enough people tonight. And even if he's been corrupted, it's Endeil who should pay. Not this Father who reminds me of home.

And yet, I know if it comes to it, I'll do anything to get out of here.

I take a step to the side, trying to get out of the light. "I don't know what you're talking about."

"The High Priest *showed* me," he says, poking his temple. "He put an image in my mind. Yes." He wags a finger at me and nods at whatever realization he's just made. "There's no mistake. It's your face I see in my head. The High Priest told us all what you've done."

Oh, did he? "It's not me. Whatever he said, it wasn't true." I'm edging along the wall, keeping my eyes on him, my heart beating like mad.

Lightning arcs between the Father's hands. It makes a sharp *CRACK*. "He said you're the wizard killer."

Okay, so maybe that part's true. "You don't want to hurt me. The Fire wouldn't want you to—"

"Don't you dare speak its name!" he shouts, and then he points his hands toward me, releasing the lightning.

I dive to the floor. The blast crashes above me. My mind reels with spells. Spells to twist the bones in his hands until he can't use them. To turn him to dust.

But I'm not sure if I could do that last one. Not without more energy sources.

I scramble to come up with something else as I hurry to my feet. My fingers are still clamped around the candle, holding it painfully tight. I don't reach for my knife. It would be kinder than the spells—involve less suffering—but I don't know if I can get close enough now to use it.

He screams for help and shoots another blast of lightning at me. Words form on my lips. Lungs to ash. The spell's still fresh in my mind from earlier. It's also quick, thorough, and there's no screaming. It would put an end to this. No more magic, no more trying to kill me.

But I can't. I *can't*. I manage to dodge the lightning, but just barely, and it sears my left shoulder. I cry out. The pain breaks my train of thought. Another spell floats to the surface of my mind, and I grab it. It's only a few simple words, and then all the candles in the room snuff out at once, plunging everything into darkness.

I run while I have the chance. Before the lightning arcs again in his hands. He chases after me, only following as far as the church steps. By then I'm already around the corner.

He'll put out an alert, to the other members of the Church in Newhaven, and they'll be looking for me. And now Endeil will know I'm in town. But for the moment I just breathe. I'm safe enough here, in the shadows.

There's still a searing pain across my left shoulder. And my hand hurts. I look down and realize I've still got the prayer candle in a death grip.

And that's when I notice that it's lit. The same candle that wouldn't light for me earlier, that the Fire denied me. Now a tiny flame flickers at the end of it.

Whatever that means.

CHAPTER TWENTY-SEVEN

Hadrin stands awkwardly in the hallway the next afternoon, his arms pulled tight to his sides, as if he's afraid of accidentally touching anything. He looks around, his face twitching in disgust, like stepping foot inside the old house is beneath him. Like he left it for a *reason*.

Though I know him well enough now—or, at least, I think I do—to know that it isn't the house that disgusts him.

"You shouldn't be answering the door," he tells me. "Not with the whole city looking for you."

I stare at him. There's a red slash on his cheek where I cut him. He doesn't quite look at me, the only sign he gives that last night actually happened. "Leora went out to run errands. What was I supposed to—"

"*Not* get yourself killed. That's what you're supposed to do." He gives me a sharp look. "You shouldn't even be here, in this house. The High Priest knows you were at that church last night. There are wanted posters of you up all over the city now, calling you the wizard killer. People are talking about it. It won't be long before he starts searching nearby houses."

"And what about the wizards? Aren't they—"

"They believe the Church attacked them last night. They don't believe the posters. After all, they don't trust the Church, and how could one person have done all that? There were no survivors to tell them otherwise. Well, only one, but they don't know that and I didn't say anything."

"You should let me heal that cut." I can do that now, since I sliced through his tattoo last night.

He marches into the dining room, ignoring me. "Come on. We have a lot of work to do."

I follow him, sitting on the edge of the dining table and swallowing down a lump in my throat. "Hadrin . . . about what happened last night . . ."

"Oh, did something happen?" he snaps. "Are we talking about when you came to the High Guild and slaughtered six wizards—"

"Seven," I correct him.

"—*seven* wizards, and then tried to kill me?! Or when you were stupid enough to stop at a *church* and get yourself recognized?"

I wince. "Never mind."

"No, by all means, let's talk about it."

"I liked you better with the sock in your mouth."

He laughs. It's short and kind of bitter, but then he sighs and some of the venom seems to drain out of him. "I had it coming."

"I get why you're pissed at me."

"Do you?" He pinches the bridge of his nose. "If you think it's because you nearly killed me . . . Well, I won't pretend to be happy about that. But do you have any idea what would have happened if you'd been caught? And at the *guild*. If even one person had managed to sound the alarm, do you know what would have happened? When you had the whole guild descending on you?"

"Yeah, I do. I would have killed them."

"Some of them. Until you couldn't anymore. Until they overpowered you. And then . . . There would have been nothing I could do then, do you understand? Maybe I could have called it off in the past, but now? There'd be no escape for you, after all your crimes against us. Especially after your killing spree last night. And I would be left with the decision to oversee your torture, to try and limit the damage as best I could, or to leave it in the hands of someone else. There's no good option there. I couldn't stand by and watch while they hurt you again. I couldn't order it to happen. But walking away, leaving you to them completely . . . I would never have forgiven myself, either way."

"You think I *wanted* to go to the guild? You saw me yesterday. I couldn't even look at the stupid building. I don't know what happened. One minute I was me, and the next, I was who I used to be." I wince a little and put a hand to my head. "Ever since Leora unlocked my memories . . . I don't always know where I am. Sometimes I think I'm still back there. That none of this is real."

"It would help if you didn't try and make yourself crazy. I shouldn't have let you get anywhere near the guild yesterday. But this will all be over soon enough, and then you can go back to— Well, probably not back to Ashbury, after everything that's happened. But somewhere else. Anywhere but here."

"And in the meantime? What if I'd killed you? Or what if it happens again?" What if Leora had woken up last night? Would she have brought me back to reality, or would I have looked at her without even recognizing her?

Hadrin's quiet for a while, just staring at his hands. Then he says, "Once this is over, you'll never have to see me again. Or this city. You won't have to think about the wizards' guild. You *will* think about it," he adds, when I start to correct him. "Of course you will. But you won't have so many reminders. And perhaps, if you like, you could find someone to block your memories again. If Leora had the power to unlock them, surely someone else out there has the ability to put that lock back in place."

"Maybe." But I still don't know how my memories got locked up in the first place. Was it my mind's way of protecting me from all the horrible things that happened? Or was it something else? Hadrin let me go, but he didn't have anything to do with me forgetting everything. He didn't even know I'd lost my memories until I told him. "I did all this work to get them back. They're part of me, even if I don't like it."

And it's not like this is the first time that reality has gotten away from me, that my past has taken over. I think of that time in the church basement with Leora. The first time I saw the chair. I wasn't exactly myself then, either. I can't imagine losing my memories again, having no idea about my past or why I feel the way I do. Especially since Leora would still know. And I'd be left to wonder why she sometimes looked at me so strangely. Or, worse, why she sometimes looked at me with pity in her eyes.

That's if I even remembered who she was. If my memories could be locked up again, wouldn't it be *all* of them? There are too many good ones. Even if I have to endure the bad ones, I've got too much to lose now to give them all up.

"I have to keep them," I tell Hadrin. "I'll leave this city, if Leora will come with me. If she still wants to. You said there are wanted posters now?" Leora's going to see them. And even if she doesn't, she's going to hear someone talking about me. About the wizard killer. And when she hears about what happened at the guild . . . she won't believe the Church did it. But will she believe *I* did?

"Never mind what's going on outside," Hadrin says. "We've got work to do. And the less time I have to spend in this house, the better."

"I don't know what you think you're going to teach me. I already know how to cast. I *did* almost beat Endeil."

Hadrin raises an eyebrow at me. "Oh? Did you *really*?"

I glance away. "At first. I almost had him." Or at least I thought I did, until he used his magic on me. Until I was writhing on the floor, completely in his control.

"You mean when you took him by surprise. You can't count on that next time. And what happened after that?"

I bite my lip, not wanting to answer. "He made me remember. I thought I was there, in that room again. By the Fire, it even *smelled* like that room. He knew exactly how to break my concentration."

"Perhaps if you hadn't let him look inside your head before. But then we wouldn't even be in this mess now, would we?"

I glare at him. "I had to do it. You didn't exactly give me any other option."

"It doesn't matter now. What matters is he knows too much about you. And if it worked for him once, he won't hesitate to do it again."

"He's powerful. He has a direct line to the Chasm. But if I'd come across him last night . . ." I would have been a match for him then. I would have drained every person there in order to kill him. The monster would never have been distracted by a vision of the chair. The monster doesn't believe he ever left it. "I'll have to over-power him. But I don't know if I'm strong enough."

"*You* don't think that you're strong enough? The same person who marched into the guild last night, leaving a path of death and destruction in his wake?"

I shake my head. "That wasn't me. Not exactly. But what if that's who I have to become to stop him? And . . . what if I can't come back from it?" That's what he was afraid of, when Leora unlocked my memories. That it would change me, that I would only be the weapon and not the boy at all. It's what Leora was afraid of, too. Not that she knew who I was before, but that this new version of me wouldn't love her.

Hadrin folds his hands together on the table. "You're stronger now than you were then. I know you don't believe that, especially after last night, but you are. And I won't lie. Defeating him is going to be difficult. But I believe you can do this."

"And when I have to become the monster in order to stop him, what then?"

"You won't. You're strong enough now. You—"

"Wishful thinking. You let me go that first night in Ashbury, when I almost killed you. I asked you why you would let a killer go free, and you said it was arrogance. Or sentimentality. Well, which one is it now? We both know if I fight him, I could win. But only if I give in and become the weapon, the one *you* made me to be. A cold-hearted killer with more destructive magic than should ever exist at all, let alone in one person. And it felt good, letting so much energy flow through me last night and watching those wizards fall, unable to even touch me. Not one laid a finger on me. *Not one.* It was the only time I've been safe. In my entire life, it's the only—" My throat tightens, and I pause, unwilling to lose it in front of him. "If I have to become the weapon to defeat him, I will. Because the alternative is that he kills me, and then Leora dies, too. I won't let that happen. But if I win, I know who'll walk away from that fight—you and I both do—and it won't be the boy. It will be the monster."

Maybe that's how it was always going to end. Maybe it was inevitable. The last three years have been a brief rest before the final hour, when my past catches up to me and I become what I was supposed to be all along.

"You don't know that," Hadrin says, but he stares down at his hands on the table, shaking his head.

"No, but I have a pretty good idea. And if that happens, promise me you'll—"

"Don't you dare ask me to kill you. You know I can't do that. Not with your life intertwined with hers. And, even if it wasn't, what makes you think I could?"

"So lock me up. Sew my mouth shut. Take away the knife. Just *keep me away from her.*" I squeeze my eyes shut, remembering the Fire's warning, the image of her sobbing and drenched in blood.

Hadrin's staring at me now.

"Do you understand?" I ask him.

"Yes," he says quietly.

"Don't wait. When I fight Endeil, if I come back, don't wait to find out who I am. Because as soon as you see me, it will be too late. She won't want to leave me. She'll want to believe I could really come back, and she'll hold on to that hope until it's too late. But you can't let her. So promise me you'll—"

The front door opens, followed by the sound of rustling baskets and Leora's footsteps. "Az?" she calls.

"In here."

There's more rustling as she sets the baskets down. I smell fresh bread. She rushes in, but she stops short when she sees that I'm not alone. "Dad." She gapes at him, then at me, then back at him again. "You're in the house."

"So I am." He doesn't look at her when he says it.

"You haven't stepped foot in the house in . . ." She pauses, doing the math. "It's been almost six years."

"I had business to attend to here."

"He was helping me," I tell her. "To prepare." I give Hadrin a look that says, *Promise me.*

He nods, just once.

"So," Leora says, "he hasn't been in the house since he abandoned my mother and me six years ago, not even when she died, not even when I needed— I'm his own *daughter*, and now he's here, helping you? I guess I shouldn't be surprised. He's always chosen you over me."

She makes it sound like we've both just betrayed her. I feel guilty, though I don't know that I've done anything wrong. Was I not supposed to let him in? It's not like I could leave the house. Not with everyone looking for me.

Hadrin gets to his feet. "I was just leaving." Then, to me, "Don't do anything stupid. It's going to be all right. *You'll* come through this."

His meaning isn't lost on me, even if I don't believe it.

He mutters some lame good-bye to Leora on his way out. She watches him go, shock and anger mixing on her face. Then she turns to me. "What in the Chasm was that all about? I can't believe he was *here*. He wouldn't come here for me, but he'll come here for you?"

I don't know what to tell her. He should have been there for her. I hop down from the table and slip my arms around her.

I breathe her in, feeling her heart beating next to mine. After I fight Endeil, I'll never hold her like this again. Either I become the weapon or he kills me. Either way, *I* don't come back. And I hope, for her sake, that I'm the winner in that fight, as long as Hadrin keeps his promise.

She rests her head against my chest, and for a moment, the only sound in the world is our breathing. And then she says, "Az, I saw the posters."

My muscles go tense. "Right. Hadrin said there were . . . Did it . . . did it look like me?"

"Close enough." She pulls away, taking a step back so she can see my face. "The High Priest is calling you the wizard killer. He says you attacked the guild last night."

It takes all my effort not to flinch, not to look away. "So?" I'm hoping she'll say that she doesn't believe a word of it, but, more than that, I'm hoping she'll ask me if it's true and get this over with. Because if she asks me right now, if she actually *says the words*, then I'll tell her. The truth will come pouring out of me. And she'll hate me, and I'll hate me, but at least this secret won't twist inside me anymore, as hot and sharp as my obsidian.

I won't have to die keeping this secret. And maybe when I tell her who I really am, she'll run, and I won't have to worry about

Hadrin keeping his promise to me. I won't have to worry about her holding out hope for someone who won't exist anymore.

She opens her mouth to ask a question we both know she'll never be able to take back.

"Say it, Leora. Whatever you have to ask me, just *say it.*"

"I already know everything I need to," she says, turning away from me. "What would I possibly need to ask?"

CHAPTER TWENTY-EIGHT

The wizard's daughter is asleep in her bed. In the room with the blood on the floor. The boy's blood. No, it's her blood, too. But it might as well be his. He stands over her, watching her sleep, not sure how he got here. All he knows is that the wizard's daughter lies before him, vulnerable and alone.

His life and her life are linked together. Or so the wizard said. He would want the boy to believe that if she died, he would die, too. But she doesn't have to die to cause the wizard pain.

She breathes in and out, slow and steady, never knowing that a killer watches her. That the boy her father tortures is here, noticing the way her eyelids flutter as she dreams, or the way moonlight plays across her unprotected throat and down the front of her nightgown. There's something so familiar about her.

The wizard's daughter shifts in her sleep, pushing the blanket away, the nightgown clinging to her, the moonlight revealing bare skin and soft curves. The boy's face gets hot, and he looks away, knowing instinctively that he shouldn't be seeing anything that's normally underneath her clothes. If she were to wake up right now, he would feel ashamed of what she might think of him, standing here, watching her like this. But the boy also feels like he knows every inch of her, like he's known her all his life. And, more than that, like he's known her intimately.

It's impossible. The boy can't know this girl. He doesn't know anyone except wizards, not even a wizard's daughter. And she belongs to the *wizard, the one who deserves to die the most. He deserves to suffer. And if that means the girl has to suffer, too, then so be it.*

The boy should do it now. He should hurt her while he has the chance. But he hesitates, watching her a little longer, even though he knows there can be no room for sympathy. Even if she didn't ask to be a wizard's daughter—his flesh and blood—no more than the boy ever asked to be his experiment. Her fate is already sealed, because of what the wizard has done to the boy. Because of all the pain the wizard has caused him. The wizards thought he could be a weapon, and now he will be. They even thought they could control which of them he hurt, by marking themselves with that spiral tattoo, the same as the one on his wrist. But no one thought to mark the wizard's daughter.

Maybe the wizard never thought the boy would be here, hovering over her while she slept. The boy never would have thought so, either. He doesn't know how long he'll have before the wizards come for him. They could have set this up on purpose to see what he'll do. Will the boy be tamed by the innocent girl they've thrown in his path? Or will he become more of a monster than they ever imagined?

But the wizards never taught the boy to have mercy. Even if she was marked, that wouldn't stop him from hurting her. The boy doesn't need spells to slice into her, bit by bit. Or to ignore her screams, begging him to stop. Because this is to punish the wizard. To make him raw and dead inside. And the boy knows he could endure anything to make that happen.

And he doesn't know the girl. She's nothing to him. She could be just like her wizard father, for all he knows. She might deserve this.

The boy won't kill her. He and this girl bleed from the same wounds.

At least according to the wizard. The boy isn't sure he believes it, because if it was true, she wouldn't have that peaceful look on her face. She wouldn't be so trusting, sleeping with her door unlocked, waiting for just anyone to come in and take what little she has left of herself.

But she's not like the boy. She still has all of herself to lose, which means she has enough to spare. More than the boy could ever hope to have.

And if it turns out that the boy and the girl really do bleed together, then at least it will be her who feels the pain this time.

The boy reaches for the knife at his waist. He doesn't know why the wizards would let him have it now. It must be a test, and they must be watching somehow. He wonders if the wizard knows they've thrown his daughter to the wolves. Or wolf, just the one, since it's only the boy here.

Only the weapon the wizard made.

Even if the wizards are watching, no one's come to stop him. A thrill runs through his stomach and up his spine as he imagines the knife cutting into her. The ecstasy of the blade touching her body, lighting every part of him on fire. Slicing slowly across her skin as he prolongs the whole process, drawing out the pleasure of knife against flesh.

But even the boy feels sickened by that. His ears burn with shame. The wizard's daughter might be innocent. She's not a wizard. Only the means to get to one, and hurting her isn't supposed to be fun. And not so . . .

So intimate.

No, this has to be calculated. Not ruled by the knife's desires. Or by the boy's. So he reaches over to the other side of the bed, where it looks like another person has slept recently. Like she wasn't alone. The boy wonders if the wizard knows what his daughter's been doing.

But it doesn't matter. The wizard will have reasons to worry about her soon enough, and whoever was in the bed before . . . he's not here to protect her now. It's only her and the boy. So he takes the pillow from the far side of the bed and slides the casing off. He wraps it around the knife hilt, to shield himself from its fire. So the boy will be himself the whole time, knowing exactly what he's doing to her.

He thinks about tying her down first, like the wizards do to him. Not so she doesn't get away—he could chase her through the dark and catch her again if she did—but so she doesn't hurt herself. Not any more than necessary.

But in the end, the boy is too impatient. Too afraid of losing his nerve. So he grips the knife and brings the blade down toward the soft, tender flesh of her stomach.

———

Sick. Cold. Shaking. I sit at the dining table, my hands folded in front of me, trying not to think about anything. It's morning and the sun rose a while ago and I was sitting here then, too. Tasting the lingering, sour burn of vomit in my mouth. My stomach's empty and cramping—from throwing up, from being hungry. From the overwhelming feelings of disgust and self-loathing.

I try not to think, to just be numb. I don't dare move. Not after last night.

It wasn't me. I would never think those things. I would never *do* those things.

Or at least that's what I tell myself.

I was wrong before. All this time, I thought I was the boy *and* the monster. Coexisting at the same time. But I was wrong. I was the boy. Only the boy, no matter how many wizards I killed. No matter how many times I enjoyed it. What I was last night . . . *that* was the monster.

And now I'm what, exactly?

I press my hands flat on the table, thinking about all the awful things I've done with them.

Maybe what the wizards did to me . . . maybe I deserved it all along. I thought they made me what I am. But what if that's who I always was, and that's why they did what they did?

Leora's footsteps echo down the hall, and then she pauses in the doorway, yawning. I have my back to her. I don't look up. I don't say anything.

"Hey, Az," she says. There's a smile in her voice. A warmth when she says my name. Neither of them should be there, but she doesn't know that. She has *no idea.* "How long have you been up? Don't tell me my father's got you meeting him at the crack of dawn now. Wouldn't that be just like him? He's not happy unless he's annoying everyone, trying to control them. You don't have to listen to him, you know. I mean, I know you know that. But if you— Az?" There's a hesitation in her voice this time. "Is something wrong?"

My world is broken. Not as broken as it could have been, if I'd gone through with it last night. If I hadn't woken up to find myself hovering over her, the knife in my hand. And I wasn't even touching the obsidian that time. I can't blame what I did on its influence. It was me, thinking those things. Watching her sleep and wanting to hurt her.

No, not wanting to hurt her, exactly. But I was going to do it anyway. I had wrapped up the knife so its fire wouldn't seep into me, so I could torture her in cold blood.

Leora sits at the other side of the table and peers at me. The smile on her face melts away. "You look like you've been to the Chasm and back. Bad night?"

"You should never have let me touch you." I want my voice to sound empty. Cold and unfeeling. Not a monster or a boy, just nothing. But instead it sounds so *alive* and so *hurt.* "How could you have ever let me put my hands on you?"

"*What?* What are you talking about?"

I flip my hands over, staring at the lines in my palms. How many times have they been stained with blood? "Let me tell you a story, Leora. Once upon a time, there was a boy. An orphan. Innocent, probably. As far as I can tell, but it was so long ago, and my memory's still a little fuzzy. But one day the wizards got their hands on him. They poked and they prodded and when the time was right, they started the real stuff. They bound his hands and his feet while they cut into him and let his blood spill all over in sacrifice. But once wasn't enough. That was just the beginning. They wanted him to be a monster."

She shakes her head and tries to reach for my hand, but I pull it away. "It's okay. It's over now. You're not—"

"No. The story's not over. To turn him into a monster, they had to keep hurting him. In lots of different ways. Sometimes they broke his bones. Sometimes they made him go for days without sleeping. They always helped him heal up afterward. A broken toy wouldn't have done them any good. Sometimes they were even nice to him, for a few weeks or so, to make him wonder if maybe things would get better. If maybe that really was the last time they'd hurt him. But it was a trick, just to make their next torture session that much worse. And it worked. They opened up a link between him and the Chasm. They used violence and suffering to channel its spells into him. They thought they'd be able to use them—to use *him*. But you know that part already."

"Yeah, I do. I know this story. You don't have to finish it."

"They turned him into a weapon. Into a monster. And then one day he escaped. The head wizard, the one who started the experiment in the first place, wasn't the heartless bastard he wanted to think he was. He was supposed to kill the boy and end the experiment. But his conscience caught up to him, and he secretly let the boy go."

"See," she says, "it has a happy ending. The boy got away. The wizard realized his mistake. You can stop there."

"Something happened to the boy, so he couldn't remember anything. Well, almost. But it didn't change the fact that he was a weapon. A killer who liked hurting people. No, not people. Wizards." I pause there, wondering if this is the point in the story where she'll see me for what I really am. Her eyes will get wide with terror, and she'll say this is it, she never wants to see me again, and I won't have to tell the rest of it.

But Leora just bites her lip, her hands clenched into tight fists, and waits for me to continue.

"The boy left the capital and ended up in Ashbury, where the head wizard's daughter lived. They were linked. Maybe he was drawn to her. Maybe it was coincidence. It doesn't matter. The Church took him in. They knew he was a killer, and they took him in anyway. And the girl . . ."

"The girl fell in love with him," Leora snaps, as if she thinks I'll try to argue otherwise. "But that's her story to tell, not yours."

"He fell in love with her, too. To her, he was innocent. He liked that. But the whole time he knew her, the whole time she thought he was just an altar boy—"

"Az. Whatever you think you need to say, you *don't* need to say it. All right? I mean," she adds, her voice dropping to a whisper, "do you think I'm stupid?"

"Of course not." But she wants to see the best in me, even when it's not there. "There's just something you should know."

"Are you going to make me spell it out for you? I *know*."

I shake my head. My chest aches with what I'm about to say, but she deserves to hear the whole truth. She deserves to know what the boy who shares her bed is capable of, while he's still here, while he can still tell her. "If you knew, you would have left already, Leora. You think I don't know *you* well enough to know that?"

"You're the wizard killer." The words drop from her mouth like stones.

It hurts to hear her say it.

If she had any lingering doubts, the look on my face must clear them all away, because she nods and says, "That's what I thought."

"How long have you known?"

"I don't know. The whole time I've known you? Just now? Somewhere in between. I guess I've been piecing it together for a while—I just didn't realize I was. And it's not like you tried to deny it yesterday. I mean, if it wasn't you, you shouldn't have had to. But . . . I knew."

"There's more to the story."

"Az, don't. I know the rest. The boy was the wizard killer, but the girl loved him anyway. That's all that matters."

"The boy was the wizard killer. He killed so many, he lost track. And the girl didn't know how much he *liked* it. How he enjoyed every second of causing them pain."

"And the girl *still* loved him, even knowing that. That's how the story ends, so just stop already!"

But I can't. She said she loved me enough to break her own heart for me. I said I'd do the same, and I meant it. "And then the boy got his memories back. Slowly, at first. He thought that the memories didn't change him, but they did. Sometimes, he couldn't remember where he was. He thought he was back at the guild, being tortured again. And when that happened, he didn't remember the girl anymore. I mean, he knew who she was. That she was the wizard's daughter. But he couldn't remember all the time they'd spent together. That she was his best friend. That he *loved* her."

"So you don't always remember me. But you know who I am now, don't you? You love me *now*, don't you?"

"Yeah, I do. That's why I'm telling you this. Because the story's not over. Because when he thought he was back there, being tortured, and when he didn't remember who she was—who she was *to him*—he became a danger to her. And she sort of knew that, but she didn't want to admit it. Because she loved the boy so much, she thought she could ignore the monster."

"Az. I'm warning you. *Shut up*."

"But the monster tried to hurt her. To get revenge on the wizard who hurt *him*. And one night, while she was asleep—"

"No!" She slams her hands down on the table. "What in the Chasm is wrong with you? Why would you *say* something like that?"

"I would have killed you, Leora." Admitting it out loud makes my chest feel raw. Raw and dead, like I wanted Hadrin to feel. "I would have settled for just making you suffer." Hadrin thought linking us made me a danger to her. But maybe I was already a danger to her, and the linking spell between us is the only thing keeping her even remotely safe. "But don't get me wrong. I would have killed you if I could. And I would have—" My throat tightens, and it takes all my effort to say the words, to give her my one last truth, the one that might actually be enough to save her. "I would have *liked* it."

She gapes at me. Finally seeing me. Emotions flicker across her face. I watch little bits of her shatter, piece by piece—the boy she thought she knew, the one she thought she loved, crumbling away.

The silence stretches out between us, until I think she's never going to speak again. I clear my throat. "I should leave." I don't know where I'll go, but I shouldn't be here.

She swallows. "You didn't kill me, Az. You knew who I was."

"It still makes me a monster."

"*They* were the monsters. My father tortured you for years. I remember the day I bled all over. I didn't know it was from your wounds at the time. But when I look back on it now . . . What they must have *done* to you . . . They deserve whatever you did to them."

"Don't make excuses for me, Leora. I know they deserved it, but you didn't. You can't be with someone like me."

She scowls. "Don't tell me who I can be with."

"I could have killed you."

"No, *you* couldn't have. You're still my best friend. You're still the boy who climbed that apple tree just because I dared you. The only person who ever really understood me. You have to be, because I still need him. Whatever part of you would have hurt me, that isn't you!"

I told her my truths, and she still sees only the boy. She thinks the monster is something separate, not really part of me. "It is me. Stop pretending it isn't. The more I remember about my past, the more I forget about my present." I rub my face with my palms, wishing for this to be over. "And one of these days, that boy who's your best friend won't be here at all."

Tears well up in her eyes. "*No.* The Fire doesn't sacrifice people. It wouldn't have done this if it meant I was going to lose you!"

"The Fire has nothing to do with this. I'm going to forget you, Leora. It's only a matter of time, and—"

"You're not going to forget." She says that like she knows for sure.

"I lost my memories before, and almost everything about myself. I still don't know why, and that means it could happen again. I'll lose my mind."

"It won't happen."

"You don't know that. You don't know what they did to me, what I'm—"

"No, I mean, you won't lose your memories again. I, uh, sort of know how you lost them."

"You what?" I was supposed to be the one revealing secrets, not the other way around.

"When I unlocked your memories. I told you, it was like I found this door. And I saw where the door came from. It was the Fire, Az. The Fire blocked your memories."

———

"Why didn't you tell me?" I finally ask Leora, after staring at her for a while in disbelief. Disbelief in what she said, and in what she did. I kept my secrets because I thought she'd hate me. Because I liked who I was in her eyes. But I don't understand why she'd keep something like this from me.

"I was going to. At first. But the Fire put that locked door there to protect you."

"To protect *me*, or everyone else?"

"Maybe both. To keep the spells you got from the Chasm locked away. And so you wouldn't have to remember all the bad things they did to you."

"And you know all this how?"

"I *saw* it. It was just a flash. Just this warm feeling when I used my power on you. The Fire had put the lock in place, but it also let me unlock it. It *wanted me to*. Because you need the spells, because you're the only one who can stop Endeil."

"You're saying the Fire wants me to . . . what? Fight the *Church*?"

"No, just the High Priest. He's corrupt—he might still be the head of the Church, but he doesn't represent it anymore."

"What else did you see?"

"Nothing. But, Az, I didn't tell you because I knew you would worry. I mean, a primal force puts up a wall in your head to keep the bad stuff from getting out? That's pretty serious. And then I undid it. And I know you asked me to. I know the Fire wanted me to do it. But it just made everything too real. How bad everything must have been for you, and how powerful those spells must be. How *dark*. I didn't know how to tell you that I knew. And I didn't know how you'd react to finding out it wasn't just some spell or some trauma that blocked your memories, but the Fire itself. Especially since you've got this chip on your shoulder about it."

"About what?"

"The Fire. About how it's never deemed you worthy of a power."

"Yeah, well, wizards don't get powers."

"You're not exactly a wizard."

"Right. I'm worse. I've not only used spells, but spells from the Chasm."

"It's not fair. None of that was your choice."

Maybe not at first. But now? "The Fire has a lot of reasons to condemn me. I've made my peace with that. You should, too."

"Oh, *right*. That's why I didn't want to tell you, because you'd see it as some kind of punishment. Some sign that you're . . . I don't know . . . not on good terms with the Fire. And you've got enough to worry about as it is."

"So, the Fire *wants* me to use these spells? Spells that came straight from the Chasm? It wants me to kill Endeil?" And here he thought he was still its favorite. But me? It never favored me—only condemned me. And now it wants me to sacrifice myself to save everyone from the High Priest. And I'll do it. Whether it's the punishment I deserve or my chance at redemption, I'll do it.

"The High Priest is that dangerous," Leora says. "So if you have to use those spells, then yes. But I think what the Fire really wants is—"

The front door slams open, interrupting her. We both turn to look toward the living room. I'm on my feet, moving to get between her and whatever threat might be coming toward us. I thought I'd have more time, but Endeil must have found me already. My hand instinctively reaches for the knife, though realistically I know it's my spells I should be using, preparing to give myself to them, to let the past take over. But I'm not ready for that. I'm not ready to become someone else completely, to lose Leora, and myself. So I don't call up the spells, not just yet.

But it's only Hadrin who appears in the doorway. His face is ghastly pale, almost green. He's limping, dragging one foot. His robes are filthy and smeared with grime. There are scrapes across his knuckles and along one side of his face.

Leora gasps, and all I can do is gape at him. He looks so unlike himself.

"Well, don't just stare at me like idiots," he growls. *"Help me—"*

And that's as far as he gets before he collapses.

CHAPTER TWENTY-NINE

"Hold still," I tell Hadrin, trying to get a better look at his foot.

He flinches, even though I haven't put my hands on him yet. "Don't touch it."

"I *have* to." If he wants me to heal him, anyway. He's almost lucky that I cut through his tattoo the other night. Otherwise, I'd have to do it now. Or else let him suffer.

He pushes me away, grimacing.

I glance over my shoulder, exchanging a look with Leora, who has her arms folded in frustration. "Just do it, Az. He's being such a baby."

Hadrin grits his teeth. "I can hear you, you know. I'm not so old and feeble that you have to talk about me as if I'm not in the room."

Leora clenches her fists at her sides, looking like she wants to kill him. Like it's taking a lot of effort for her not to. "Heal him, Az. *Now*."

I put my hands on Hadrin's broken foot before he can protest again. He cries out, and I ignore him, concentrating on casting the spell. But I take some pleasure in the fact that he's the one screaming at my hand.

The spell takes more energy this time than it has in the past, and I'm drawing from all three of us before I realize it.

Leora gasps in surprise and steps back.

I open my eyes—I don't remember closing them—and focus on using only my own energy.

"Sorry," I tell Leora when it's over.

"It just felt weird," she says. "That's all."

"Please, don't anybody ask me how I'm doing," Hadrin mutters. His face is still pale and shiny with sweat.

I reach for his arm, to heal the tattoo. It should work again, if I heal it. I'm the one who broke it, and . . . he's going to need it.

But he jerks his arm out of my grasp. "Save your energy."

"What happened?"

"It was Endeil." He puts a hand to his head, wincing, and I can't tell if he has another injury or just a headache. He makes a face as he stands up, gingerly testing out his foot, seeming almost shocked that he can put his weight on it. He eases into a chair at the table. "The High Priest came to the guild. He had a royal decree from the king and queen to—" He coughs and tries to clear his throat. I move to go get him some water, but he shakes his head. "Listen to me," he says, his voice still slightly hoarse. "He had their permission to take over. To come inside and throw us out. Endeil convinced the king and queen that he was afraid we would retaliate, after what *you* did—what the other wizards believe the *Church* did. He's the one with the power now. Whether they believed him or not, they granted him permission to attack us. He came there with his army."

"His *what*?" I say.

"The people he's turned into . . . that he's given new powers."

I picture a whole army of Rathes, ready to use the Chasm's magic. "How many?"

"Enough," he says, wincing again as he sits up straighter. "They came in fighting. We fought back, of course, but they didn't even *ask* us to leave, they just—"

I raise an eyebrow. "You think the wizards would have abandoned everything if only they'd asked first?"

"*No*, of course not. For the Fire's sake, boy, don't be an idiot! Try and pay the least bit of attention. It's bad enough you nearly killed me. That you nearly got *yourself* killed. Then the High Priest's army throws me out of my home, severely injuring me in the process. And I drag myself all the way down here, in excruciating pain, and now I have to deal with your *stupidity* on top of everything else!"

I flinch. "I didn't mean—"

There's a loud *smack* of skin on skin as Leora slaps Hadrin across the face, startling both me and him. "Don't you *dare* talk to him like that!"

"Leora . . . ?" I can't believe she just did that.

"And don't you dare apologize to him, Az." She doesn't take her eyes off of Hadrin as she says it. "Not after everything he's done."

Hadrin touches his cheek, stunned.

"You tortured him for years. You made his life a living nightmare. You're *lucky* he didn't kill you, then or now. For the Fire's sake, he just *healed* you. That's more than you deserve, but he did it anyway, and you act like you don't even care!"

"Are you quite done?" Hadrin says.

Leora's eyes flash. "No, not even close. You knew, didn't you?"

"Knew *what*?" he asks, but his eyes dart toward mine, guessing what she must mean, or something close to it.

"What he was. Is. He kills people." She makes a point of not looking at me, avoiding my reaction. "You *knew*," she tells Hadrin, "and you didn't think to tell me."

"Last I checked," he says, "you weren't a wizard. You weren't in any danger."

She doesn't correct him. "You should have cared enough to *want* to tell me. To *worry* about me!"

"If you'll remember, I wasn't crazy about the two of you getting together. I did tell him to stay away from you, as much good as that did."

"Don't pretend like you don't know what I'm getting at," she says. "You've always cared about him more than me. *Always.* And now I discover you're more worried about someone finding out the truth about him than you are about my safety. If you really cared, if I was in any way as important to you as he is, you would have said something. To *me*, not to him. Even if you thought he wouldn't hurt me, how could you keep a secret like that from me? From your own daughter? Once you knew we were together . . . And you should have known I could keep this secret. You should have trusted me with it."

Her words sting. She says them to him, but they're meant for both of us. And no matter who she says them to, they still cut me.

"I care about both of you." Hadrin doesn't look at either of us as he says it, as if admitting it is too much for him, even though he told me the same thing the other day. "And now isn't the time to discuss this. We've got—"

"No. If I had been the dangerous one, if *I'd* been the one hurting people, then, Chasm take you, you would have told him. You would have done anything to keep him safe!"

"First you accuse me of treating him badly," Hadrin says, speaking slowly. "And now you accuse me of putting him above you? What kind of argument is that?"

"It's the truth." A tear slides down her cheek.

I try to put my arm around her, but she steps away. "No." Now she's furiously wiping away tears with her sleeve, as if no one will notice she's crying as long as she keeps up with it. "I can't . . . I can't *be here* right now." She turns away, running for the door.

"Leora, don't!" I shout. Even though only minutes ago I was telling her she should stay away from me.

But she doesn't stop, and I hesitate, not sure if I should go after her. She's mad at Hadrin for keeping secrets, but it's not like I was honest with her this whole time, either. Maybe she's not as okay with that as she said. Or maybe it just hadn't caught up to her yet.

"She'll be back," Hadrin says, his voice quiet. Ashamed. "She's never liked letting me see her cry."

"It's more than that."

"She'll get over it."

But I hope she doesn't, for her sake. I sit down at the table, running my hands through my hair. "She has a point, though. Why didn't you tell her?"

"As if either of you would ever listen to me."

"She might have. She knew I was your experiment, but she didn't know what that meant. What I'd done."

"And take the one thing she loved away from her? I'm not as heartless as she might think. Besides, I was under the impression

271

you only killed wizards. That you had at least a little bit of control over yourself. Was I wrong?"

"No," I lie. "But—"

"It's not as if you were in any hurry to tell her yourself."

"I should have told her a long time ago."

"You can berate yourself over that later. Right now, you have to get ready to fight Endeil."

"What, now?" *Not now.* I'm not ready. I said I'd do it, but . . . By the Fire, I thought I'd have more time.

"Yes, *now*. He overthrew the High Guild. He marched in there and started attacking. Like someone else I know. The entire guild tried to fight him and his army, to protect what's ours, and we failed. Did you think I showed up like this, all battered and broken, because I tripped down the stairs? I woke up in the middle of the night to a battle going on. I barely escaped with my life!"

"So he wants to destroy the wizards. I can't say that I blame him." Even if I know what he's doing isn't right. And even if I know it won't end there. He'll corrupt everyone with his magic, until they're all touched by the Chasm. Until they're all shadows of who they used to be.

"He's gotten more powerful. You know he's not going to stop, that it's not about us or the Church anymore. You need to fight him *now*."

"I didn't get to say good-bye to her. I didn't—I *can't*"—I rub sudden tears from my eyes—"I can't go while she's mad at me. I can't leave and never come back without saying good-bye!"

"You don't know that you won't come back from this," Hadrin whispers. But he doesn't sound at all sure about it.

"The whole guild tried to fight him, and they lost. The *whole guild*. So, no, I'm not coming back. I'll just wait. Until she comes home."

"And tell her what? That you're leaving? You think she won't be mad at you when you tell her she's never going to see you again?"

"I . . . Fire take you, why does it have to be *now*?"

"Because he's there, at the guild. He's just fought a long battle. We can take advantage of that."

"I'll lose myself."

Hadrin closes his eyes. "I would take your place if I could."

"But you weren't the one in the chair. So it has to be me. I'm the one who has to go in there and not come back, because of your mistakes."

"This is your chance to stop him, Azeril. It might be your only one. You have to take it."

I get up from the table. My hands are shaking. I turn away, so Hadrin won't see. "I can't. I'm not ready to not be me. I'm not ready to forget her. I'll *never* be ready for that, but, damn it, I don't want to go. Not yet. Can't I have one more day with her? Just—"

"Azeril."

There's a hitch in his voice as he says my name. He's staring at something. At my right arm. I follow his gaze, looking down at the flesh, and what I see turns my whole body to ice and makes my hair stand on end.

Because there, written in blood, are the words, *I'VE GOT HER.*

And then we both watch as more letters appear. I hold my breath, not daring to move the entire time. The first message was bad enough, but the second . . . The second makes me glad, for once in my life, that I was made to be a weapon. The only one that can stop him.

Because the second line says, *IN THE CHAIR.*

And I know, with more certainty than I've ever known anything, that Endeil is going to die today. No matter where I have to go to find him.

No matter who I have to become.

CHAPTER THIRTY

I don't look this time as we approach the guild. I keep my head down, telling myself it's so there's less chance of someone recognizing me and trying to report me to the High Priest. They wouldn't know that he's already got me right where he wants me, walking up to his new front door. Or what's left of it. But really it's because I don't want to think about what's going to happen when we get there. I don't want to think that these are my last moments as myself.

So instead I think of Leora, as painful as that is, remembering how she came up to me on my first day of school when no one else would. Everyone was talking about me, the new kid that Father Moors brought in from the streets, ragged and wild. They whispered about me in the halls, but no one had the guts to actually speak to me. No one except her. Rathe wasn't there yet, though I like to think he would have been another exception. And maybe Leora did it just to show everyone up, not expecting to become my friend. Or maybe we really were drawn to each other, because of the spell Hadrin had cast years before.

"Is there any chance you can lift the bond between us?" I ask Hadrin. "Because if you can, now might be a good time."

"Lift it? You're asking for miracles. I don't know how to lift your curse—and don't look at me like that, because it *is* a curse—any more than you do."

"Okay, but you could do what you did before. To block the link from working."

"I needed her mother's energy for that, and she's no longer here. She was"—he clears his throat—"she was never sickly before I cast that spell."

I stare at him. "You ki—"

"*No.* My actions might have ultimately led to her . . . illness. It was a powerful spell, but I had no idea it would have that effect on her. I would have at least warned her if I could. But she saw Leora covered in blood that day and she would have done anything to fix it. Both of us would have. She was a willing participant. But after that . . . I saw what it did to her. What *I* had done to both of them, and I couldn't stay."

"And then I undid it. By kissing her."

He scoffs. "Oh, I think you did plenty more than that. But, yes. The two of you made a connection, and that counteracted it. And if I'd ever dreamed she would take up with you, with my experi— With the one boy I was trying to protect her from. If I'd known that, I would have . . ." He rubs his face, looking tired. "I don't know what I would have done. Probably any warning I gave her only would have driven her right to you."

I can feel the wizards' guild looming above us. This is where we were before, on Market Street, when I noticed the spire. And I know it's there now, a long gray spike towering in the sky, like a beacon for lost souls, trying to draw them back inside its clutches. Calling back all the monsters. Or at least just this one.

We reach the top of the hill, turning a corner, and there it is. The sight of the guild hits me full-on. It's a giant gray stone building, several stories high, and spans the entire block. Ivy grows across the walls. It looks like a school, or a place for stuffy old men to sit in cushy chairs and decide how the world should be. Unpleasant, maybe, or boring. But ultimately harmless, and not somewhere where people get tortured in the basement.

No, not *people*. Person. Me.

Hadrin glances over, watching to see what I'll do. I get the feeling he'd go in alone if he had to, even knowing what the outcome would be. At my most powerful, I stand a chance against Endeil. Hadrin wouldn't last five minutes.

And we're still a few streets away from actually *being* there. No one's noticed us or recognized us. A small voice in the back of my head whispers that we could still turn around and not do this. While I'm still me. While I can still make that decision. We'll figure out some other way to save Leora and stop Endeil.

"You'll go around the side," Hadrin says. "Not the front entrance. He'll be expecting that. There's another door on First Street, down a little set of stairs. I think you're familiar with it—it's the same one you escaped from." He reaches into a pocket of his robes and pulls out a tiny golden key. "You'll need this."

I tell myself to hold out my hand and take the key, but nothing happens. A tremor of fear runs up my spine. Then something in me crumples, and I know—I *know*—that I'm going to run. My teeth clamp down on my tongue. And this is what it comes down to. Either I'm too terrified to even approach the building, or I'm the ruthless killer, carving out a path of destruction and murdering anyone who gets in his way without a second thought.

But I won't become him until I have to. I won't let that part of me take over until there's no other choice. I can make it a little farther, I can stay *me* for that much longer, because it has to be me who goes into that basement. It has to be me who saves Leora. Even if that's not who comes back out.

Hadrin must see how scared I am. I expect to hear him snap at me at any moment. But he waits, saying nothing. And then a minute later the wave of fear has passed and I'm still here. My hand shakes as I finally hold it out for the key.

"The stairway won't be guarded," he says. "Not many of us had access to it. And if it is . . . Take out anyone who gets in your way."

"The side entrance," I repeat numbly. The path of my escape. "And where will you be?"

"At the front of the building. Creating a diversion."

"A diversion?"

"I'll demand an audience with the High Priest. He'll refuse at first, but I know a few things about him and his so-called gifts and where they come from. Things he doesn't want anyone shouting at the entrance to his new palace for everyone to hear. Not," he adds, "that anyone here will listen to a wizard who's obviously bitter about being cast out of his home. But it will be enough to attract his attention for a few minutes at least. The less focus he has on you and her, the better. Leave the door unlocked behind you. I'll catch up, one way or another."

"That might not be a good idea. Hadrin, if I don't see you again—"

"You'll see me," he says. "You know what you have to do?"

I nod. And despite what he said, I know this might be my last chance to say something to him, while I'm still me, though I'm not sure what. I can't forgive him. I can't forget what he's done to me, even if . . . "It's not a fairy tale," I tell him. "Redemption. It's real."

He makes a *hmph* noise in disbelief, but he smiles a little. "Good luck, Azeril," he says softly. Then, without looking back, he walks off toward the front of the guild.

"Good luck," I say, though he's already too far away to hear me. "We're both going to need it."

———

The stairs aren't hard to find, even though all I can see from the street is a bit of railing that descends below ground, to the sunken basement. The narrow staircase and cramped entryway look forgotten and unimportant, a place you'd never go unless you had business there. They'd be easy to miss, but I remember exactly where they are. Now my hand shakes and my chest feels tight as I fumble with the key, trying to unlock the door.

This feels so *wrong*. I should be going the other way. Out, not in. This entrance leads directly to the basement, the home of all my nightmares. The place where they broke me, where I lost myself before. Where I'm going to lose myself again.

The key clicks in the lock. It's so dark in the basement that I can almost pretend this isn't happening, that I'm not here, in the place I said I'd never go back to. And it's a good thing this entrance isn't guarded, because if there was anyone here, surely they'd hear the ragged way I'm breathing, or how clunky my footsteps sound, even to me.

Normally I'd be moving silently, a killer lurking in the shadows, but I keep imagining things in the darkness as I creep through the hallway. A flash of blue robes. Someone darting away as soon as I look in his direction.

Hallucinations. There's no one in blue robes left, not after Endeil took over. And if there are and they're hiding down here, then they have no interest in turning me in. Though if they do . . .

I put a hand to the rough stone wall to steady myself, to stay grounded in reality. I could cast a light to banish the imagined visions, but if there *is* anyone down here, it would give me away. Plus, I don't need light to find where I'm going. My fear makes my thoughts scatter, but I focus on a couple of spells, ready if anyone jumps out at me, wizard or priest.

They don't. It's just me, all alone down here. And in a way, that's almost worse. It leaves me with only my thoughts and my imagination, filling in the gaps with things that aren't there. Whispers in the distance. Overheard conversations from long ago. And I know my hold on reality is slipping.

I think of the rats in the basement of the church when Leora and I went exploring. It was only a few weeks ago, but it feels like forever. Everything's changed since then.

Leora's words echo back to me. *I'm not afraid of anything.* I smile a little and imagine she's with me now. Rolling her eyes and saying, "Come *on*, Az. What are you, scared of the dark?"

The thought of her is like a flame pushing back the darkness. I breathe a little easier. My footsteps feel a little lighter.

And then I turn a corner and come to the door. *The* door. I can't see it, but I know it's there. I cast the light, because it's now or never. It gives off a pale glow against the heavy oak, flickering off the set of sliding iron locks, the kind that could only be opened from the outside. They weren't always there. When the wizards started their experiments, there was only one lock. They thought that would be enough, that I would never be able to overpower them. Most of the time, they were right. There were only a few times when the extra locks were necessary.

The metal sliders look rusted, as if they haven't been used in years. They probably haven't. I put my hand on the cold brass knob. The spell to make the door wither and decay is already at the surface of my mind, though it would be much slower, not nearly as powerful as before, when I had all those wizards to draw from. But then I turn the knob, not locked after all, and the door swings open.

The familiar smell of old, rotting blood and damp, moldy earth nearly chokes me. The chair sits there, in the middle of the room, the straps hanging from it. Exactly how I left it three years ago, as if no time at all has passed. My vision blurs, and my heart races so fast, I think it's going to explode.

But the chair is empty. There's no one here.

Just the boy. The wizards forgot to strap him down and lock him in. Their mistake. One they'll regret, as soon as they come back for him. Maybe this is a test. Maybe they didn't really forget him at all, but are waiting to see what he'll do. But they left him with the knife again, which was wrong of them. If they want to live, anyway. The boy, alone in the darkness, with this obsidian, sharp as death. His spells might not work on all of them, but the knife will. Always. Though sometimes, sometimes, they send in wizards without the mark. To see what he can do to them. How far he'll go. Sometimes they stop him, before he kills them. Sometimes they don't.

It's a punishment. For the ones who screw up. And the boy always knows which ones they'll let him kill, because they're the ones who don't know anything about him or this experiment. They're the ones who won't live to tell about it.

No. I shake my head, coming back to myself. Not yet. I can't be *him* yet. I'm not a prisoner. I'm here to find Leora.

My heart's still pounding, but I try to stay calm as I survey the room again. Empty. No sign that anyone's been here. "Leora?" I whisper, though I know she's not here. And I have this terrible feeling that things have already gone horribly wrong. Though I would have known if Endeil had hurt her, if he'd . . . Well, I'm alive, aren't I? So she is, too.

Then the door slams shut behind me.

"Hello, Azeril."

I spin around, my hand hovering over the hilt of the knife. "Rathe."

He grins at me. That creepy, hollow grin. The dark spots under his eyes have gotten darker since I last saw him. His face has thinned out, too, so that it's almost skeletal. And the hunger in his eyes has only gotten more desperate. He's still wearing the red robes of the Church, though he must know where his power comes from by now.

I take a step back. He doesn't have a knife this time—not that he'd be a match for me even if he did. And still he takes a menacing step forward.

"How do you like being back?" he asks, laughing a little. "The High Priest told me all about it, you know. About what happened here. To *you*."

"Where is she?"

"I thought we could play a game. Since we're such *good friends*."

"I asked you a question."

"And if I told you the answer, you might try to leave. Then where would all the fun go?" He takes another step toward me.

I unsheathe my obsidian. Its familiar burn makes me feel a little safer, more like I'm in control of the situation. Though I'm not quite sure what I expect to happen.

I hold the knife out where he can see it. A warning. "Don't come any closer. Just tell me where she is."

"I thought I could sit here, in this chair. Like before. And *you* could—"

"*No.*" By the Fire, he's really lost it.

The grin on his face widens. "What's wrong, Az? Don't you want to hurt me?" He takes another step.

Damn it. "I *said* don't move!"

"Or you'll what?" he whispers. "Kill me?"

"If I have to."

"Well, you do. Have to."

I watch his hands, waiting for him to reach for a weapon I haven't noticed. But he doesn't. "The door locks from the outside," I remind him. "I could leave and lock you in here."

"No, you couldn't. Because if you let me live, I'm going to bring him back."

"Bring who back?"

"The High Priest. When you kill him. Rathe wouldn't have done it, but *I* will. I'll have to. How many times can you fight him, Azeril? How many? Because I haven't found a number yet where they don't come back."

"Rathe, listen, you don't—"

"Rathe isn't here anymore!" His face twitches, and his nostrils flare in and out. "He had to leave. You killed him that day, with the High Priest. And now I'm all that's left."

I didn't kill Rathe. I *didn't*. But I study this shell of what he used to be, and I wonder if any of the old Rathe is still in there, or if he's completely gone.

"It was so easy for you then," he goes on. "It should be even easier now."

"I'm leaving, all right? Just stand over there and—"

"And let you walk out of here?" He crosses the last bit of distance between us and puts himself directly in front of the knife. "Not before you finish what you started. Rathe trusted you, and you killed him."

"No! Rathe, listen to me. I know you're still in there."

He takes one more step, walking right into the knife, letting the tip press against his stomach. "Do it," he whispers. "Get it over with already."

Sweat prickles down my back. It would be so easy, just one quick movement, and then the knife would be tasting his flesh. But . . . that's the knife talking, not me.

"I know what you think," I tell him. "But I really was your friend, Rathe. Remember all those times we were late to candle service? You always made up the stupidest excuses. Like when you said there was a lost dog in the courtyard and you had to stop and find its owner. Or when you said the girls stole all your robes so you couldn't get dressed."

"That one was true."

"Yeah. The *first* time. But the Fathers never believed a word of it."

"And you loaned me your dirty robes." He smiles a little, lost in memory. Then he shakes his head, like none of that matters. But for a moment, I saw him. The old Rathe isn't gone. Not completely.

"Those days are over," he says and lunges toward me.

I can't tell if he's attacking me, or trying to impale himself. I sidestep, evading him. He screams and reaches for me, his fingernails biting into my arm. And I wonder if I really should do it. If he's right and all that's left is for me to kill him.

"Do it," he says, as if he can read my thoughts. His voice comes out a rasp. "*End* this."

But there's hope for him. I saw it. I force myself to sheathe the knife, even though I hate not having my obsidian between us. Maybe it would be kinder to do what he wants—and maybe if I don't finish him off, I'll lose the fight with Endeil. But Rathe's my friend. And he's still in there, somewhere, and . . . hurting him was what got him into this mess.

"If you won't do it, I *will*." He lunges for me again, this time grabbing for the knife.

I hear the door open behind me, and dark flames suddenly erupt across Rathe's chest. Recognition flashes in his eyes.

I cry out, but it's too late to stop this. The flames grow higher, burning darker. Rathe reaches for me even as his body disintegrates. My last image of him is his terror-filled eyes and his mouth forming the words, *Kill him*. And then he's gone. A pile of ash that used to be my friend.

My hand falls to the knife hilt. I don't have to turn around to know who's behind me, but I do anyway.

"You made me break my favorite toy," Endeil says. He has Leora. One arm is around her neck, his hand holding those same dark flames to her mouth, keeping her silent. "And now I'm going to break *yours.*"

CHAPTER THIRTY-ONE

My lips start moving before I have time to think about it. A spell to twist his bones, to make it so he can't hold on to her. So he'll be in too much pain to use his magic. Just one spell, not too strong. Not enough to change me. Not while he still has Leora.

Endeil holds up his free hand, throwing a wall of dark flames between us. It pushes against my magic, trying to stop me. I push back, though it feels like the equivalent of trying to walk through a stone wall. And it's that night in his office all over again, with him so easily overpowering me.

"Az!" Leora screams, managing to free her mouth. She squirms and kicks at him, struggling to get away.

Endeil grips her throat. "Stop," he says to me. He's still got his other hand up, controlling the flames, pressing them closer and closer toward me.

I keep casting, though he seems completely untouched by my spell. Sweat beads on my forehead from the effort of keeping up so much energy. And none of it's even getting to him, blocked by that stupid wall of flames. Cold, dark flames that feel like they're sucking all the life out of the room.

"Stop," he says again—sternly but calmly, not at all threatened—"or I kill her."

And I hesitate. Not because I could ever think of letting him do that, but because I know if I stop casting, this might as well be over. I'll have lost before I even started, and there'll be nothing to stop him from hurting her. But I'm not getting anywhere as it is. And if he kills her, I die, too, and then it really is all over.

I stop casting then, letting the words to the spell trail off. "Let her go."

Endeil sighs, already bored with me, but he eases his grip on her a little. "Or you'll what?"

"Az, run!" Leora shouts. "Don't—"

Endeil grips her throat again, cutting her off. "I'm waiting. Tell me how you're going to kill me. Go on. How are *you*, who couldn't even stop someone like Rathe, going to kill *me*?"

"He was my friend. I chose not to kill him."

"And are you going to *choose* not to kill me, too? I know what's in your head, Azeril. I know every move before you're going to make it, and, let's face it, I've overpowered you twice now."

"With trickery. Not in a real fight. Let her go and we'll find out whose magic is actually stronger."

He laughs. "You think I don't know what you're trying to do? It won't work."

"Let her go. I'll do anything you want." At least until she's out of here, away from both of us. And then he's as good as dead.

"Ah. There's the apprentice I know." He smiles. It's that same sick smile he wore the first day we met.

"Az, no!" Leora says, before Endeil throws her to the ground.

"Leora!" I move toward her, but Endeil's already encircled her with dark fire. The flames climb higher, until I can only catch flickering glimpses of her behind them.

"I looked inside her head, too, you know," Endeil says. "Very enlightening. That's how I knew how to send my message. And do you know what else? I know what she thinks about you. All the *doubts* she has."

"Don't listen to him!" Leora says, but her voice sounds far away, fading in and out, like there's a gust of wind stealing her words.

I glare at Endeil, looking him right in the eye. "Leora loves me."

"But still she *doubts*. Do you know how much time she's spent wondering if she can actually be with someone like you? Her father's psychotic experiment?" He taps his fingers together. "It's even worse now, after you told her all your secrets."

I glance at Leora. Her face is pained, though from his fire or from his words, I can't tell. She's saying something, but I only catch fragments of sound.

"And no matter what she told you earlier, she's worried it's not safe for her to share your bed. You killed all those wizards. You nearly killed her. Obviously you can't control yourself."

"That's not true." Except that it is, no matter how much I don't want it to be.

The dark flames cast an eerie greenish glow across Endeil's face. "She would never admit how terrified she is of you. She wants to believe she still loves you, but you're not at all who she thought you were."

I catch a glimpse of her, but the flames distort her face, so I can't make out her expression. But it looks troubled. Guilty.

"So," Endeil says, "knowing what she really thinks about you, are you certain you want to save her? Are you sure you'd do anything? Because you told me you would once and you lied. And if you lie to me here, she is dead. Do you hear me?"

"Yes," I tell him. I don't have to wonder if what he says about Leora is true or not. Because it doesn't matter. I love her. What she thinks of me or what he says about either of us doesn't figure into that. I love her, and I'd do anything to save her. "Whatever you want."

"Then, please," Endeil says, "sit down. There's only one chair, but what kind of host would I be if I didn't offer it to my guest?"

I glance over at the chair. I don't think I can make myself move any closer to it.

But Endeil snaps his fingers, and the circle of flames closes in on Leora. She cries out.

"Sit. Down."

I do. It feels so familiar. The cold, rough stone, stained with my blood. I thought I'd never be here again, that *no one* could make me. I vowed that no one would ever have that much power over me again, that I would die first. But here I am.

"Put your arms in place," Endeil says.

I know I'm walking down a dark road that I won't be able to turn back from. But I do what he says, because he has Leora. Then he snaps his fingers again, and the straps close over my wrists and ankles.

And I try to hold still, to stay calm, but I can't breathe. Something inside me breaks, leaving me wild and terrified. For a moment I can't remember why I'm here, if it was the wizards who forced me here or someone else. I struggle to stay *me*, because if I forget . . .

If I forget, I won't know who Leora is anymore. I won't have any reason to do what Endeil asks, and then he'll kill her.

I keep my eyes focused on her, trying to stay grounded, to not give in to the mad terror.

"Better," Endeil says. He lowers his hand, and the flames surrounding Leora let up a bit.

Enough for me to see that she has tears streaming down her face. "Don't listen to him!" she says. "For the Fire's sake, *do something*! Use your magic!"

Endeil just grins. "I don't think she understands how this works, do you?"

I give Leora a wobbly smile. Trying so hard to make it seem like it's going to be okay. But it's not, and my jaw starts shaking again, ruining my efforts. If I cast something, he'll stop me. And then he'll kill her. All I can hope to do is buy us more time until Hadrin arrives. If he's still coming. If him showing up will even make a difference. But maybe he can get Leora out of here. And then I can finally give in and become the weapon I was always meant to be.

"You could have just killed me," I tell Endeil. "But you didn't."

"If you think I harbor warm feelings for my former apprentice, you're wrong. Killing you would be too quick. This is a punishment for betraying me. You were a terrible apprentice and now you're a traitor."

He lifts a finger, pointing it at me. Something sharp and burning presses against my stomach. I look down and see that it's my own knife, unsheathed and controlled by Endeil and that dark fire of his.

"It's amazing how precise you can be with obsidian when you don't need to touch it," he says. "I couldn't have done it on my own, that first time. But every time I bless someone with a new gift, my own power strengthens."

"You can still stop this," I say. I feel blood trickling down my stomach and smell my own burnt flesh. A sob escapes Leora, and I wonder if this is how it happens. That vision I saw. Maybe I should just give in now, become the weapon, because if me and Leora are both going to die, I'm taking him down with us. "You can still be saved."

Endeil laughs. He laughs so hard his eyes water. "I can be *what*?"

"If you give up the Chasm. If you pray to the Fire, maybe . . . maybe it will forgive you. Someday. And you'll—"

"Someday," he says, making a face. "You think I would give up all this power for maybe *someday* finding the Fire's forgiveness?"

"You were its favorite once, remember? You thought we both were."

For a moment, there's that familiar look in his eyes. The wistful look he got whenever he talked about being the Fire's chosen one. Of having some great destiny. But it's only there for an instant, and then he scowls. "And you're so sure it has forsaken me now."

"Yes." I close my eyes, feeling the knife—my *own* knife—dig into my skin. Deeper this time. Maybe I shouldn't be pissing him off. Maybe dragging this out is only going to make it that much worse. But I have to try.

"Just because it's forsaken *you*," he says.

But I'm not so sure it has anymore. Leora said the Fire was protecting me all this time. It could have just been trying to keep the Chasm's spells at bay, to keep hidden what the wizards never should have dredged up. But it still kept me safe from all the dark memories that might have destroyed me. It let me have a few good years. And then there was that candle that lit for me the other night at the church. Not right away, not until I fled, sparing that Father's life. But it happened, and that has to mean something. I hope.

"I never touched wizard magic," Endeil says, the knife jerking and digging in deeper. "I— *You.*" He suddenly whirls around, glaring at Leora. "What do you think you're doing?"

Leora's hand is out, frozen in place. She looks like she was trying to touch the dark fire surrounding her. Like she was trying to unlock it.

Before she has a chance to say anything, Endeil reaches into the circle and grabs her by the arm, yanking her toward him. "I can make him bleed just as easily with *you* in that chair," he snarls.

Leora spits in his face. "Then do it. There's no saving you. You're already too far gone. So it doesn't matter what you do—Az is still going to kill you."

Rage flares on his face. He raises a hand to hit her.

And that's when the boy loses it. Trapped in the chair. Screaming. Like before. Like a thousand times before.

The priest hits the girl, and the boy's mouth fills with blood. It makes his words taste like metal as he casts the spell to turn the priest's lungs to ash. The priest is no tattooed wizard, but he guards himself with his magic, so the boy takes the energy from the girl. Too much. She cries out, looking at him for mercy. Like he's hurting her. Like he should stop.

But the boy is in the chair, and he will kill the one who put him there. And the priest is fighting against him, using his magic to block the boy's. So the boy takes more energy from the girl, because she's the only source besides himself.

"You promised," the priest says. He grabs the girl by the throat and squeezes. Starting to strangle her.

The girl tries to say something that sounds like the boy's name, but it only comes out a choked gasp. She's going to die. And the boy switches spells, trying to make the leather straps on the chair decay before the priest finishes her and comes for him.

And then the wizard appears in the doorway. He throws a handful of herbs in the priest's eyes and chants a spell. Fire scorches the priest's skin, and he screams and lets go of the girl. The dark flames disappear, and the knife clatters to the floor as all the priest's attention goes to the fire trying to consume him. He swipes at the wizard, first with a wave of his hand, then with a wave of his magic.

The girl puts a hand to her throat and gasps for breath. Then she rushes over to the boy. "It's going to be okay," she lies, touching a hand to the straps on his wrists. They fall away as soon as she does, and he pulls his hands back. She touches the ankle straps, too, and then he's free.

She tries to grab his arm, but the boy jumps out of the chair, snatching up the knife and warding her away. "You shouldn't have done that," he says. No one has ever helped the boy before.

"Az, I had to. He was killing you."

She thinks he means something else. She uses his name—part of it—but she doesn't know him, otherwise she wouldn't have freed him. "Who are you?"

She looks into his eyes then, startled. Like he should already know. And then she looks afraid.

The wizard's spell comes to an end. He screams as the priest recovers and throws dark fire at him.

The boy sheathes the knife. "You should run," he tells the girl. He's never told anyone to run before. Not unless he was going to chase them.

"You know me better than that," she says, even though it's not true, because he doesn't know her at all.

And still, part of him wants her to stay. He doesn't know why.

Then the priest has the wizard against the wall. The boy casts the spell to destroy the priest's lungs. If he can't breathe, he can't use magic. He can't put the boy in the chair again. He can't steal the wizard from him, killing him before the boy gets a chance.

But the boy only gets a few words out before the priest coughs and whips around, his eyes full of hatred. He holds out both hands, summoning up a wall of dark flame.

The boy concentrates harder, drawing more energy from the people around him. Until the girl standing too close to him turns pale and the wizard cries out, still slumped against the wall. So many people have tried to stop the boy. The wizards gave him the magic— made him pay in blood—*and then wouldn't let him use it. But he uses it now. He won't stop until he's killed the priest. And the wizard. And if the girl is stupid enough to stay in the room while he drains her, after he told her to run . . .*

The boy hopes he doesn't have to drain the wizard yet. He wants to save him for last. To put him in the chair and make him suffer.

He shouldn't be able to drain the wizard at all, but he remembers cutting into him, slicing the tattoo.

You've become like a son to me.

The words flash in the boy's head. A memory of the wizard saying them. Meaning it. His stomach twists and his magic falters.

"You think you can beat me?" The priest laughs. "You with all your spells. Even knowing where they come from, you try to lecture me on the Fire? I don't care if it has forsaken me—I still have all the power I need!" There's a whoosh as the wall of flames grows and moves toward the boy and the girl. The floor cracks, a giant fissure opening up, like the Chasm itself is trying to swallow the room.

The flames grow higher and move to circle them. The boy draws from the girl and the wizard and now even himself, but it's not enough. He could kill them all and it wouldn't be enough, not with that crack in the floor feeding the priest endless power.

The boy seeks out more energy, feeling for more sources, farther away. There are more people in the building, far above them. His muscles burn and his head feels like it's on fire, all without touching the knife. It's harder, because they're not in the room. But he does it anyway. There must be several dozen people he's pulling from now. He'll kill them all. He'll be the only one who walks away from this.

Then the girl moves closer to him. She slips her hand into his, their fingers automatically intertwining. As if they've done it a million times before.

And he doesn't want to remember, but he does. Suddenly he remembers crying at her bedside when he thought she would die. He remembers telling her he loves her.

Lying in her bed, letting her trace his scars.

Falling from an apple tree.

Kissing her.

The boy concentrates harder on the spell, focusing all the energy he's drawing from everyone near enough. Everyone except the girl. He won't be the only one to walk away from this.

The dark flames die down as the boy's magic overpowers the priest's. The priest struggles for breath, the boy's spell finally taking hold.

In a few more moments, there won't be a priest. A few more words of the spell, and he'll—

The priest is on his knees, but he shoots out a new blast of flame. A desperate attempt to save himself. And it works. The force of the flames sends another whoosh of air through the room. The flames push the boy's spell away, letting the priest breathe again. Letting him live. The giant crack in the floor widens. The chair tilts to one side, sinking toward it. The crack is big enough that a person could fall in.

The boy doesn't want to think about how deep it goes, as if the Chasm was really there, in the room with them.

The priest gets to his feet, his face red, a fevered look in his eyes. But he's nowhere near spent. Or maybe he is, but the Chasm isn't.

The girl squeezes the boy's hand. "Keep . . . going . . ." she pants.

And he realizes he's drawing from her again. From her and the wizard, who's kneeling on the floor. The wizard, who put him in the chair. Who let him go. Who thinks of him as a son.

It won't be enough. No matter how many people are in this building, no matter how many the boy draws from, it won't ever be enough to stop the priest and the Chasm. The girl will die for nothing. The only person who ever truly helped the boy. The girl he loved in another lifetime. In a dream. One he's woken up from, but that still feels so vivid.

"Are you ready to give up?" the priest asks. As if he could go on for days like this.

The boy is the one the priest wants. Maybe he can't beat him, maybe he'll die here, but the girl doesn't have to. She and the wizard could escape.

He remembers something else about her. About the spell the wizard cast long ago. The wizard said he couldn't sever the link between them, that he wasn't powerful enough.

The boy isn't powerful enough, either. Not on his own.

And that's when he does the unthinkable. He stops casting altogether.

The priest's flames encircle them, tugging at what energy he and the girl have left, trying to suck them dry.

"Giving up?" the priest says.

The boy falls to his knees. He closes his eyes. "Please."

"Yes?" the priest asks, because he thinks the boy is talking to him. Because he expects him to beg.

But that's not happening, not this time.

"Please," the boy says again, praying to the Fire. "Please sever the bond between me and Leora." The wizard isn't strong enough to break the link, and neither is the boy, but surely the Fire can do what they can't. If it will listen. When he speaks again, he's not sure if it's him talking, or the part of him that's still living in the dream. "I know I don't deserve any favors, but you can't want her to die."

"What are you doing?" the priest demands.

The wall of flames inches closer.

"Az, no," the girl sobs. "You have to fight him."

But the boy doesn't listen. It's over. "I loved her," *he tells the Fire.* "A weapon can't love, but I did. And now she's going to die, because of me—"

"Azeril," *the wizard warns from across the room.*

"—and I don't care what happens to me, but please let her live. Please keep her safe from all the monsters, even me. Especially me."

"You can stop that," *the priest says.* "It's not going to work. And if you don't stop, I'll kill you."

The boy gets to his feet. He stands in front of the girl, holding his arms out. "Let him kill me. Just keep her safe. I don't care what happens to me, as long as she lives."

"Az, don't," *the girl cries.* "You can't do this! You can't just let him win!"

"This is foolishness!" *the wizard says.* "I won't stand here and watch you do this!"

"Then take her and run." *The boy glances over his shoulder at the girl. Their eyes meet. Hers are pleading with him. Begging him not to do this.*

Memories of her come back to him in bits and pieces, in floods and waves. "I love you," *he tells her, because right then he does. He remembers what it feels like to be a boy and not a monster. To feel her heart beating next to his.* "Don't forget that."

"You're making me sick," *the priest says. Then he holds up a hand, and the boy's obsidian flies out of its sheath and stops in front of him. The priest aims it right at the boy, the edges of his mouth curling in a grin.*

The girl screams the boy's name. The wizard swears.

The boy doesn't flinch. It's fitting, him dying the way he killed so many. He just wishes the girl didn't have to watch.

But the knife doesn't hit him. It's like it runs into an invisible wall a foot away from his chest and falls to the ground.

"No," the priest breathes, gaping at the boy, just as shocked as he is. The priest gives up on the knife and hurls a ball of dark flame, as if he'd only chosen the wrong weapon. It hits the invisible barrier and veers to either side of the boy, completely missing him.

Then there's a warm feeling in the boy's head. It starts out as just a flicker, a sort of tingle, and then burns brighter. New energy seeps into his limbs. The priest's dark fire doesn't seem so oppressive, and it feels like a huge weight lifts from his shoulders.

An image burns in his mind, like it did when the Fire sent him that warning before, about the girl. About her sobbing and covered in blood. Only this time what he sees isn't a warning. The Fire shows him an image of himself, his hands glowing with a white light. A light so bright it purges away the darkness.

And it's more than an image. It's a question tugging in the boy's mind, weighing all his spells, all the power the wizards gave him, against one single gift from the Fire. Asking him to choose between them, between revenge and mercy, darkness and light.

The boy always chose to hide in the darkness before. Even in the dream. The wizards never taught him mercy, only bitterness and pain. He might never have ventured out of the shadows if it wasn't for the girl. The one who freed him from the chair. Who didn't run even when she was afraid.

All these thoughts flash through his head in only an instant. One quick flicker, and then he's making his decision. Choosing light over darkness. Order over chaos.

Love over revenge.

There's a burning feeling in my head, and then I blink, not sure where I am for a moment. *Who* I am. I remember being in the chair, watching Endeil raise his hand to Leora, and I remember giving in to a fight I didn't think I'd come back from.

I was the weapon, and still I chose to save her.

I look down and see my palms are glowing. The white light is real and blinding. And I don't know if the bond between me and Leora is severed, but I do know the Fire wants us to win this fight.

An invisible barrier still holds back Endeil's magic, but now I meet his gaze, and for the first time tonight, I see fear there.

"Wait," he says when I take a step forward. The barrier moves with me. My hands glow brighter. "You can't do this. It won't work. The Fire still favors me. The Fire and the Chasm both."

"It doesn't work like that." I hold up my hands.

He holds up his, but not to attack. He's trying to ward me off. "No, don't—"

But he's too late. There's nothing he can say to stop me. The white light gets bigger and brighter, spreading out from my hands. It's so bright it makes my eyes water, but I don't blink or look away. The light grows until it fills the room. This room that was once so dark, so full of nightmares. The chair is just a chair in its light. Ugly and stained. But inanimate. A piece of old furniture.

The light reaches its peak. It flows into Endeil, and he cries out, but it's more of a sob than a scream. And I feel the darkness leave him. The Fire purging out the Chasm, cleansing him of whatever damage it did.

And then it's over. The light vanishes, leaving Endeil huddled on the floor. I stagger, suddenly dizzy and drained.

Leora grabs my arm to steady me. "Az," she says, "what in the Chasm just happened?!"

"Not the Chasm, Leora," I tell her, feeling like I could sleep for a week and it wouldn't be enough. "The Fire."

———

"That might have been the stupidest thing you've ever done," Leora says. But she throws her arms around me, hugging me tight and pressing the side of her face against mine.

I half hug her back, half lean into her, ready to collapse. "But it worked." I feel a lingering warmth from the Fire's magic. And . . . I can feel the white light inside my palms still. A light to banish the darkness. Channeling the Fire's power to defeat Endeil might have been a onetime thing, but the light wasn't. "I gave up all my spells. I chose mercy, and light, and the Fire gave me this gift."

Now I have the ability to undo what I started when I let Endeil look inside my head. I can heal all the people who've been corrupted by his magic. Everyone except Rathe.

Hadrin waits until I've stepped back from Leora before putting a hand on my shoulder. He hesitates, trying to find the right words. And then he gives up and hugs me instead.

I share a surprised look with Leora. This is the last thing I ever expected to happen here, in this room, with the chair. Not to mention a giant crack in the floor and the newly healed High Priest huddled in the corner.

Hadrin pulls away, as if he's ashamed of his display of affection for me, and says, "Your curse? Is it lifted?"

"I think so," I tell him. "It feels like it is, but . . . I'm not in any hurry to test it out."

"Let's go," Leora says. She wraps her arms around herself, as if it's freezing in here. And I catch a glimpse of the letters that Endeil carved into her arm and feel a pang of sadness and guilt. The physical wounds will heal. But I wish she hadn't had to go through that. There's a bit of blood welling up from one of her wounds, but my arm is clean. So I guess the bond really is broken.

She catches me staring at her and says, "It's okay. I'm fine."

"You say that now, but—"

"I wasn't the one in the chair. I can take it. And"—she shakes her head—"all that stuff he said, about me being afraid of you—"

A high-pitched scream interrupts her. There's a flurry of movement as Endeil rushes toward us, my obsidian in his hand. He has this crazed look that I must have had a million times. It happens in the span of a heartbeat. He cries out and leaps at me, the knife aimed directly at my heart. And obsidian never misses.

My last thought is that at least Leora is safe. At least the bond is broken.

But then Hadrin jumps in front of me. The knife sinks into his chest. He kicks Endeil, throwing him off balance. Endeil tumbles backward, pulling the knife with him. It clatters to the ground as he trips and falls into the crack in the floor.

Hadrin stares down at his chest, holding his hands to the wound as blood pours out. He sinks to the ground.

Leora kneels beside him, trying to stop the bleeding and muttering incoherently.

"You didn't have to do that," I tell Hadrin, my voice choked.

"But I did," he says softly. "I always knew I'd die by that knife."

If I still had my spells, I could heal him. But I gave them up, and now I can't do anything to stop this. It's not fair. Except that it is.

Leora's sobbing now. Covered in blood and sobbing. Just like in the vision the Fire showed me of her.

I'd assumed it would be because of me. And maybe it could have been. It came so close to being me.

Hadrin glances up at her. His eyes are glassy, the light in them fading. "I'm sorry," he says. His voice is so weak, I almost don't hear it. But I know Leora does.

She nods. "It's going to be all right. Do you hear me? You're going to—" But she doesn't finish. The light in his eyes goes out completely.

Leora's shoulders heave. Tears pour down her face while blood soaks her clothes. I put my arms around her, trying to hold her while she clings to him. To the father she thought didn't love her. To the one I thought didn't love me.

"How could you *do* this?" she says, shaking him, her voice thick from crying. "You weren't supposed to leave me!"

He wasn't. *I* was. He was supposed to keep her safe, because I was never coming back. But I lost myself and I still came back, and now he's the one that's gone.

He said he would take my place if he could.

Hot tears flood my eyes. I never thought I'd be crying over a wizard. Especially not him. I let go of Leora and take his hand. Lifeless but still warm. He survived my visit the other night, only to still die by my knife. At least it was quick. At least it wasn't what I'd planned for him.

"I'll miss you," I whisper, because it's true. Even though it's too late.

I let go of Hadrin's hand and put my arms around Leora again, and this time she lets go of him and buries her face in my neck.

Then there's a groan. Coming from the crack in the floor behind us. Leora glances up, hearing it, too. And I see Endeil's hand, clinging for dear life to the edge.

And I think there'll be plenty of time to comfort her *after* I kill him.

"Az, no!" Leora shouts as I get up and take a step toward him. She jumps up, putting a hand on my arm. "Don't do it." Her face is red and wet with tears. Smears of blood cover her hands and the front of her clothes. "You chose mercy. That's why the Fire gave you that gift, isn't it? Don't ruin that. Not for him."

"Yes," Endeil says. He struggles to keep his grip on the edge of the floor. "Help me up. Be merciful. Listen to her." As if he didn't choose to attack me, even after I'd purged him of the Chasm. This was all his choice. He was corrupt from the beginning. I think back to the first day I met him and how eager he was to get inside my head.

I peer down, seeing only a vast darkness beneath him.

"I didn't say he should *help* you," Leora tells him, anger burning in her voice. "I just said he shouldn't be the one to *end* you."

Endeil's eyes go wide as Leora's foot comes down on his fingers with a loud crunch. He screams and slips from the edge, disappearing down into the blackness.

I stare at her, a little shocked, a little amazed.

"What's the matter?" she says. "You've never seen a killer before?"

CHAPTER THIRTY-TWO

The scents of pine needles and fresh earth fill my nose as Leora and I make our way up the narrow path that leads to the mausoleum in Ashbury. It's the same path we walked a few weeks ago, when we went to visit her mother's ashes. Only now we're here during the day. The graves we pass on the outskirts of the church grounds, the ones with wizards buried in them, are no longer new. The wizard killer has officially retired. Even my obsidian is gone. I tossed it into the same crack Endeil disappeared into. I hate that it's gone—I still long for it—but I made my choice. And with my spells and the knife gone, maybe I can be a normal person, leading a regular life.

Word has also spread that Endeil wasn't the High Priest everyone thought he was, making what he said about me being the wizard killer less credible. Everyone knows he had a grudge against me, his apprentice trying to expose his evil, and it doesn't hurt my case that I've been using my ability from the Fire to purge away all the "gifts" Endeil gave everyone.

I mean, I'm still not the innocent apprentice people think I am. But I'm working on making up for it.

I took Hadrin's advice and got out of the capital. Father Moors was kind enough to let us stay at the church while we're in town, even though we're not students anymore. I think he feels guilty for the part he played in all this. He knew Endeil, back when he was an acolyte here. And it was here, in the Church of the Sacred Flame, that the High Priest's corruption started to spread. Father Moors might have known my secrets, but he didn't know what Endeil was truly capable of until it was too late.

The king and queen are officially funding the High Guild's renovation, though they're not admitting any fault for giving an insane high priest so much power. The Church has its seats in court back, too. They're also in the process of naming Endeil's successor from one of the other priests, who all claim they had no idea what he was doing, of course. And the Guild is too busy recovering from the attack to continue their search for me. It seems that the war between the wizards and the Church is over, at least for now.

Leora holds an amber-colored urn with Hadrin's ashes in it. He should have been buried in the Fire-forsaken ground. He was a wizard, after all. But in the end, I'm not sure he deserved that. Not that his sacrifice erased all his sins or all the hurt he caused, but . . . it certainly went a long way. He died so I could live. Maybe to make up for what he'd done to me, or maybe because he really did care. About me and Leora.

The graveyard looks so different during the day. The smells of earth and pine are the same, but the path looks like just any normal path, nothing sinister or creepy about it.

"I know he and my mother didn't always get along," Leora says, "but I want them to be in the same place. Is that crazy?"

I shake my head. "Of course not."

"Do you think the Fire will . . ." She trails off. The Fire might not let him be laid to rest inside the mausoleum. We might have to bury his ashes.

Leora glances at the graves of wizards as we pass. Last time we were here, she was wondering if one of them was her father's. Not realizing that I was the one who'd killed them. "Az," she says, "what the High Priest said—"

"Don't call him that."

"He *did* look into my thoughts, and what he said about me being afraid of you . . . That was true." She bites her lip. "He made it sound worse than it was, but I had those thoughts, Az. Those doubts. Just for a moment, but—"

"You don't have to tell me. I can't blame you for having doubts." Or for being afraid.

"I want you to know that I might have thought those things, but that's all they were. Just thoughts. I trust you. I'm not afraid of you."

"Or of anything," I add.

She punches my arm. "I might have exaggerated when I said that. The truth is, I'm terrified of losing you. When he put you in that chair, I thought . . . I knew he was going to kill you, Az. And nothing else mattered. By the Fire, if you had died, I would have, too, even without the curse."

My chest feels warm and kind of achy. But it's a good ache. Not the longing for something you can never have, but the feeling of loving someone so much that no matter how close you are to them, it can never be enough. "You don't care who I was? I mean, do you really think a person can change?"

We arrive at the door to the mausoleum. Leora hugs the amber urn to her chest and doesn't answer me. She holds her breath as she prepares to cross the threshold. Hoping—praying, like I am—that the Fire will allow Hadrin's remains inside.

I slip my hand into hers. We step inside together. At first I feel empty and cold. There's nothing, and I think we're going to be rejected. There'll have to be one more grave, after all. And then a gentle warmth washes over us as the Fire gives its approval.

Leora finds her mother's urn on the shelf and sets her father's next to it. She smiles at them. It's a bittersweet smile, remembering the good times along with the bad.

She takes an unlit prayer candle from the box on the floor and hands me one, too.

"Please, protect him from the darkness," she says.

I say it along with her. Thinking about Hadrin. About the darkness that he gave me, and that he tried to save me from. Because of him, I'm alive. And I have Leora.

And when I look down, flame flickers to life on her candle. And on mine.

She smiles at me. "Not defective this time, I see?"

"Funny, now that I'm not an altar boy, it works just fine."

"You asked if a person can really change, Az. Well, I think you have your answer. But you know what?"

"What, Leora?"

She takes my hand again, her fingers interlocking with mine. "I wouldn't change a thing."

ACKNOWLEDGMENTS

I wrote the first version of this book about eight years ago. It was all I talked about back then, and I'm pretty sure I was completely insufferable. Thanks to all my friends who put up with me anyway. And thanks to everyone who read and loved this new version, especially Chloë Tisdale, who never gave up on the story; Karen Kincy, who helped me with endless problem solving; Jennifer Cervantes, who saved me from having no title; and Kevin Wolske, who liked all the really dark parts.

ABOUT THE AUTHOR

 Chelsea M. Campbell grew up in the Pacific Northwest, where it rains a lot. And then rains some more. She finished her first novel when she was twelve, sent it out, and promptly got rejected. Since then she's written many more novels, earned a degree in Latin and Ancient Greek, become an obsessive knitter and fiber artist, and started a collection of glass grapes. Besides writing, studying ancient languages, and collecting useless objects, Chelsea is a pop culture fangirl at heart and can often be found rewatching episodes of *Buffy the Vampire Slayer* or *Parks and Recreation*, or dying a lot in *Dark Souls*. Visit her online: www.chelseamcampbell.com.